HEARTWARMING

Her Cowboy Sweetheart

New York Times Bestselling Author

Cathy McDavid

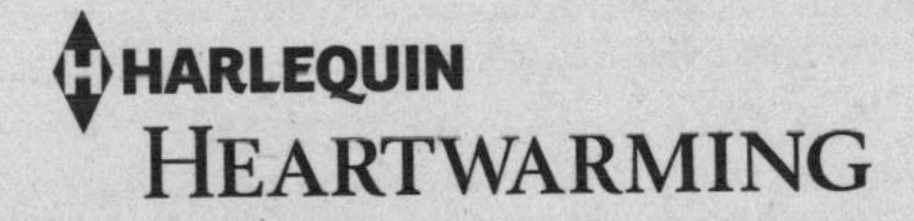

HARLEQUIN®
HEARTWARMING™

ISBN-13: 978-1-335-88969-0

Her Cowboy Sweetheart

This edition published by arrangement with Harlequin Books S.A.

For questions and comments about the quality of this book, please contact us at CustomerService@Harlequin.com.

Harlequin Enterprises ULC
22 Adelaide St. West, 40th Floor
Toronto, Ontario M5H 4E3, Canada
www.Harlequin.com

Printed in U.S.A.

“Hmm. Let me give it a try.”

He sauntered toward the mare, prompting Carly to pause. She might not be interested in him, but that didn’t make her immune to the confidence he exuded, the mirth twinkling in his chocolate-brown eyes and the crooked grin that hinted at mischief.

Speaking softly in Spanish, he approached the mare and foal, exhibiting the slow, easy manner she found so appealing. At the same time, there was an undeniable determination and deliberateness that surfaced in moments like this. Under different circumstances, Carly’s insides would have melted in response.

“That’s right,” he murmured, stroking the mare’s neck and scratching her between the ears.

The mare visibly relaxed. Her foal appeared equally mesmerized and, surprise, surprise, stood quietly beside her mother, watching JD’s every move.

Just like Carly.

Dear Reader,

I always have mixed feelings when a series comes to an end. I've loved living in my Sweetheart Ranch world these past couple of years and will be sad to leave it (for now—who knows what the future may bring?). But I'm also excited about what comes next and the new world I'm creating.

Carly and JD's story is one that's close to my heart. They are both dealing with huge challenges, emotional and physical. I think most of us have been there at some point in our lives, struggling with an intolerable situation or facing a health crisis, and can relate to Carly and JD. That they ultimately overcome their challenges and find love at the end of their journey is deeply satisfying to me.

Oh, yeah, and there's an adorable baby boy and equally adorable dog that will surely make you smile with their charming antics.

Warmest wishes,

Cathy McDavid

PS: I love connecting with readers. You can find me at:

CathyMcDavid.com
Facebook.com/CathyMcDavidBooks
Twitter: @cathymcdavid
Instagram.com/CathyMcDavidWriter

Since 2006, *New York Times* bestselling author **Cathy McDavid** has been happily penning contemporary Westerns for Harlequin. Every day, she gets to write about handsome cowboys riding the range or busting a bronc. It's a tough job, but she's willing to make the sacrifice. Cathy shares her Arizona home with her own real-life sweetheart and a trio of odd pets. Her grown twins have left to embark on lives of their own, and she couldn't be prouder of their accomplishments.

Books by Cathy McDavid

Harlequin Western Romance

Mustang Valley

Cowboy for Keeps
Her Holiday Rancher
Come Home, Cowboy
Having the Rancher's Baby
Rescuing the Cowboy
A Baby for the Deputy
The Cowboy's Twin Surprise
The Bull Rider's Valentine

Harlequin Heartwarming

The Sweetheart Ranch

A Cowboy's Christmas Proposal
The Cowboy's Perfect Match
The Cowboy's Christmas Baby

Visit the Author Profile page
at Harlequin.com for more titles.

To Mike. I can't wait for this next exciting phase in our wonderful life together.

CHAPTER ONE

CONVINCING STUBBORN OFFSPRING to cooperate was nothing new for Carly Leighton. Hardly a day or hour passed when she didn't engage in a power struggle with her adorable but often temperamental year-old son.

This particular youngster, however, was different. Born three months ago, she stood with all four legs braced in a defiant stance and her hind end pressed firmly into the round pen railing.

"It won't hurt you," Carly cooed. "I swear."

The foal glared at her with huge, suspicious eyes. Both ears lay flat against her head as her feather duster tail flicked back and forth.

"See?" Carly held up her latest originally crafted horse necklace. Late-morning sunlight reflected off the intricately woven silver chains and ruby glass beads, splintering into a hundred shimmering fragments. "Totally harmless."

The foal stomped a tiny hoof, her way of refusing, and then nose-butted her mother in a bid for reassurance. The sturdy brown mare paid no attention. She was much more interested in the group of students jumping their mounts over low fences in the adjacent arena. Not five minutes earlier, she'd willingly allowed Carly to place a similar necklace on her, one with a matching brow band that dipped to a point in the center.

"Your mother doesn't mind." Carly took a small step forward and lifted the necklace a few inches higher.

The foal turned her head away, much like Carly's son did when he resisted her efforts to wash his face.

"Two pictures. Okay, three. That's all I need for my website."

These pieces of horse jewelry were Carly's latest creations, finished just last evening after she'd put her son to bed. Many of her orders came from her website, and she strove to keep her catalog fresh with a steady stream of new offerings.

When not working at Sweetheart Ranch—she'd been hired this past spring to manage their new wedding boutique Monday through Friday—she sold her original handmade horse jewelry at craft fairs, livestock shows, rodeo events and holiday bazaars. The extra money came in handy since Carly's was a one-income household. *Her* income.

Her ex-husband didn't pay child support and that was just fine with her. She'd gladly agreed to the condition when he abdicated his paternal rights. Someday down the road, she might have to allow him into her son's life. Rickie was bound to ask questions when he was older, and she'd cross that bridge when she came to it. But until that day, she wanted nothing whatsoever to do with the man.

Pretending he didn't exist was the only way she could forget the terrors he'd inflicted on her and the emotional damage he'd caused. The momentary reprieves were too short, however. Fear and worry always returned, burrowing into their hiding place deep in her heart.

"Be good," she told the foal, checking her jeans pocket for how many apple slices and carrot pieces remained, "and I'll give you another treat." Taking one tentative step after the other, she lifted the necklace toward the foal. "That's right. Good girl."

Without warning, the foal squealed and twisted sideways, colliding with the round pen railing. The resulting loud clang startled the mare, and she darted away, the foal prancing beside her as if electricity ran through its slender legs. Carly stepped out of the way while the pair made two full circuits of the round pen before finally slowing.

All the commotion triggered another squeal, this one from Carly's son. He sat buckled in his stroller, which she'd parked just outside the round pen gate in close visual range. He wasn't happy about the arrangement, preferring to be part of the action rather than an observer.

"Shh, honey bun. Mommy will be done soon."

His protests increased in volume, upsetting the foal even more. Carly was about to abandon her efforts and take pictures of just the mare, when a familiar male voice hailed her.

"Hey, I didn't know you were here."

Help, it seemed, was on the way.

She turned and produced a wide smile for JD Moreno, head barn manager here at Powell Ranch, the largest horse facility in Mustang Valley. His constant companion, a tricolor Australian shepherd named Hombre, hurried to the round pen fence. Squeezing his head between the two bottom rails, he stared at the mare and foal, his tongue lolling.

One word from JD and the dog would have climbed in with the horses. He liked nothing better than herding—anything from sheep to cattle to horses. Carly had once seen him nipping at the heels of a group of small children visiting the ranch.

"Last-minute decision," she said, explaining her presence. "My friend said I could use her mare and foal for models. As you can see, it's not working out like I'd hoped." Her gaze traveled from her still-squalling son to the skittish foal.

"How about I give you a hand?"

"I won't say no."

JD started toward the gate. When Hombre whined, he stopped and leveled a finger at the dog. "Stay."

Hombre obediently sat but continued to whine softly, a bundle of nervous energy.

Carly assumed JD would enter the round pen. Instead, he stopped first at the stroller and bent over Rickie.

"How's it going, Rico?" he asked, using his pet name for Rickie.

Instantly, her son stopped fussing and lit up like a starburst. Arms and legs flailing, he babbled a string of nonsense syllables. Carly mentally translated. *Hi, JD! I'm happy to see you. Please play with me.*

JD removed his scuffed cowboy hat and plunked it down on Rickie's head. "Can you hold on to this for me while I help your mama? I'd appreciate it."

Rickie giggled and pulled on the sides of the hat, distorting its shape. JD didn't appear to mind and, after cuffing the boy gently on the chin, he unlatched the gate.

Like Carly, he was also relatively new to town and new to his job. Perhaps that was why they'd become fast friends.

Plus, he was safe. JD had made it clear from the beginning that while he liked her very much, he wasn't in the market for a romance—which was fine with her since she wasn't ready, either. Not that his dark good looks weren't appealing. They were. Extremely. But the timing wasn't right.

Perhaps someday down the road, when their respective lives were less complicated, they could act on their mutual attraction. Until then, they were better off remaining in the friend zone.

"Foal acting skittish?" He entered the round pen and shut the gate behind him.

"She refuses to wear the necklace. I'm afraid if I'm too aggressive, I'll upset her and won't be able to get any decent pictures."

"Hmm. Let me give it a try."

He sauntered toward the mare, prompting Carly to pause. She might not be interested in him romantically, but that didn't make her immune to the confidence he exuded, the mirth twinkling in his chocolate-brown eyes and his crooked grin that hinted at mischief.

Speaking softly in Spanish, he approached the mare and foal, exhibiting the slow, easy manner she found so appealing. At the same time, there was an undeniable determination and deliberateness that surfaced in moments like this. Under different circumstances, Carly's insides would have melted in response.

While she stood and watched, he approached the mare.

"That's right," he murmured, stroking her neck and scratching her between the ears.

The mare visibly relaxed. Her foal appeared equally mesmerized and, surprise, surprise, stood quietly beside her mother, watching JD's every move.

Just like Carly.

He reached an arm out toward her. "Here, give me the necklace."

She did and was even more impressed when he slipped it over the foal's head with no more resistance than a slight head bobble.

"You're a miracle worker," she whispered. "At least with horses and little boys."

"I don't know about that."

He stayed beside the mare and foal for another couple minutes, continuing to stroke the mare and talk to both her and the foal. Then he slowly backed away.

That was Carly's cue to move in and snap

some pictures with her phone. She took them in rapid succession, hoping one or two would be usable. Horses weren't very good about holding still or following instructions on how to pose. She feared there were too many shadows at this time of the morning but kept snapping away. Afternoon would have been a better choice, but she was busy and Rickie didn't tolerate the heat well.

"Are those necklaces new?" JD asked from where he waited by the gate.

"My latest and greatest."

"They're pretty."

"Thanks." She didn't know how much he appreciated them. Men weren't usually into accessorizing their horses. Not like women, who were Carly's main customers. Besides loving her decorative necklaces and "earlaces," they hung her charms on manes and tails and placed bejeweled bracelets around ankles. "I wanted to get a few new designs finished and uploaded to the website before the horse show next weekend at WestWorld."

Carly was fortunate to have weekends off. Especially with June, the busiest month of the year for the popular Western wedding venue, looming right around the corner. Sweetheart Ranch was open on Saturdays and Sundays, but someone else manned the boutique. That allowed Carly the freedom to spend time with her son and her parents and to work on her side business. Her parents frequently accompanied her to wherever she was selling her horse jewelry, helping her with setup and sales but mostly watching Rickie.

"There's a good chance I'll see you there," JD said.

"Yeah? Don't tell me. You've entered some reining and trail classes."

He chuckled—a nice rich, appealing sound. "No, but a few of the ranch's regular customers have. I drew the short straw among the wranglers."

"You sound like you don't mind."

"I have no other plans."

She wondered, did he miss his family in New Mexico or spending every weekend on the rodeo circuit? He'd given up both when he moved to Arizona. "Stop by my booth and see me if you have a few spare minutes. The vendor area is just inside the main entrance."

Carly marveled at how easily she'd extended the casual invitation. She'd once doubted that would be possible again. Her ex-husband had stolen her trust in people and so much more.

Snapping one last picture, she pocketed her phone and removed the necklace from the mare. When the foal trotted off, she said, "I may need your able assistance again."

JD obliged. After putting the halter back on the mare, he slipped the necklace off the foal with almost no trouble.

"Show-off," Carly teased.

"My one talent."

That wasn't true, and they both knew it. JD had been in contention four years running for a World Championship in both bull and bronc riding, finishing in the money but not quite earning the title. That was before his troubles started this past winter and he'd been forced to quit.

Once they exited the round pen, he took over leading the mare and foal while Carly pushed Rickie in his stroller a safe distance away. JD had yet to reclaim his hat despite the boy having fallen asleep.

Hombre scurried after the mare and foal, diving at their feet and yipping loudly. The mare retaliated by throwing out a kick, but Hombre was much too fast and deftly dodged her flying hoof. JD whistled to the dog, who reluctantly trotted back to him.

"We're working on training," he said by way of explanation. "We obviously have a long way to go."

"Not entirely his fault." Carly smiled when

the dog came over to nip at the stroller wheels. "He's young and doing what he was bred for."

At the maternity pasture, Carly rewarded the mare and foal with the remaining treats before JD released them. Hombre bolted into the pasture and took chase. JD whistled, calling him back before the pregnant mares and those with foals scattered. For once, the dog listened.

He rewarded Hombre with a head-scratching. "Good boy."

"The horses don't mind nearly as much as they pretend they do," Carly said. "To them, it's a game."

"Yeah, but what if he got hurt? Or one of the horses? I can't let that happen."

They turned simultaneously to leave, Carly pushing the stroller. Three steps later, JD unexpectedly swayed and knocked into her. The next instant, he moaned and pitched forward.

She caught his arm and instead of him face-planting on the ground, he dropped slowly to his hands and knees. Alarm shot through her.

"JD! JD! Are you okay?"

THE FIRST THING JD heard when the cotton batting surrounding his head finally lifted was Hombre's insistent barking. Next was Carly's sharp...scolding?

Wait. When did she ever raise her voice? Never. Not even with Rickie.

"No, Hombre," she shouted. "Be quiet."

"It's okay," JD croaked.

Hombre didn't stop. He wouldn't until JD reassured him. Reaching out an arm, he gathered the dog into a hug.

"Good boy," he said.

Hombre licked his face over and over, further rousing JD.

Carly knelt down beside him and cradled him with her arm. "You all right?"

"Just embarrassed."

"Oh, my God. Don't be. It's not your fault."

He didn't need to explain to her what had happened. She'd witnessed this before, unfortunately—though not to this extent. His Meniere's Disease seemed to always pick the worst possible moments for an attack.

Once, he'd collapsed in the middle of an elevator full of people. Another time, he'd thrown up at the table while having breakfast with his rodeo buddies. He doubted he'd ever live down that humiliation. The worst had been when he staggered from the arena after being thrown two-point-six seconds into his bull ride. Everyone assumed he'd been injured, and they'd called the medics. He'd had to explain he was simply dizzy and disorientated.

Soon after, JD had gone to his first doctor. Two months and two new doctors later, he had a diagnosis. Turned out, his condition wasn't life-threatening. It was, however, lifestyle-altering. Extreme sports were out of the question, and that included rodeo. Just swimming in the ocean or riding a bike down the street could be dangerous.

Worst of all, he may have to give up driving altogether if the attacks worsened in frequency and severity. And a romantic relationship? Out of the question. How could he get involved with someone when he had no idea what the future held for him, work-wise or health-wise? That seemed unfair—even if the woman was willing.

Honestly, he'd been lucky to wind up at Powell Ranch, taking over the job of head barn manager from his good buddy Tanner Bridwell, who'd recently returned to bull riding after a year off. JD hoped for the same outcome: to pick right up where he'd left off.

The only drawback was leaving his family behind in Las Cruces, New Mexico. He missed them, accustomed to returning home regularly during breaks on the rodeo circuit. Between his new job and inability to easily travel, he wouldn't be heading home anytime soon. Another reason to resent his new limitations.

Patting Hombre's head, he pushed himself to his feet, wishing his legs weren't so wobbly. Carly gripped his arm, surprisingly strong for such a tiny person.

He tried not to notice her proximity and how much he liked it. As always, he failed.

Not for the first time, he wondered what had gone wrong in her marriage. If she'd been his wife, and Rickie his son, nothing short of world disaster would have made him leave her.

Except it was the other way around. *She'd* left her ex-husband. And from what little she'd shared with JD, for good reason. He admitted to being curious about the details but hadn't pressed her. If she wanted him to know, she'd tell him.

"Go slow," she warned, still supporting him.

"Thanks. And, please. No posting this on social media."

"What!" Her brow rose, emphasizing her expressive green eyes. "I swear… I—"

"I'm kidding." He smiled down at her.

"JD." She gave him a playful jab in the ribs. "Oops, sorry. I shouldn't have done that."

"I'm fine." He was. Thanks to her. "Is Rickie okay?"

"Still sound asleep. I can't believe Hombre's barking didn't wake him." She let go of JD and grabbed the stroller handle.

Together, they headed toward her car. Hombre trotted along, not at JD's heels but weaving back and forth from one distraction to another. When he wasn't herding, he was investigating.

"I didn't mean to snap at you earlier," JD said. "But his barking helps me to focus when I have an attack."

"You didn't snap. And now that I know about Hombre, I won't try to hush him next time."

Next time? JD hoped there wasn't one. "Too bad I can't take him everywhere with me."

"What if he was a certified service dog?"

"He doesn't have the personality or the restraint. He gets excited when there's a lot going on and forgets to listen. Kind of like having doggie ADHD."

"Aw." She cast Hombre a sorry look. "Poor guy has a short attention span."

As if to demonstrate, the dog went from digging at a spot beside a rock to chasing a bird foolish enough to land nearby to spinning in a circle. All in a matter of thirty seconds.

"Yeah, but he still has a lot of puppy in him." JD had gotten the dog five months ago from a rescue organization. "I'm hoping he'll settle down as he gets older."

At her car, they lingered, chatting as if neither of them was quite ready to part. Carly parked the stroller in the shade and adjusted the cover, making sure Rickie wouldn't get overheated.

He really was a cute little kid, thought JD. And pretty well behaved. Not that JD had much experience. He hadn't lived near his sister since long before her kids were born, and none of his former girlfriends had been mothers.

Not that he considered being a single mother a deterrent to dating. Were their situations different, he'd ask Carly out in a heartbeat.

"Have you changed your mind about surgery or implants?" she asked.

"No, though I may have no choice. Especially if I suffer any significant hearing loss, which can happen. For now, I'm self-managing with medicine and coping techniques." Except he wasn't managing. Not well, anyway, as today had proven.

"What kind of coping techniques?"

"The usual. Exercise and diet. Limiting my salt and caffeine and alcohol. I also use a pulse generator."

"Does it help?"

"A little. Balance exercises, music therapy and meditation work better."

"Meditation?" A smile pulled at her mouth.

"I get it. Hard to imagine a big lug like me sitting cross-legged on the floor listening to soothing music and chanting while I imagine myself inside a blue aura."

"Do you?" She laughed. "Chant and imagine a blue aura?"

He laughed along with her. "I'm not telling."

"I think it's great." She retrieved his hat from atop Rickie, plunking it down on JD's head. "And you're not a big lug. Not a lug, anyway."

Huh. If he didn't know better—and he *did* know better—he'd think she was flirting.

Clearing his throat, he said, "The thing about Meniere's Disease, it's a vicious cycle. Stress can trigger an attack, but having the condition is what causes me the most stress."

"Because you're worried you'll have an attack?"

"That. I also don't sleep well, my social life is practically nonexistent and half my free time is eaten up with managing my health."

He skipped the part about being unemployed for months before he landed the job at Powell Ranch and how he'd only been hired because his buddy Tanner vouched for him. Being a walking liability and answering yes to the question about having a physical condition that could potentially affect his job made getting hired next to impossible. Neither did he mention his dismal dating prospects.

"Who knows if I'll ever live a normal life again?"

"You will," Carly assured him. "You said yourself you're making progress."

"Not as fast or as much as I'd like." With each passing week, a rodeo comeback felt less and less obtainable.

"What will you do if you can't ride bulls and broncs anymore?"

"That's a good question. I've never wanted to do anything else."

"You must have considered a career path once you retired from the circuit."

"Not enough, obviously." He shook his head. "Poor planning on my part."

Every occupation he might have pursued, like ranch manager or horse trainer or bull-riding instructor, was inconceivable for someone who couldn't sit a horse without the risk of falling off. He supposed he was lucky. There were some people with his condition who became housebound or even bedbound.

"Oh, gosh." Carly checked the time on her step tracker and opened the rear door on her car. "I need to run. I promised my parents I'd be there by noon."

"Lunch again?"

"Are you kidding? I don't dare miss it."

She spent every Saturday with her parents,

rain or shine. It wasn't just so Grandma and Grandpa could see Rickie. Carly had spoken of her traditional parents and her strict, ultra-conservative upbringing. She'd been raised with certain expectations that had continued even after she grew up and moved away. Regular weekly visits were one of them.

JD watched as she loaded a sleeping Rickie into the car seat, grinning when she double-checked each buckle. He then helped her collapse and stow the stroller in the trunk.

"I'll see you around, then," he said when they were done.

She closed the trunk and swiped her hands together. "On Monday for sure. At the boutique," she prompted when he stared at her blankly.

"That's right."

He'd agreed to pick up the bolo ties and cuff links for Tanner. In two weeks, Tanner and his fiancée were getting married at Sweetheart Ranch. The bolo ties and cuff links had been specially ordered to match the groom and groomsmen's Western attire. JD had been deeply honored when Tanner asked him to stand with his brother and was happy to help.

"I'll call you if by chance the shipment doesn't arrive," Carly told him and slid in behind the steering wheel.

He retreated a few steps, intending to wait and wave while she pulled out. Except the ground suddenly shifted beneath his feet and his stomach dropped to his knees.

"JD? Are you all right?" Carly's voice sounded twenty feet away.

"Yeah." He swayed, and Hombre suddenly appeared at his side, barking insistently.

"I've got you," Carly said.

He felt her hand gripping his arm hard. Wasn't she in her car?

A wave of nausea hit. *No*, he silently hollered. *Not again!*

Concentrating on Hombre's barking, he blindly reached for the nearest solid object to anchor himself. Finding one, he closed his eyes and counted his breaths. All kidding aside, meditation techniques did sometimes stave off an attack. And they did today.

Inch by inch, the thick fog vanished. Little by little, the ground beneath his feet stabilized. Bit by bit, his stomach settled.

"Better?"

He opened his eyes and was surprised to find Carly's face inches from his and his arm wrapped around her. Concern filled her expression as she studied him intently.

"I'm fine," he muttered.

What was wrong with him today? Two attacks not twenty minutes apart. Could it be the heat? Temperatures had been higher than usual for May. Stress? No. He wasn't under any more than usual. That one beer he'd had with his buddies last night at the Poco Dinero Bar and Grill? Unlikely. If alcohol were the culprit, he'd have had an attack last night, not sixteen hours later.

"Maybe you should go lie down for a while," Carly suggested.

"No."

He wasn't sure his ego could take any more hits. First, he'd nearly passed out in front of a woman and then she'd suggested he lie down.

"JD," Carly pleaded. "You need to take care of yourself."

Her voice contained the same worried quality his mother's always had when he called her before every rodeo. Only his mother used his given name, Juan Diego, and added *mijo* on the end.

"I will."

"Promise?"

He removed his arm. "This is becoming a habit."

He'd meant the remark as a joke. But when their gazes connected, the sudden shock of awareness coursing through him was anything but funny.

They stayed rooted in place for several seconds, with JD caught in Carly's magnetic pull and unable to escape. Why hadn't he ever noticed that the color of her eyes changed from hazel to jade in the sunlight? Or that tiny mole above her left eyebrow?

"You are one gorgeous woman, Carly Leighton."

Her smile slowly dimmed, and she backed away, her hand falling to her side.

"I'd better go."

"Sure. Right. Drive careful." He, too, backed away, murmuring, "What an idiot," under his breath as she drove away.

He could blame the Meniere's Disease for his unintentional slip, except that would be a lie. JD had merely spoken out loud what he'd kept trying not to think about since the day he and Carly had met.

CHAPTER TWO

JD COULDN'T REMEMBER the last time he'd felt so completely out of his comfort zone. Maybe when he'd taken his cousin to her obstetrician appointment because her husband was stuck at work. Or when his then girlfriend had insisted they go on a pottery painting date. The paintbrushes he was used to holding were fat and thick and the kind used on houses or barns. Not ceramic figurines.

Everything in the Sweetheart Ranch wedding boutique was like those tiny ceramic figurines—small, delicate and breakable. If he moved a fraction too fast or an inch the wrong way, he'd be reaching for his wallet to cover the replacement cost of whatever he broke.

He didn't dare imagine the resulting wreckage if he had an attack and went down here. He'd almost refused his friend Tanner this favor for fear of embarrassing himself.

Not for the first time today, JD resented his affliction and the effects it had on every aspect of his life. Thank goodness there weren't any customers in the boutique.

His gaze traveled the large room with its floor-to-ceiling display shelves. Carly was nowhere in sight. So much for accomplishing his task quickly and getting the heck out of there.

It was then he noticed a silver plaque on an antique-looking desk that read Be Right Back… Have a Look Around. Beneath the words were two interlocking wedding rings.

JD did look around—for a seat. He figured the safest place for him was remaining perfectly still with his arms crossed over his chest.

The only available chairs, other than the one behind the desk, were at a table in the far corner of the boutique. Between here and there stretched an endless obstacle course of mannequin heads wearing long sheer veils, glass cabinets containing garters and stockings, and frilly, lacy undergarments. An entire section was dedicated to different miniature couples in various poses and combinations, everything from the traditional bride and groom to cartoon characters. He even spotted a saguaro cacti couple. Another section held cake toppers, according to the sign. Printed beneath the description was a warning to please not touch. No problem there.

He considered waiting for Carly in the parlor. Better yet, on the bench in the foyer, close to the door should he start feeling dizzy. Anywhere else at Sweetheart Ranch's sprawling country house other than the boutique.

The next second, he squared his shoulders. He'd made a promise to Tanner, and he wasn't about to let anything interfere. His friend had yet to return from Kingman—the Andy Devine Days Rodeo was his last event until after he returned from his honeymoon. JD had considered the dangers of a wedding boutique when he'd agreed to run the errand, but couldn't say no. Not to Tanner. And besides, he'd get to see Carly.

JD had been unsure what to expect. In all his twenty-nine years, he hadn't once entered a wedding boutique or, for that matter, come close to saying I do. Sure, there'd been a couple long-term relationships that might have gone somewhere…until they hadn't. His fault. Every woman he'd dated had grown weary of a boyfriend who was gone most weekends, missed important dates like birthdays and anniversaries, and spent several weeks, if not months, every year laid up from injuries.

"Hi. You waiting for Carly?"

He spun and automatically removed his hat, stopping himself in the nick of time before he knocked into a velvet-lined tray holding an assortment of gloves.

"Ah, yeah. I am." Recognizing Molly Caufield, he smiled.

He'd met Sweetheart Ranch's head of guest relations once before when delivering rental horses for a trail ride wedding. Since the two neighboring businesses weren't competitors, they enjoyed a friendly relationship and often referred clients to the other.

Molly recognized him, too. "You're JD. One of Tanner Bridwell's groomsmen."

"Yes, ma'am. I'm supposed to pick up some bolo ties and cuff links." He shifted uncomfortably. The room had shrunk to half its size with the addition of another person.

"Ah." Molly's glance cut to the stack of boxes behind the antique desk. "I'm going to let Carly help you with those. I don't want to mess with her system. She's a stickler for detail."

"No worries. I'll wait."

"She mentioned the two of you have become good friends."

JD was unsure how to take this remark. Molly could simply be making conversation, or she could be warning him that Carly was vulnerable and didn't need any potential problems.

If the latter, she was wasting her time. He'd been giving himself the same lecture these past two days. Ever since his filter had malfunctioned and he'd called her gorgeous. Based on her immediate withdrawal and hasty exit, his plan to act as if his momentary lapse of judgment never happened was a good one.

"She's pretty special," he said to Molly. "A genuinely nice person."

"That she is. Still fragile on the inside, however. It's only been a year and a half since her divorce, and her ex is a real piece of work."

Okay, definitely warning him off. JD didn't disagree. He often saw the vulnerability Carly tried to hide.

"I would never hurt her," he assured Molly.

"Of course not. I wasn't implying that."

"You have nothing to worry about."

Her demeanor gentled. "I apologize if I spoke out of turn. Even though Carly's only worked for us a short time, she's already like a member of the family. We adore her, and are a bit overprotective."

"I understand. I'm protective of her, too." He didn't have to be told what her ex had put her through to know he'd go to any lengths to ensure her safety.

"She's lucky to have you for a friend." Molly's eyes shone with a respect that hadn't been there when she first greeted him.

"I'm the lucky one."

Conversation stopped when, at that moment, Carly entered the boutique, showering JD and Molly with a bright smile. Unlike him, she glided around every potential obstacle with grace and ease and confidence.

"Hello! Hope you weren't waiting too long."

Feeling Molly's eyes on him, JD strove for nonchalance. Inside, he lit up like a kid at a birthday party. "Just got here, in fact."

"And I'm just leaving." Molly checked the clock on the wall. "We have two weddings today, and I'm running late. Nice to see you again, JD."

She hurried out of the boutique, leaving JD and Carly alone.

"Sorry I wasn't here when you arrived." She squeezed in behind the antique desk. "I've had one customer after another since we opened this morning. Thought I'd starve before I got a chance to eat lunch."

"Is it always this busy?"

"No, thank goodness. But June is fast approaching, the most popular month of the year to get married. Can you believe we have nearly forty weddings scheduled? I've sold three guest books and feather pen sets in the last hour alone."

"How do they fit all those weddings in? Assembly line?"

"No. That would be a nightmare to coordinate, what with setting up and the cleaning afterward. They're spread throughout the day. Sunrise weddings, sunset, midnight..."

"People actually get married at midnight? Seems a little hard on the guests."

"I imagine it is." Carly laughed and motioned him closer. JD advanced carefully, mindful of every step.

"I haven't opened it yet." She bent and retrieved the package from the stack. "I was waiting for you."

Her warm tone dispelled any worries that his big mouth had cost him their friendship. She was the same Carly as always, no hint of awkwardness or ill ease.

Using a small utility knife, Carly sliced through the package tape and removed the smaller boxes inside buried beneath layers of bubble wrap.

"You don't need to take everything out," he said. "I'll just grab the package and be on my way."

"Better make sure the company sent the correct order. We don't want to discover at the last minute that you're short one bolo tie or the cuff links are the wrong style."

He supposed she was right.

"Let's see what we have here." She opened the first white box.

Nestled inside on a bed of cotton lay a gold bolo tie with a large ruby-colored gemstone set in the center. JD recalled being told about the color and style of the bolo ties, but he hadn't been able to picture them.

Carly let out a small gasp of delight and gingerly lifted the tie from the box, laying it across her open palm. "So pretty. And it goes perfectly with your shirts."

JD was a throw-on-the-first-clean-thing-he-found kind of dresser. But even he could see how well the tie matched.

The wedding shirts were a deep maroon, chosen to complement the black Western-cut tuxedos they'd rented from the upscale men's clothing store in Scottsdale. Tanner's bride, who'd gone with them, had accused JD, Tanner and Tanner's brother, Daniel, of looking like a band of outlaws in their all-black attire. Then, she'd kissed Tanner full on the mouth as if she hadn't cared who saw them.

JD had forgotten about the bolo ties and cuff links but not that kiss. He'd been genuinely happy for his friend and, admittedly, a little jealous. Maybe one of these days, once his Meniere's Disease had improved, he'd find a woman who would kiss him like that.

"Now for the cuff links." Carly opened another box and removed a pair of gold-and-zirconia cuff links in the shape of a horseshoe. "I love them!"

JD waited while she inspected every box. Only when she'd assured herself the order had been correctly filled did she reassemble the package. Except for the last box.

"You should try on a bolo tie."

"I'm sure it'll fit. They're adjustable."

"What if the clasp is broken?"

He highly doubted that.

"Come on, JD." She gave him a look he suspected was the same one she used with her son when he put up a fight.

"Fine." He reached for the tie only to realize he had nowhere to set his hat.

She correctly read his confusion and said, "Here. Give it to me."

Pivoting, she hung the hat on a peg by the mirror. JD slid the bolo tie over his head and tucked it beneath his collar. His work shirt felt shabby next to the shiny gold and sparkling gemstone. Fiddling with the clasp, he attempted to adjust the tie's length, but his big clumsy fingers hindered the task.

Carly came out from behind the desk. "Let me."

Before he could refuse, she stopped in front of him and reached for the tie. Her fingers, much smaller and defter than his, tugged and pushed and pulled. More than once, they brushed lightly against his chest like butterfly wings.

He held his breath. Then, he didn't, inhaling the flowery scent of whatever lotion or shampoo she'd recently used.

A naturopath doctor he'd seen on the recommendation of his cousin had suggested aromatherapy as a stress reliever. JD had refused and not returned to the doctor for a follow-up visit. Meditation was one thing, smelling a bunch of lotions and oils another.

Carly had him reconsidering. With his attention riveted on her, there was no chance of an attack.

Retreating a step, she inspected her handiwork. "Wow. Very handsome."

The tie. She couldn't be talking about him. He struggled to swallow, his throat suddenly bone-dry.

"Thanks for your help," he croaked.

"Of course. My pleasure." Her features brightened on the last two words as if she had indeed enjoyed herself.

Helping people was her nature, he reminded himself. And her job. He wasn't receiving special treatment.

Slipping off the tie, he changed the subject

to a safer one. “You make any new pieces of jewelry for the horse show this weekend?”

“I wish.” She resealed the delivery package and presented it to him. “Been having some trouble building my new display.”

“What’s the problem?”

She escorted him through the boutique door and into the parlor where wedding receptions and luncheons were held. “Apparently, while I’m good at making jewelry, those same skills don’t carry over to larger projects.”

“I’m handy with a hammer and pliers. I could be your assistant.” The offer was out before JD realized it.

“That’s awfully nice of you, but I can’t impose.”

He should relent, but he didn’t. “What about tomorrow evening?”

“Okay, but only if you let me fix you dinner.”

“Deal.”

They reached the foyer where Molly sat behind the registration counter, another antique from the looks of it. Thankfully, she was on the phone and unable to do more than cast them a curious glance.

Outside, JD and Carly traded air-conditioned comfort for sweltering heat. They bid goodbye on the large veranda that ran the entire length of the house. During the walk to his truck, he commended himself for not blurting another unintentional remark.

All he had to do now was stay the course tomorrow night. Shouldn't be hard. It was just building a jewelry display and a casual dinner between friends. Perfectly innocent.

Why, then, did it feel a lot like a date?

CASSEROLE NEARLY DONE, oven temp lowered to warm: check. Salad prepared and chilling in refrigerator: check. Baguette on counter ready to slice: check. Garlic butter also on counter softening: check. Array of beverages on hand: check. Rickie playing contentedly in the middle of the kitchen floor with wooden spoons, pans and plastic cups: smiley face. Clean kitchen before JD arrives: check.

Should she set out candles? What about music?

"Now you're being ridiculous," she murmured, only to place a silk flower arrangement in the center of the table.

During the three months she and JD had known each other, not once was there such a definitive… What to call it? A moment, she supposed. No, spark was a better description. She'd spent much of the last few days replaying those few seconds and overanalyzing every detail.

Did this mean she was ready to start dating again? What about JD? Was he ready?

He'd experienced the same spark as her. She'd seen the flash in his eyes, instantly recognizing it for what it was. But he'd been adamant about his unwillingness to bring a ton of baggage into any potential relationship.

Carly couldn't agree more. She had her own baggage to contend with. Unresolved baggage, according to her parents and best friend Becca. They insisted that her pretending she hadn't suffered at the hands of her ex, Pat, didn't make everything go away.

The thing was, Carly preferred not to dwell on the past. She'd much rather look to the future. Plus, she had a young son who depended entirely on her. She had to be strong for him.

Returning to the kitchen, she considered how best to handle this sudden change between her and JD. Yesterday at the boutique, she'd pretended ignorance. Well, not entirely. She'd had no reason to insist he try on the bolo tie. But she'd wanted to see if their shared spark at her car was an isolated incident or, possibly, a figment of her imagination.

It hadn't been either of those. Carly's skills weren't so rusty she couldn't tell when a man found her attractive and—dare she say it?—wanted to kiss her.

Would she have kissed him back if he'd tried? Likely. With that slow, easy manner of his, JD was surely a good kisser, and Carly wasn't made of stone.

But then what? They'd have both awkwardly retreated and apologized, regretting their actions and the potential demise of their friendship.

She watched Rickie crawl across the floor, pushing an overturned pan in front of him. He got as far as the corner where the two lower cabinets joined, wedging the pan in tight. Unable to move it forward or sideways, and not yet understanding the concept of reverse, he plopped down on his bottom, screwed his face into a mask of anger and frustration, and let out an earsplitting wail.

Carly started to move. The sight of her son's expression stopped her cold. Whenever his temper flared, Rickie's resemblance to his father during those stormy days was uncanny, and she went weak with worry. What if he'd inherited Pat's tendency to…

No, Rickie wasn't like his father. All babies his age were prone to tantrums. It was normal and something he'd outgrow. Especially without having Pat around as an example, thank God. Nurture trumped nature—she'd see to it.

Crossing to where Rickie sat, she bent and

lifted him into her arms. His wailing gradually decreased to a whine.

"Hey, little man. What's all the fuss about?"

His response was a string of nonsense syllables that ended with "Mama."

"How about we put you in the playpen? Mommy needs to get ready before our company arrives. You be a good boy, okay?"

She carried him to the middle of the family room where the playpen stood surrounded by stacks of toys and picture books. Until an hour ago, there'd been two loads of clean unfolded laundry strewn on the couch, a pile of shoes in the corner and parenting magazines scattered about.

Lowering Rickie into the playpen, she handed him an activity ball and turned on a musical teddy bear that played a dozen tunes in a row.

Satisfied he was safely contained and happily occupied, she headed toward the bathroom, where she sprayed styling product on her hair while simultaneously finger combing the short strands. Next, she applied fresh mascara and lipstick. Not to impress JD. She'd go through this same routine for anyone. She would. Really.

Deciding a clean shirt was in order, she rummaged through her closet, discarding most options for one reason or another before settling on one. The fact she picked her most flattering shirt was totally irrelevant.

While putting away the pots and pans, her phone rang from where she'd left it on the kitchen counter. The distinctive ringtone identified the caller as Carly's friend Becca, who also happened to own the mare and foal she used for horse models.

Shooting Rickie a quick glance, she answered with a bright "Hey, you. What's up?"

"Calling to say hi before your big date."

"It's not a date."

"Yeah. Sure. Whatever you say."

"Becca!"

"Tell me he's not utterly gorgeous."

Funny that she picked the same word JD had called Carly. "You're right. He is."

"You bet I'm right. Chocolate-brown eyes. Chiseled features. Dark and brooding."

"JD isn't brooding."

"Let's change that to has a great smile. And his voice. That incredible accent..." Becca gave an exaggerated moan. "I could listen to him all day long."

JD did have a great voice. Especially when he spoke Spanish.

"Not a date," Carly repeated.

"Relax, will you? No judging here. I think it's high time you tested the dating waters."

"It's too soon."

"Then go slow. JD's the perfect guy for that. He's in no rush, either."

"He's in no rush because he's not interested," Carly said. "In me or anyone."

"Are you sure about that?"

She recalled the way he'd leaned in and the intensity radiating off him when she was adjusting the bolo tie.

"Even if he was interested, he's not going to act on it. Not now."

"All right, all right," Becca grumped. "Message received. I'm done nagging you. But if not JD, pick someone else. There's no shortage of good-looking eligible men in Mustang Valley. Hello, we're a horse-and-cattle town. We draw cowboys like bees to nectar. Oh, oh! What about the horse show this weekend? Plenty of pickings there."

"Dating is a big step." Carly gnawed her lower lip. "A big scary step."

"Did it ever occur to you that by not dating, you're letting Pat continue to control your life?"

She hadn't. But, then, neither had Carly imagined the turn her life would take.

During her and Pat's first year together,

they'd experienced the kind of ups and downs normal for most newlyweds. The periodic argument followed by making up. Marriage was an adjustment, after all, with a steep learning curve.

Things changed during their second year when he lost his job and couldn't find another one. His drinking, previously restricted to weekends, had intensified, becoming daily. Then, the drunken, angry outbursts had started. Yelling. Name-calling. Throwing objects. Punching holes in walls. He was always sorry afterward and repaired or replaced whatever he'd broken. Everything but Carly's damaged heart.

Her pregnancy had come as a surprise—she and Pat hadn't been planning on children anytime soon. Nonetheless, Carly was delighted. She'd always wanted children. Pat, on the other hand, took the news poorly. He'd only recently landed a new job, and they were deeply in debt after his five months of unemployment and alcohol spending sprees.

He'd *celebrated* the news of her pregnancy by getting into a drunken fistfight in a bar parking lot. After he returned home, driving when he had no business being on the road, Carly had confronted him. That was when he'd grabbed her by the arm and shoved her into a wall hard enough to rattle her teeth.

Everything changed for her in that moment. While Pat had been passed out on the bed, she'd escaped to Becca's house. It had taken him until the next afternoon to sober up enough to track her down. His fury had known no bounds. In his warped thinking, Carly should have stayed put until he told her otherwise.

"Do you ever think about that day?" she asked Becca, not needing to specify.

"Sometimes."

"I'm sorry I involved you."

"I'm not." Becca's voice shuddered. "I hate to think what would have happened if you'd been alone with him when he went on his rampage."

"I used to tell myself he'd never hurt me. Not physically. Walls, yes. Windows, sure. But that he loved me too much to lay a hand on me." Carly's throat constricted with fresh pain and grief and also guilt. For involving Becca and allowing Pat to get away with his abuse for much too long before taking action. "I was wrong. He was very capable of hurting me and anyone who got in his way. Like you," she choked out.

"Trust me, I'm glad I was there. If he'd

smacked you the way he did me, you might have lost the baby."

"Have you recovered?" Carly often worried her friend still grappled with the consequences. "That had to be traumatic. I was traumatized just watching it."

"I'm fine. No nightmares or hang-ups." She snorted with disgust. "The SOB's not worth my mental and emotional anguish."

"You'll get no argument from me."

"What about you?" Becca asked, concern tinging her voice. "Are you having nightmares?"

"Are you kidding? I'm fine."

"You went through a lot, Carly. A few counseling sessions or a support group might really make a difference."

"With my schedule, I don't have time."

"That's a terrible excuse."

"I have you and Rickie and my parents. That's all the counseling and support group I need."

"You're avoiding again."

"Probably."

Carly closed her eyes. With very little effort, she could see the vivid red stain on Becca's cheek. Pat had backhanded her when she bravely put herself between him and Carly. The second Becca recovered from the blow, she'd called 9-1-1. Pat had been too infuriated and too focused on Carly to realize what Becca had done—until the police arrived, and he was carted away in handcuffs.

The moment had been a defining one for Carly, and she'd vowed to escape Pat and her miserable marriage. No child of hers would be raised in a toxic environment or grow up fearing his or her parent's wrath. She'd been forced to wait until after Rickie's birth to finalize the divorce and custody, but she'd moved in with Becca almost immediately after that terrible day and they both quickly obtained restraining orders against Pat.

"If not for you, I don't know where I'd be." Carly wandered over to the playpen and patted Rickie's downy blond hair. Other than when he was crying, he looked like a miniature version of her.

"I can't tell you how glad I am he agreed to abdicate his rights, even if you did give up child support. You and Rickie are better off without him."

"You didn't have to drop the charges. He assaulted you."

"He assaulted both of us and should have been punished for what he did." Conviction rang in Becca's voice. "But since dropping the charges got you and Rickie free of him, I'd do it again. A hundred times over if necessary."

"You're a good friend." Tears sprang to Carly's eyes, and she blinked them away. "I can't ever repay you."

"No need. You've had my back since sophomore social studies class."

"Nothing compares to what you've done. You gave me a place to stay until after Rickie was born, introduced me to the owner of Sweetheart Ranch and helped me find this house."

Moving had turned out to be the best decision Carly could have made. She and Rickie were thriving in the peaceful, friendly town.

"I had an ulterior motive," Becca said. "I wanted you and Rickie close to me."

"I wish Pat didn't have my address. Can't be avoided, I guess. But I swear, if he ever violates the terms of our divorce and comes sniffing around, I'll see he suffers the consequences."

"Thatta girl! Stay strong."

The timer on Carly's oven went off, giving her a start. She'd set it as a reminder for herself.

"Oops, I've got to run. JD will be here in ten."

"Call me tomorrow and let me know how your non-date goes," Becca insisted. "I can't wait to hear. Every juicy tidbit."

"There won't be any."

"You say that now."

Carly disconnected after saying goodbye and executed a last-minute sweep of the kitchen and family room. Talking about Pat always released a flood of negative emotions. She compartmentalized them, as was her habit, and stowed them away rather than let them ruin her evening with JD.

Hearing Rickie's sharp yelp, she rushed to investigate. He'd abandoned his toys and now stood, holding on to the playpen's side and bouncing excitedly. At thirteen months, he still wasn't walking, though he did a lot of "cruising" from one piece of furniture to the next. His pediatrician had repeatedly assured Carly that Rickie would start walking when he was ready. She had no reason to fret.

Her biggest fear was that he'd take his first solo step while at day care and she'd miss the greatly anticipated milestone. As much as she longed to be a stay-at-home mom, she needed the income her two jobs provided.

If her horse jewelry business continued to grow, she might one day be able to turn it into a full-time job. If not, she'd gladly remain at Sweetheart Ranch. She loved managing the boutique. Having a small role in the best day of couples' lives had gone a long way toward restoring Carly's faith in the institution of marriage.

"Hey, little man. What's wrong?"

Rickie's wide grin revealed six front teeth. "Mama. Mama. Bah-boo."

"Let's wait on the bottle until bedtime."

Apparently understanding her, he wrinkled his brow and let out a disgruntled I'm-hungry squawk.

"Okay, you can have a cookie."

"Cah-cah. Cah-cah."

"Hmm. We need to practice that word. Someone's going to get the wrong idea."

Smiling, she went to the kitchen and fetched two teething biscuits—what she called cookies. She'd already fed, bathed and dressed Rickie in his pajamas. That way, she could give him his bottle and put him to bed with little disruption to dinner or building the jewelry display.

Rickie's face lit up at the sight of the teething biscuits. He reached eagerly with one hand while holding on to the playpen with the other one. "Me, me, me."

"Here you go."

He stuffed the first biscuit in his mouth and began gnawing. Most of the second biscuit dissolved into a mush that ended up on his face and hands rather than in his tummy. When she returned from the bathroom with a warm, wet washcloth, she found him shaking the sides of the playpen in an attempt to climb out. Before long, he'd succeed. Another milestone reached. They were coming in rapid succession.

"You made quite a mess of yourself," she crooned, wiping his face and hands clean.

As she was rinsing out the washcloth in the bathroom sink, the doorbell rang.

"Right on time," Carly said and speed-walked to the front door.

From the family room, Rickie hollered a string of nonsense syllables. He'd recently figured out that a ringing doorbell signaled visitors. And not being the shy type—he loved people, and they generally loved him—he couldn't contain his excitement.

Peering through the peephole, Carly caught sight of JD removing his hat and smoothing his rumpled brown hair into a semblance of order. Was he nervous?

If yes, he wasn't alone. Carly tried to tamp down her anticipation as she turned the knob.

"Hi." She went still, unable to stop staring. He'd dressed up for the occasion, donning a short-sleeved Western shirt to go with his pressed jeans and polished boots. "You look… nice."

She'd resisted her first impulse to say *handsome* even though it was true.

"Hope you don't mind." His smile turned apologetic. "I brought a guest with me. He can stay in the backyard if it's a problem."

Guest? Backyard? Problem? Carly looked around, confused.

When JD's guest stuck a wet brown nose out from behind his legs, she laughed and swung the door wide.

"Come on in, you two."

CHAPTER THREE

CARLY GESTURED FOR JD and Hombre to follow her into the family room. There, they were greeted by Rickie's excited babbling. Hombre zoomed straight to the playpen, his tail wagging and a happy dog grin on his face. Much to Rickie's delight, Hombre jumped up and placed his front paws on the playpen's side. Rickie promptly grabbed the sides of the dog's head with his chubby hands and tugged on his fur.

"Down, Hombre," JD scolded. "Come here."

The dog ignored him, having eyes only for Rickie. He lapped at the boy's face, reducing Rickie to a puddle of giggles.

"He's fine." Carly delayed JD with her hand when he started toward the playpen. "Rickie loves dogs. I'm hoping to adopt one when he's older."

"Feel free to borrow Hombre anytime."

"I may take you up on that offer."

She didn't worry that the dog might hurt Rickie. The two had interacted often at the ranch, and Hombre, despite his young age, instinctively tempered his enthusiasm with small children.

"Enough, Hombre. Down."

"I really don't mind," Carly said.

"He's not supposed to jump on furniture. That's one of the bunkhouse rules." He leveled a finger at the dog. "Sit, or you're going outside."

Hombre lowered his ears and stepped gingerly down.

"That's better."

Carly liked that JD didn't use force with the dog. "Thanks for coming tonight."

"Thanks for dinner. Whatever you're cooking smells great."

"Just a casserole."

"No such thing as just a casserole to a man who survives on mostly takeout pizza and packaged dinners."

"It's ready now if you're hungry," she said.

"You can't hear my stomach growling?"

She made her way to the kitchen. Keeping an eye on her guests and son, she transported food from the oven and refrigerator to the table in the adjoining dining area.

"No, Hombre. Leave It."

Poor JD. Try as he might, he couldn't control a determined one-year-old and a dog with puppy tendencies.

Carly stifled a laugh as she watched Rickie toss a plush frog out of the playpen and onto the floor. Hombre dove after the toy and, front feet dancing, returned it to Rickie, who immediately tossed the toy again.

"Hombre! I said Leave It."

The dog reluctantly obeyed, turning miserable eyes on JD.

"Let him have his fun," Carly said.

"He'll tear the toy to pieces."

"It wasn't expensive." And, now coated with dog slobber, it needed laundering, anyway.

Clutching the playpen railing, Rickie stooped and selected another toy. Then another. He tossed each one onto the floor, sending Hombre into a frenzy. Disobeying JD, the dog collected each new toy and dropped it in an ever-growing pile.

JD shook his head dejectedly. "What am I going to do with you, boy?"

"You know, he's pretty smart. Have you considered enrolling him in obedience school?" Carly set a pitcher of iced tea on the table. "Might be a way to direct all that excess energy into a productive outlet."

"I need to do something. He's going to get me fired."

Carly doubted that. She'd met JD's boss. He'd impressed her as a reasonable person.

"One of my regular customers is a dog agility instructor. She gives classes at the park in town. If you're interested, I'll give you her number."

"Dog agility? Is that where they train dogs to go through tunnels and leap fences?"

"There's more to it than that, so my customer says."

"Really? When's her class and how much does it cost?"

"I'll tell you what I know over dinner. Let's eat before the casserole gets cold."

Carly grabbed Rickie from the playpen and carried him to his high chair at the table. She no sooner secured the safety belt than he started slapping the tray with his palms. She quieted him with some banana slices. He'd already eaten and probably wasn't hungry. But if she left him in the playpen, he'd cry through the entire dinner.

JD waited for her to sit first. Old-school manners, she noted. Her dad would like that, being old-school himself.

The round of toy-tossing must have worn out Hombre, because he lay on the floor beside JD's chair. That, or he was hoping for a handout. He got one, too. From Rickie, who flung a piece of banana onto the floor.

Carly feigned exasperation. "I'm not sure which one of us has the bigger troublemaker."

Conversation continued to flow easily, as it always did with her and JD. Besides telling him more about her customer's dog agility sessions, they discussed the new summer schedule at Powell Ranch and the upcoming mustang auction. Carly mentioned that the owner of Sweetheart Ranch had hired a contractor to build two new honeymoon cabins on the far hill, bringing the total to eight.

When Rickie knocked his sippy cup onto the floor, JD retrieved it before Carly—or Hombre—had a chance. Definitely old-school manners.

"Be careful with that, Rico." He set the cup on the tray.

Rickie showered him with an openmouthed smile, revealing the last half-chewed banana slice. Fortunately, JD had a strong stomach.

"You're really good with him," Carly commented.

"I like kids. Always planned on having one or two of my own one day after I retired from rodeo. And found a woman willing to put up with me. Now, I guess, that'll depend on if I improve."

Her heart cried for JD. She couldn't imagine being afraid to hold Rickie because she might become suddenly dizzy and drop him. And if his condition persisted, it would be hard for him to share his passion for rodeo and riding with his child. Also with a wife.

She hadn't been completely honest when she told Becca there was nothing between her and JD. But she really needed to make sure they didn't progress beyond a spark. Anything else wouldn't be fair to either of them.

"You will get better. It's just a matter of time." Carly redirected the conversation. "You like working at Powell Ranch, don't you?"

"Yeah." He buttered a slice of bread. "The work's physically demanding, but I'm learning a lot about the business side of running a big horse operation."

"You still having trouble with that one wrangler?"

"Not lately. We finally got to the root of the problem."

"Which was?"

JD shrugged. "I'm the new guy, and that doesn't always go over well with employees who've been there a long time. We talked. He understands I'm not going anywhere and neither am I going to change a system that's not broken."

"I'm glad."

"Me, too. As far as jobs go, it's not a bad one. I can't beat the benefits. Regular wages and health insurance. Free roof over my head. Try getting that riding bulls and broncs for a living."

"Any chance you could stay on permanently?" she asked.

He pushed his empty plate away. "I haven't asked."

Because he'd be settling. She could hear the resignation in his voice, see it in his eyes. JD wanted nothing more than to return to the circuit, and she didn't blame him. Rodeoing was his love. His reason for getting up in the morning.

"No rush," she said. Though true, her answer sounded like a hollow platitude.

JD didn't respond.

Clearing the table and washing the dishes went swiftly with two pairs of hands. Normally, at this time, Carly would snuggle with Rickie on the couch and read to him or sing songs before putting him to bed. No chance of that—he was wide-awake and ready to party.

"Where's the display rack?" JD asked.

"On the patio. This way." In the light of the setting sun, Carly showed him a sketch of what the display rack was supposed to look like.

"No matter which way I attach the individual frames, they sit crooked. And the rack itself is unsteady. I'm afraid it'll topple once I load it up with jewelry."

JD examined the drawing and the display. "I think I see the problem. Where are your tools?"

"In the caddy on the chair."

While JD worked, Carly supervised Rickie. He pushed around his favorite toy, a toddler-sized shopping cart filled with plastic food. Every few steps, he'd stop and reach into the cart for a milk carton or an orange and give it to Hombre. The dog immediately returned the object to the cart. Both boy and dog were enthralled with the game, and Carly was enthralled with them.

When she wasn't watching her son, Carly observed JD. He had an amusing way of crinkling his brow when concentrating. And for a man with big calloused hands that were used to stacking fifty-pound bales of hay, shoveling muck from stalls and holding on to the back of a wildly bucking bull, he was rather adept at fastening thin wires and screwing in tiny hooks.

Did he realize he mumbled to himself when he worked? Each time he leaned back to evaluate his progress, he asked himself a question that he then answered. And each time Carly smiled to herself.

He finished sooner than she'd expected. She'd been contemplating putting Rickie to bed when JD abruptly stood, hammer in hand, and shook the display rack to test its stability.

"You're a genius!" Carly also tested the rack, impressed that the now-straight picture frames barely moved.

He pointed to the blocks. "Those need painting."

She lowered her gaze to the wooden two-by-four pieces he'd used to extend the display's feet. "I can do that. No problem." She'd add vines and flowers or stars and moons for a pleasing visual effect.

He began gathering tools, returning them to the caddy. "Let me put this away for you." He lifted the rack.

"I keep everything in my workroom." Carrying Rickie, she showed JD to her converted spare bedroom.

"I'm impressed. You've made the most of the available space."

She laughed. "What a nice way of saying I'm an obsessive neat freak."

The room was filled with her worktable, storage bins, design boards and, thanks to JD, her attractive and well-functioning display rack. All organized and stored with meticulous efficiency.

"These are cool." He studied the wall where she'd hung pictures of horse models wearing her jewelry. "Is this one from the other day?" He indicated a mare and foal.

"It came out better than I expected. I uploaded the picture to my website the next day and I already have two orders for the necklace."

"I don't know how you do it all." He smiled, an admiring light in his eyes. "Work full-time. Raise a child. Run a side business. I can barely take care of myself and a dog."

She wasn't battling a chronic health condition. That had to take a tremendous toll on him, time-wise and energy-wise.

"I have a lot of help. Rickie's in day care during the week, and my parents come with me to almost every sale. If you stop by my vendor booth this weekend, you'll meet them."

Carly had mentioned JD to her parents in passing as someone whose path she occasionally crossed. If he did stop by her booth, they might read more into the relationship and, in a way, they'd be right. But after tonight, she was more determined than ever they remain strictly friends. Neither of them needed more grief in their lives.

Rickie shoved his balled fists into his eyes and started crying.

"Someone's finally getting tired."

"I'd better hit the road." JD reached for his cowboy hat. "It's getting late."

In the living room, Carly set Rickie on the floor. Hombre immediately went over to him and licked his face. Rickie stopped crying and reached for Hombre. Using the dog as leverage, he hauled himself to his feet.

Carly sighed. "I swear, that dog has the patience of a saint."

"He has a good temperament, that's for sure."

The next instant, Hombre lowered his head and spun. Rickie lost his grip and swayed unsteadily, his face contorting into a scowl. Carly held her breath, expecting him to plunk down onto the carpet, his diaper-padded rear end cushioning the impact. To her shock, he took a tentative step forward in the direction of Hombre. Then, a second one.

"He's walking!" Her hand flew to her mouth. "JD, look!"

He grinned. "How about that?"

Rickie accomplished four more steps before falling onto his bottom and letting out a cranky sob. Carly's heart filled with joy. She hadn't missed seeing his first step. And all because of Hombre. And, she added, JD.

"I can't believe it." She scooped Rickie into a hug when his sobbing increased. Squeezing him tight, she kissed him soundly on the head. "What a good boy. You're walking."

The next moment, her phone rang.

"Thanks again for dinner." JD started for the door. "Call me tomorrow if you need help with anything else."

"Wait one sec." Balancing Rickie on her hip, she extracted her phone from her pocket and blinked in first surprise and then shock at the name on the screen.

"Everything all right?" JD asked.

"I don't know." She debated answering as a dozen possibilities occurred to her at once. "I'm worried this can't be good."

Maybe she should let the call go to voice mail and check the message later, giving herself time to prepare.

JD stood there watching her. "Carly?"

Finally she put the phone to her ear, every nerve in her body humming with anticipation.

"Hello, Evelyn."

"Carly. Hi. How are you?"

She would have recognized her former mother-in-law's voice even if she hadn't read the name on her phone display. "I'm fine. A little surprised. It's been a while."

Evelyn skipped over the remark and asked, "Is that crying I hear?"

"Yes, well, it's our bedtime."

Carly sent JD a look. He nodded at the front door, and she shook her head, mouthing, *Stay*. Just in case the news was upsetting, she didn't want to be alone.

"I've forgotten what it's like having a baby in the house. How is little Patrick?"

Carly tried not to cringe at Evelyn's use of Rickie's full name. Another of Pat's divorce conditions was that their son be named Patrick after him and his father. Carly had relented but once Rickie was born, hadn't been able to bring herself to call him either Pat or Patrick and definitely not *the third*. She'd wanted Rickie to have his own identity, one separate from his father. She also didn't want to be reminded of Pat every time she spoke her son's name.

Rickie had been a few days old when the nickname came to her. First Rick, and then Rickie. The playful version suited him.

"He's great," she told her former mother-in-law, glad her nervousness didn't show. "Growing like a weed."

"I can only imagine."

A long pause followed, during which Carly's

anxiety increased. “Evelyn? Is something the matter?”

“I called because Patrick Sr. and I would like to see little Patrick. Soon.” There was no mistaking the subtle insistence beneath her casual tone.

“Um…of course.” Carly took a second to digest the request and slow her thrumming heart. Her agreement with Pat stated that he have no contact with Rickie until the boy was eighteen. The same condition didn’t apply to Pat’s parents. “How about I call you tomorrow when I don’t have my hands full? We can decide on a day and time.”

“We’d really like to see little Patrick this weekend. If it’s not too much trouble.”

Nudging until she got what she wanted. It was Evelyn’s specialty. Her sweet disposition, cheery countenance and frequent good deeds belied a will of solid steel. When Evclyn wanted something, she went after it with single-minded determination.

And though her motives were mostly good, they could on occasion be self-serving or, when it came to her son, misguided. Carly hadn’t caved to Evelyn’s wishes after Rickie’s birth. The result had been Evelyn severing all contact in an attempt to call Carly’s supposed bluff. It hadn't worked, no doubt to Evelyn's surprise and disappointment.

Carly took a calming breath before answering. She'd initially suspected Evelyn had called to give her bad news about Pat. Another bar fight like when they were married. A DUI charge. An automobile accident with injuries. In comparison, a visit with Rickie was a favor she could easily grant.

"I'm sorry, Evelyn," she said. "I'm busy this weekend. But I'm free the following one."

"*All* weekend?"

"I've rented a vendor booth at the West World horse show. I'll be there both Saturday and Sunday."

JD had taken up residence at the front door, leaning a shoulder against the jamb. Hombre sat at his feet. Both appeared uncomfortable and eager to leave.

"That's perfect!" Evelyn exclaimed. "We'll watch little Patrick for you."

"No!" Carly swallowed and tried to temper her voice. She couldn't bring herself to leave Rickie with Evelyn and Patrick Sr. for a few hours, much less for two full days. Despite being Rickie's grandparents, they were virtual strangers to him. "Thank you, but I'm bringing Rickie with me to the horse show."

"Is that wise?" Evelyn's tone cooled. "Won't you be too busy to watch him?"

"Not every second. And my parents will be there."

Carly immediately wished she could take back her words. Before her divorce, her mom and Evelyn had been good friends for almost thirty years. After Carly left Pat, sides were chosen. She'd felt guilty over the demise of such a close friendship. That hadn't stopped her from doing what was best for Rickie, however.

"We'd rather not wait," Evelyn said. "It's been ages."

More nudging. Carly dug in her heels.

"What about one evening this week?" she offered. "If you can come early. Rickie's in bed by eight."

"Possibly. I'll call you tomorrow when you're not so busy."

That had been Carly's suggestion in the first place. But all she said was, "Good night, then."

"You look a little rough around the edges," JD commented after she hung up.

"That was Pat's mother. She and his dad want to visit Rickie."

"You okay with that?"

"Mostly." She rocked Rickie, more to calm herself than him. "They haven't contacted me or seen Rickie since right after he was born. Their choice. Not mine. They were unhappy about the divorce and against Pat abdicating his rights. They accused me and Becca of lying about what happened so I could gain full custody of Rickie."

"People change. Maybe they're ready to make amends."

"Maybe. And, honestly, they're not bad people. They can be very generous and were good to Pat and me. Their one fault is they're blind where he's concerned. They see him as they want him to be, not as he is."

"Will they attempt to influence Rickie against you? When he's older?"

It was just like JD to hit the nail on the head. "Not so much against me but in favor of Pat. If I agree, there'll have to be ground rules. No talking about me or Pat or our marriage."

"Sounds reasonable."

She walked JD to his truck, sending him off with a one-armed hug and Hombre with an ear-scratching. At some point, Rickie had nodded off in her arms, his head resting heavily on her shoulder.

Thoughts of her and JD's evolving relationship were far from her mind as she readied Rickie for bed. Instead, she dwelled on her phone call with Evelyn.

Why, after a bitter parting and more than a year with no contact, had she suddenly called with a request to visit Rickie? Carly had been too disconcerted at the time to ask. Now the question ate at her.

As much as she wanted to give Evelyn the benefit of the doubt, she couldn't silence the niggling reservations. Whatever Evelyn wanted, it was more than a simple visit with Rickie. Carly was convinced.

"KEEP A FIRM grip on the reins but not too tight," JD told the young rider while buckling her horse's chin strap.

"I will." She drew in a thready breath and straightened her spine.

"Give him his head on the poles but pull back when he's crossing the bridge. Be confident. If you're not, he'll sense that and refuse to listen or, worse, spook."

"Thanks, JD." She patted her horse's neck with her free hand and glanced around. "This is my first trail class competition, as I'm sure you can tell."

"You'll do fine. There's no obstacle on this course you haven't practiced a hundred times at the ranch. Just stay focused. Skywalker here will do the rest."

The striking sorrel, with his three white

stockings and matching blaze down the center of his face, stood calmly, taking in the surrounding commotion. He had a lot more experience than his rookie rider and was already a seasoned competitor long before the teen's parents purchased him this past winter.

This pair was one of three under JD's watchful eye at the horse show. They'd arranged with Powell Ranch for him and the head wrangler to transport their mounts, tack and equipment to WestWorld and, in the case of this young rider, provide coaching. JD was glad to oblige. He liked the teen. What she lacked in experience she made up for in enthusiasm and determination, qualities that, in his opinion, carried a competitor far. If not today, she'd soon be bringing home ribbons.

"The trickiest obstacle for you will be removing the plastic poncho from the post." JD patted Skywalker's rump. "He won't like the crackling noise. Be sure and maintain a steady pressure with your legs."

"Got it."

"I'll be watching the whole time."

"My dad's going to video me." She groaned. "That way, if I screw up, the entire family gets to see it over and over."

"Your parents are proud of you. You've

come a long way, and your hard work's paying off."

A tinny voice announced the start of the trail class.

"I should head over," she said. "My parents are waiting for me."

"Good luck, kiddo."

Turning her horse to the right, she trotted off toward the small outdoor arena where the trail and halter classes were taking place. At the same time, cheering erupted from the large covered main arena as the Western pleasure class winners accepted their honors.

JD had visited WestWorld earlier in the week in order to familiarize himself with the layout. Good thing he had—the place was the size of a small city. Besides horse shows, the multiuse event facility hosted classic car auctions, trade shows, concerts and even high school football games.

Heading in the same direction as his young charge, he quickly covered the distance from the warm-up area to the outdoor arena. He located an empty seat in a lower row of the bleachers and near the aisle, just in case he felt an attack coming on and needed to make a hasty exit.

Too bad he hadn't brought Hombre. The dog really had a settling effect on him. But he'd left Hombre in the bunkhouse—a horse show wasn't the place for him. Too many distractions. Fingers crossed he wouldn't chew the couch arm or a table leg and would instead amuse himself with the half dozen "enrichment" toys JD had left out.

Hombre didn't suffer from separation anxiety. No, it was his low boredom threshold that landed him in constant trouble. No shoe or belt or pair of sunglasses was safe from destruction if he got his teeth on it. JD had called Carly's client yesterday and registered Hombre for her next dog agility class at the park. Luckily, the woman had an opening. The price was a little steep but less than the cost of a new couch.

JD had then phoned Carly to give her the news. Yes, it was an excuse and a reason to hear her voice. She'd been excited for him and Hombre and hoped everything went well. When she'd asked how he was doing—her code for his Meniere's Disease—he'd reported that he was fine—his code for no attacks.

He'd resisted asking if her former in-laws had visited Rickie. It really wasn't any of his business. But then, without any prompting, Carly had said there'd been no word from Evelyn. She'd been initially baffled at the lack of response and then admittedly annoyed. Apparently, Evelyn had returned to no-contact status. By week's end, Carly had decided to put Evelyn from her mind. No sense losing any sleep over it.

He didn't mention his disappointment that Carly hadn't stopped by the ranch for any photos of horse models. Four days was too long. He missed her. More than he would have guessed. She, as much as returning to the rodeo circuit, was motivating him to get better. He'd make sure their status quo remained good friends, for now. But once he improved, all bets were off.

The second his young charge finished her turn in the novice trail class, he was going in search of Carly. With each name and number called, he tapped his boot heel impatiently. How much longer? Finally, the teen and Skywalker entered the arena at a measured walk.

"Slow and steady," JD murmured to himself.

It seemed as if she heard him, for she and the horse performed well. One by one, she executed the various challenges. Pole weaves. Crossing the bridge. Completing a full circle inside a small rectangle. Jumping a series of one-foot-high fences. She even managed to remove the plastic poncho from the pole without incident.

"You've got this," JD murmured under his breath.

And it seemed as if she did—until disaster

struck on the last obstacle, executing a simple loop around a stack of straw bales. Either the teen lost her concentration or Skywalker spotted something in the stands that startled him. All at once, he sidestepped and began prancing in place. His right front hoof came down outside of the boundary, costing him a penalty. Before his rider could regain control, he stepped farther out of bounds with his left front hoof. Another penalty.

They exited from the arena amid a smattering of applause, and her score appeared on the board. Ninth place. But unless everyone after her performed worse—which was highly unlikely given the level of talent here today—she wouldn't finish in the top ten. Still, she'd done well for her first time, and JD told her as much a few minutes later when he found her outside the arena with her parents.

With nothing requiring his immediate attention for the next hour, he politely excused himself and crossed the huge grounds at a brisk pace. The smell of fair cuisine tempted him as he passed the food court. Maybe on his way back from seeing Carly he'd stop for a barbecue sandwich or some fry bread.

As he drew closer to the vendor area with its many white-tented booths, he noticed several exhibitors leading or riding horses adorned with what had to be Carly's creations. Skirting a corner booth selling various leather works, a pair of hand-tooled chaps caught his eye. And if he was considering new boots or some grooming supplies, he'd have ample choices.

Carly's booth was located at the end of the south row. He spied her short blond hair first and then her unmistakable attractive silhouette.

She stood with her back to him, busily restocking the display rack they'd worked on together at her house. In the back of the booth and well beneath the shade, a woman JD guessed to be Carly's mom sat on a folding chair with Rickie standing between her knees. She attempted to interest him in a toy of some kind, but he was having none of it and struggled to break free of her grasp.

A man sat beside her, no doubt Carly's dad. Possibly sleeping, definitely resting, he reclined with his legs stretched out in front of him and his ball cap drawn low over his eyes.

Several potential customers approached the booth, and JD waited, not wanting to interrupt a sale. When they continued on after no more than a cursory look, he strode forward.

"Morning." He flashed Carly a grin. "The rack looks like it's holding up okay."

"Hi!" Carly hurried out from behind the

table to greet him. "You came! And, yes, it's working perfectly. Thanks again."

He couldn't help noticing her mom had perked up. Erring on the side of caution, he refrained from pulling Carly into a hug, which wasn't easy. Besides looking great, she smelled incredible. He could do with a little of her special brand of aromatherapy.

"How's business?" he asked.

"Not bad. Rushes and lulls, depending on when classes are starting and finishing." She reached for his arm. "Come on. Let me introduce you to the folks."

By now, her dad had roused, pushed back his ball cap and straightened from his slumped position. He, too, wore a curious expression aimed directly at JD. Make that aimed at Carly's hand on his arm.

"Mom. Dad. This is my friend JD. I told you about him. He's the barn manager at Powell Ranch. He's also the one who fixed my display rack."

Both parents stood and emerged from behind the booth, Carly's mom holding on to Rickie's hand. He toddled along beside her, eyes bright, head swiveling and finger pointing at this or that.

"I'm Russ." Carly's dad shook JD's hand. "This is my wife, Tilda."

She returned JD's smile, though with noticeable reservation. "Everyone calls me Tilly."

He tugged on the brim of his cowboy hat. "Very nice to meet you both."

Rickie broke away from his grandmother and wobbled toward JD, his chubby arms extended.

"Wow. His walking has really improved in just a few days."

Carly beamed. "He went from zero to sixty in no time."

Stooping, she snatched him up. To everyone's surprise, JD's most of all, Rickie continued extending his arms toward JD and babbling in a whiny voice.

"Did I do something?" he asked.

"He wants you to hold him."

"Hold him?"

"Go on. He won't break."

JD hesitated. He hadn't held many babies. None that he could remember at the moment. What if he felt suddenly dizzy and dropped Rickie?

"I better not."

"You can do it," Carly said as if reading his mind. "I'll be right here."

"Go on," her father grumbled. "If you don't, he'll just start crying."

JD succumbed to the pressure and took

Rickie, not quite sure what to do with him. "Hey there," he said when Rickie grabbed his hat and tugged. "Guess I should have seen that coming."

He plunked the hat down on Rickie's head, triggering an explosion of happy giggles.

"You have a buddy," Tilly observed.

"We've hung around a few times at the ranch. Though I think he likes my dog and hat better than he does me."

Carly laughed, only to hurry off when a couple approached the booth and two more people right behind them.

JD started to panic. She'd promised she'd be right there. One look at Rickie's wide-eyed face, and he pulled himself together. If he started to feel light-headed, he'd simply hand off Rickie to one of his grandparents. Having a plan in place calmed JD.

Their location helped, too. They'd moved off to the side and away from the booth. JD made sure to stand so that he could see everything around him. The trick often helped counter his bouts of disorientation and dizziness. He definitely didn't want an attack now in front of Carly's parents. His pride had suffered enough when he'd had to let the wrangler drive here. But no way would he have taken a chance with the ranch truck and a trailer full of horses on the freeway.

While Carly waited on the customers, her parents and JD continued chatting, mostly about the weather and the many stunning horses at the event. JD's glance frequently cut to Carly, noting her natural and easy manner with customers. Likable without being pushy. Probably why she did well at the wedding boutique, too.

Rickie suddenly squirmed and pointed at a passing horse and rider. "Has, has."

His grandmother brightened, clapping as if he'd solved a complicated puzzle. "That's right, Rickie. Horse. You're such a smart boy."

His grandfather grunted, appearing much less impressed.

Tilly wriggled her fingers at Rickie and spoke in that high-pitched voice people used with babies. "You want to come to Nana?"

He frowned and shook his head, the movement causing the hat to shift and sit at a crooked angle.

"You sure, pal?" JD asked. "Your grandmother's better at this than me."

Rickie twisted and wrapped his arms around JD's neck.

"He sure does like you." Tilly studied JD intently. "How did you and Carly meet exactly?"

JD took her close inspection in stride. "At Powell Ranch. Through Becca. She boards her horse and foal there. Carly also arranges with the ranch owners to use some of their horses for jewelry models, and since I'm in charge of the horses, I help her out now and then."

"Of course." Tilly relaxed, some of the starch leaving her. "That makes sense."

He supposed Carly's parents had reason to worry about her, given her recent troubled divorce. They were bound to speculate about any man in her life, especially one who appeared to be best buddies with their grandson. JD would feel the same about his daughter were he in their shoes.

Finishing with her customers, Carly sauntered over to join them. When she went to take Rickie from JD, the boy again refused and clung to JD's neck.

"No accounting for taste," he joked.

"Oh, I think he's a pretty good judge of character."

Before JD could respond, a voice called, "Carly," and then, "Tilly. Russ. Over here."

They all turned at once to see a middle-aged couple walking swiftly toward the booth. JD didn't recognize them, not that he knew any of Carly's friends besides Becca.

The same couldn't be said for Carly and her

parents. All three of their expressions registered shock.

"I don't believe it," Tilly muttered under her breath.

Carly stared in silence—confusion, uncertainty and frustration clouded her eyes.

"We can't ignore them," her mother said, her tone bordering on pleading.

At Carly's terse nod, Tilly went over to the man and woman in front of Carly's booth. After a few words, they exchanged awkward half hugs.

Carly's dad put his large hand on her shoulder and squeezed. "You okay, honey?"

She nodded, her mouth compressed to a thin line.

"I take it you had no idea."

"They were supposed to come over one day this week. She never called me back."

The couple shifted their attention to Carly. The woman's gaze immediately zeroed in on JD holding Rickie, and her eyes narrowed. "Who's *he*?" she asked loud enough for everyone to hear.

Instead of answering, Carly took Rickie from JD and returned his hat to him. Paying no heed to her son's protests, she started forward. "Evelyn. Patrick. How are you?"

Okay, JD mused. That explained Carly's

stunned reaction. Her former in-laws had shown up unannounced and from the looks on their faces, thcy were none too happy with him holding their grandson.

CHAPTER FOUR

CARLY MADE INTRODUCTIONS all around, her mouth drawn up in a smile she hoped appeared less forced than it felt. Her first impulse had been to ask Evelyn and Patrick Sr. why they'd shown up without calling first. She disliked thinking they'd ambushed her, but the possibility existed. They knew it went against her nature to make a fuss in public or in front of her parents.

Then again, Carly had mentioned the horse show to Evelyn during their phone call the other night. Perhaps she'd taken that as an open invitation and, as JD suggested, was attempting to make amends.

Given her and Patrick Sr.'s wide happy smiles, they were genuinely overjoyed to see Rickie. Carly's resolve softened one tiny degree. She'd been more than willing to remain on good terms with her former in-laws. Both for her mother's sake, since she and Evelyn had been good friends, and so that Rickie would grow up with two sets of grandparents.

Carly had missed out on that for a variety of reasons: divorce, death and distance. She'd seen her maternal grandmother yearly when she visited and the others only sporadically over the years at graduations or weddings or funerals. She didn't want that for Rickie.

Evelyn and Patrick Sr. had hurt Carly enormously. She'd accepted their unshakable loyalty to Pat, even though she believed they were wrong, and had striven to look past it. But for them to refuse all contact with Rickie? That cut to the core. Her sweet little boy was innocent. Why punish him to get back at her?

"My, my." Evelyn bounced Rickie in her arms. "Look how you've grown. Such a big boy."

Rickie plucked at Evelyn's straw hat, his large eyes roaming her face. At that moment, Carly was glad he liked most people. Another baby might have objected to being held by someone who was basically a stranger.

"You're the spitting image of your dad." Evelyn pinched his chin between her fingers. "Yes, you are."

She appeared utterly oblivious of the glances darting between everyone else, including her husband's. Rickie's strong resemblance to Carly couldn't be denied, from the color of his hair and eyes to the shape of his face. No one corrected Evelyn, however. Perhaps she saw a hint of her son in Rickie's features that everyone else missed.

Carly's mother squeezed in close to Evelyn. "He's such a good boy, too. Hardly ever cries."

"Not sure about that," Carly countered. "Just this morning he threw a temper tantrum when I tried to feed him scrambled eggs for breakfast."

"Who doesn't like scrambled eggs?" Evelyn crooned in a high-pitched voice.

"I'm surprised," Carly's mom said. "He's not usually a picky eater."

Carly didn't comment. Rather, she watched the two women, once dear friends for nearly three decades, bond over their shared grandson. She reminded herself that even though Pat's parents had sided with him, they doted on their other grandchildren and spoiled them rotten. Most certainly they'd treat Rickie the same.

"Tell me, JD." Evelyn peered up from fawning over Rickie. "How long have you and Carly been dating?"

Alarm radiated through Carly. She'd introduced JD as a friend, but, obviously, Evelyn had added "boy."

To JD's credit, he appeared unfazed. Or, he hid his reaction better than Carly.

"We're not dating," he answered with a good-natured grin. "Carly spends a lot of time at Powell Ranch where I work, and we've gotten to know each other."

"The horse facility next door to Sweetheart Ranch?"

"That's it. Carly uses the owners' horses to model her jewelry."

"I see." Evelyn managed to infuse both distrust and dislike in two simple words.

Carly silently fumed. Evelyn's curiosity about JD was understandable. Her ill manners weren't. But rather than respond, Carly ignored Evelyn's remark. Now wasn't the time or place, and she wouldn't embarrass JD any further.

By now, Evelyn had returned her full attention to Rickie—who'd grown restless during the exchange. "What's wrong, sweetie pie? You need a diaper change?"

"I imagine he's hungry," Carly said. "Hold on."

She made a quick dash to the diaper bag stowed beneath one of the folding chairs in the back of the booth. With luck, Evelyn and Patrick Sr. would leave soon. Finding a sippy cup, she filled it from the bottle of all-natural apple juice she'd brought along, grabbed a teething biscuit and then returned.

Rickie saw her and held out a hand. "Cah, cah."

"Here's your cookie." She gave him both the sippy cup and the teething biscuit. "This should tide him over for a little while."

"I'm going to head back," JD said. "Leave you all to catch up."

"Please stay," Carly blurted at the same time Evelyn said, "It was nice meeting you."

At that moment, a small parade of customers arrived at the booth. Left with little choice, Carly excused herself to wait on the four women and one reluctant man tagging after them.

To her surprise, JD did stay, and she released a long sigh. She couldn't explain why, but she wanted him there with her former in-laws. Not that she thought they'd abscond with Rickie or anything like that. But the sense of safety she always felt with JD soothed her frazzled nerves.

Even so, focusing on her customers proved nearly impossible. While she attempted lively conversation with them, her glance constantly wandered to the small gathering ten feet away. What had Evelyn whispered to her mom? Was her dad annoyed or just squinting at the sun? And the most pressing question of all, why after more than a year, and with no explanation, had Evelyn and Patrick Sr. suddenly resumed contact? Carly couldn't lay her nagging suspicions to rest.

No sooner did the customers leave, without making a purchase, than Rickie released a loud wail. Carly hurried over, discovering he'd finished his juice and dropped what remained of his teething biscuit on the ground.

"I think he needs a real lunch," she said. "And then a nap. We've had a big morning. Lots of excitement."

"We can feed him if you're busy," Evelyn offered, hope shining in her eyes.

Carly tried not to be swayed and failed. What would letting Evelyn feed Rickie hurt?

"I'll get his lunch ready." She'd packed several ready-to-eat toddler meals and healthy snacks, along with juice and milk. "You can sit on the chairs in the booth."

"I'm hungry, too." Evelyn turned to her husband. "What about you?"

"I could eat."

"Tell you what. We'll take little Patrick with us to the food court. I can feed him while we get some lunch."

Carly swallowed an explosive "No!" and said, "I'd rather you didn't," with as much casualness as she could muster. "He's not used to being away from me in new surroundings."

"We'll tag along," her mother suggested. "We need to eat, too, and I can bring you back a chicken Caesar wrap. You like those."

How like her mother to attempt a compromise while also reassuring Carly she'd watch over Rickie.

"I don't know..."

"All this time," Evelyn said, "we haven't asked you for anything."

Not just nudging, she was seriously turning the screws. Carly looked to JD, who gave her an it's-your-decision shrug.

If she refused what in most circumstances would be a reasonable request, she'd be pegged the bad person. But because of Pat's abuse, protecting her son was a primal drive she couldn't ignore. Not for any reason.

She mentally calculated the distance from her booth to the food court. Fifty yards, give or take. The longest her invisible mommy tether could stretch.

"All right. But don't be gone too long. Rickie needs his nap."

Evelyn brightened. "Wonderful."

Her mother smiled reassuringly and with a touch of apology.

Carly's concerns weren't alleviated. And recognizing the emotional damage Pat had inflicted on her didn't make her hang-ups instantly better. They were too deeply rooted.

Neither did she like being pressured. However, she did see the value of compromising in circumstances where she could exercise a modicum of control.

Under her direction, they quickly assembled everything needed for the short excursion. Several times Evelyn questioned if Carly was going overboard. She didn't offer an explanation, not caring what Evelyn thought.

The prospect of a ride thrilled Rickie, and he bounced excitedly in his stroller seat, his small fists gripping the bar. Carly bent and kissed him on the head, reluctant to let him go.

"Be a good boy for…" She hesitated, trying to remember what Evelyn and Patrick Sr.'s other grandchildren called them. Her parents had chosen the names Nana and Papa. "For your grandparents," she finished lamely.

"That was nice of you," JD said after everyone had left.

Carly fumbled with the display, holding in a sob. "Wasn't easy."

"Your parents won't let anything happen to Rickie."

She nodded. Sniffed.

"You want me to run over there and spy on them? I can text you." A twinkle lit his dark eyes.

"No. Absolutely not." Not unless they were late returning with Rickie, she silently added. Then she'd cover the distance herself at the speed of light.

Taking advantage of the lunchtime lull, she straightened up the table and restocked her displays until everything was neat and tidy. When she finished, she motioned for JD to sit in the folding chair beside her. It was a wonder her borderline frantic behavior hadn't sent him running.

"I'm probably overreacting, but Evelyn's phone call out of the blue, her insistence on seeing Rickie, and her and Patrick Sr. showing up unannounced really bothers me."

"Is she normally the pushy type? I say this only because my mom is, and I know what that's like. If she wants everyone to show up for a birthday dinner, we show up and don't dare refuse."

Carly rubbed her palms along her thighs and stared at length in the direction of the food court. "Evelyn is a bit manipulative. She wants what she wants and works to get it. My mistake was I always caved rather than argue with her. Or Pat. She usually coerced him into agreeing with her."

"Keeping the peace with family isn't a terrible thing."

"I wasn't so much keeping the peace as choosing the path of least resistance. Especially near the end of my marriage when I was just so tired of fighting all the time." Carly allowed herself a moment's satisfaction. "She was probably thrown for a loop the other night when she insisted on seeing Rickie and I refused. I'm sure she expected me to be my usual doormat self."

"Is that how you see yourself?" JD asked.

Carly drew in a deep breath. She hadn't told JD the specifics of her abuse. She disliked appearing the victim. Or, worse, having people silently judge her for what had happened. Why hadn't she left Pat when he started drinking daily? How come she'd tolerated his abuse for so long? Hadn't she noticed the signs? Why had she kept making excuses for him?

Not that JD would question those things. He was different. And he probably disliked people silently judging him for his health problems.

"I let Pat bully me for a long time before I finally stood up to him," she admitted on a sigh.

"Bully you?"

"Abuse me. Verbally and physically."

"My God, Carly." His expression filled with a concern that touched her heart. "I knew your marriage ended badly, but I had no idea."

"I don't talk about it much. Not exactly dinner conversation."

"You don't have to tell me if you don't want to."

"No. I do. Give me a second." She swallowed the painful lump in her throat, then went on to summarize the last year of her marriage, Pat's increased drinking, the night he'd shoved her and how it had ended with him backhanding Becca. "It's not easy admitting you let someone treat you the way he treated me."

"None of what happened is your fault."

"I know that. I really do." She sat up straighter. "But I did contribute."

"I doubt that."

"It's true. I've always been too amenable and compliant for my own good. In part, it's the way I was raised. My parents were very strict with me and my sisters. Dad, especially. Apparently, he was pretty wild in his day and didn't want us to get in the same trouble he had."

"They don't seem that way now. Strict, I mean."

"They've loosened up a lot since my sisters and I grew up and moved away. But when we were young..." She groaned and shook her head. "Even now, they're constantly *advising us*—" Carly used air quotes "—on what to do and then dishing out grief if we don't take their advice. They had a fit last summer when my younger sister ignored them and traveled to Italy on her own."

"Maybe they come on strong, but they love you. It's obvious."

"They mean well, for sure. But they're not always right. They were convinced Pat would make a good husband and for a long time excused his behavior."

"That surprises me," JD said, "considering how protective they were of you and your sisters."

Funny how he'd hit the nail square on the head. "I was really frustrated that it took Pat endangering my pregnancy and backhanding Becca before my parents fully accepted the danger I was in."

"Were they not aware, or did they not believe you?"

"In their defense, Pat and I hid most of the damage. Hung pictures over the holes in the walls. Repaired the broken windows and cabinet doors. Replaced shattered dishes. I was so ashamed in the beginning and did what I could to downplay what happened."

"But not later?"

"No, not later." Carly battled against a surge of old hurt. "After Pat moved out of the house and I showed them everything, they were stunned and remorseful. Since then, they've been there one hundred percent for me. They help with Rickie, of course. They also stored my stuff while I stayed with Becca. Moved me into my new place. Paid for my divorce attorney."

"I'm assuming that upset Evelyn."

"Big-time. She felt betrayed by Mom. In hindsight, I think she was grieving the loss of what she'd seen as a dream come true. Two best friends had become mothers-in-law together. Then it ended. Badly."

"Did your moms encourage you and Pat to date?"

"Oh, yeah. We went out for a short while in high school. Evelyn took the breakup harder than I did. Pat and I met again about five years ago at an anniversary party for my parents. I think because we had so many shared memories, we clicked, if that makes sense."

"It does."

"When Pat proposed a year later, I said yes. In hindsight, not because I was head over heels, though I did love him at the time. But I was ready for marriage and a family, and Pat fit the bill. He had a good job and came from a good family, and my parents adored him."

Carly stood when a customer approached the booth. When they left five minutes later, carrying a bag containing two necklaces and two bracelets, she returned to the chair beside JD. But not before checking her phone and staring in the direction of the food court.

"Must have been a shock to Pat's parents," JD said, picking up the conversation where they'd left off. "Learning their son is abusive."

"That's just it. They didn't believe me or Becca and thought I invented the story as a way to get full custody of Rickie. I'm pretty sure their opinion hasn't changed, either. Which is another reason why I question their sudden reappearance."

JD frowned. "They really had no idea the extent of his temper?"

"They had some idea, I'm sure. How could they not? Pat played sports in high school. There were a few incidents on the court and the field. Fights he got into. He once broke a boy's nose in a scuffle during basketball finals."

"That didn't concern you?"

"I didn't like it, no. But he was a teenager at the time and in a highly competitive situation. Heck, even adult professional athletes get into brawls. His parents played it down. Mine, too, and like always, I went along with them. I figured teenage hormones were responsible and that he'd changed. Matured." She let her shoulders drop. "I was wrong. And stupid."

"No, you weren't. Don't be so hard on yourself. You misjudged him."

"I *excused* him and allowed him to manipulate me. That won't happen again. Ever. With anyone."

"That's my girl."

She smiled at JD, liking that he cared about her. And also liking that he couldn't be more different than Pat.

"I should have left him when his drinking started to get out of control. After we found out I was pregnant, I naively hoped he'd change. That becoming a father would straighten him out and motivate him. Wrong again."

"You need to quit blaming yourself."

"I don't." At his stare, she admitted, "Okay, I try not to."

"For Pat's sake, I'm glad he's out of your life. I'd have a lot of trouble letting him near you or Rickie."

"Let's hope we never have to worry about that."

Another customer stopped at the booth and, with only a little coaxing from Carly, purchased three charms. She thanked the woman, being sure to stick a business card in the plastic sack.

"You think your mom and Evelyn will be friends again?" JD asked when Carly returned to her chair.

She was glad for the change of subject. Retelling the story of her failed marriage had worn her out emotionally. "Seeing them together today, I'd say it's a distinct possibility."

"How do you feel about that?"

Carly set her aching feet on a box and considered before answering. "Not great. I don't like information about me and Rickie getting back to Pat. And I guarantee Evelyn will tell him."

JD's phone dinged. He read the text message and pushed to his feet, the folding chair creaking beneath the strain. "I hate to leave, but duty calls. The reining competition starts at twelve thirty, and two of the ranch's clients are competing. I promised I'd be there."

She emerged from behind the booth with him, straining to see the food court. If there was a problem, surely her mother would call. Carly's phone had been utterly silent.

"Thanks for coming by," she said. "You going to be here tomorrow, too?"

"Possibly. Depends on how today goes and if anyone from the ranch advances to the finals."

"If so, drop by again." Carly rested a hand on his arm, liking the connection. She'd shared a lot with him today. "I forgot to ask, you ready for the wedding next weekend?"

"Are you kidding?" He grimaced. "I'm petrified I'll pass out or heave on the altar."

"Relax. Remember, stress can trigger an attack."

"I'll try." He grinned. "And my earlier offer still stands. I'll walk past the food court and text you."

He'd do it, too. "I'm fine. Thanks."

She watched him go. He really was a good friend. And wasn't that worth more to them both than a complicated and potentially heartbreaking romantic relationship between two damaged individuals?

A moment later, she was once again staring in the direction of the food court and checking the time. Only when she spotted her parents and former in-laws in the distance did the tension she'd been holding on to finally melt away.

JD SAT IN the chair closest to the large archway leading from the parlor at Sweetheart Ranch to the foyer. That put him in close proximity to the exit should he need to execute a quick escape. It also isolated him from the wedding guests and reception activities, making him feel more like an observer than a participant.

He resented the exclusion as much as he was

grateful for it. No reason to make his problems everyone else's.

"What a beautiful ceremony. I couldn't stop crying."

"I love her dress. I heard it was her mother's and that they restyled it."

"No way! Jerry, is that you? It's been…what? Four years? Five?"

"Rachel. You look incredible! Haven't aged a day." The man and woman hugged warmly.

JD yanked on his dress shirt collar. It had grown uncomfortably tight during the ceremony, and the constant pressure still refused to lessen despite his efforts. On top of that, his stomach pitched and rolled every few minutes.

Breathe in, breathe out. Again.

Meniere's Disease wasn't responsible for his discomfort. He knew from experience that his intense worry about *having* an attack was what fueled his current restlessness, sweating and upset stomach.

You made it through the ceremony. Only one more hour to go. If he lasted that long.

His pal Tanner's wedding to Jewel had proceeded without a single hitch, other than several out-of-town guests overindulging at the previous night's rehearsal dinner and not feeling their best today.

What mattered to JD was he hadn't thrown

up. Neither had he lost his balance and face-planted on the floor. Not yet, anyway.

In his left hand, he held a small squishy ball, which he rhythmically squeezed in time to his breathing. Both were coping techniques he'd used before. Whether or not they actually worked, he couldn't say for sure. But doing *something* felt better than doing nothing. Loosening his bolo tie sure hadn't helped.

"Don't you just love this place?" a guest gushed. She held a champagne flute in one hand and balanced a plate of hors d'oeuvres in the other. "Sweetheart Ranch. Could there be a better name?"

"Have you seen the boutique?"

"Not yet."

JD's glance cut across the parlor and in the direction of the boutique. Carly wasn't working today—she had weekends off. Otherwise, he'd have been in the boutique right now. She had the same calming effect on him as Hombre.

He'd talked with her earlier in the week but only for a few minutes. She'd brought Rickie to the ranch after work one day in order to let him run around the grounds and burn off some excess energy. JD had been busy with a team penning practice and unable to do more than let her borrow Hombre for a game of throw the stick.

"Would you look at that," a guest said. "Aren't they so sweet?"

"Now I'm going to start crying again." Her friend fanned her eyes.

They weren't referring to the newlyweds. Tanner's brother and best man had pulled his wife into a fond embrace and kissed her on the cheek. Normally, two people hugging at a wedding wouldn't stir that much of a reaction. But Daniel and his wife were the exception.

Having a cancerous tumor removed from his brain had darn near cost Daniel his life. Sadly, the victory had come with a steep cost. He'd been left with a bum leg, as he called it, and a Swiss cheese memory, also his words.

Even with those, and other huge challenges, and the possibility of his cancer returning, Daniel lived a fulfilling and productive life with the love and support of his wife, children, family and friends.

"You're an idiot," JD mumbled, directing the remark to himself, not Daniel.

What right did he have feeling sorry for himself just because he had to deal with a nuisance health condition? Meniere's Disease was easy compared to Daniel's struggles. About time JD pulled up his bootstraps and stopped feeling sorry for himself.

Better yet, get out of the corner. He'd barely

started to rise when his stomach pitched again. He sat, feeling betrayed by the body that had once been strong and fit and had propelled him to within reach of a world championship title.

Earlier this year, Tanner had returned to his rodeo career after taking a year off. JD was glad for his friend. He was also a little jealous, but he suppressed the annoying twinge. It would do no good.

"Hey, bud. How goes it?"

JD swiveled to see Owen Caufield meandering over. "All right." No need to spoil Owen's mood by listing his problems.

"Nice wedding." Owen lowered himself into the empty chair beside JD.

"*Very* nice wedding."

"You did good."

JD shrugged, thinking again of Daniel's battle with cancer. "I managed. That's what counts."

He and Owen sat in silence, observing the guests, which was just fine with JD. Perhaps Owen sensed his need to concentrate distraction-free and willingly obliged him. He knew about JD's condition. Owen owned the local feed store, and he and JD often talked when JD stopped by to make purchases for the ranch. As a former rodeo champion, Owen understood better than most JD's frustration with his inability to return to the circuit.

The difference between them was Owen had chosen to retire from competition. JD had been forced to leave, and the blow still hurt.

"How are things at the ranch?" Owen asked JD. "Ready for the wild mustang auction next month?"

"Getting there. The Powells are donating use of the entire facility to the sanctuary, which means a lot of work to prepare."

"They're mighty good people."

"They are. They've been really accommodating to me, considering I can't do everything a barn manager should be doing."

JD recalled them having to send a wrangler along with him to the horse show at WestWorld because he couldn't be trusted on the freeway with the truck and trailer. His bruised ego had yet to recover, and he was certain some of the wranglers resented him for what they saw as special treatment.

"You thinking of staying on?" Owen asked.

"We'll see." JD wasn't yet ready to commit. Not until he felt like he didn't have any other choice.

"Time for the toast," someone called out. "Everyone grab a glass from the trays coming around."

A trio of young women in black slacks and white shirts appeared. Circling the room, they distributed glasses of champagne. JD and Owen both stood when they neared.

"Which one's the sparkling cider?" JD asked. He wasn't taking any chances.

The young woman pointed, and he took a glass.

"If you don't mind—" Owen selected his glass "—the bride requested I join her and the groom for the toast."

"See you Wednesday morning. I'll be in to pick up that order of salt blocks and mineral supplements."

"Bring coffee with you."

"Can do." JD nodded.

As was tradition for the best man, Tanner's brother, Daniel, made the toast. He started with anecdotes about him and Tanner as children and progressed to their rodeo days together. He then talked about his brother's steadfast support during his darkest days battling cancer and ended with the incredible and inspiring love Tanner had found with Jewel.

He raised his glass, his other hand holding himself steady with his cane. "I may have the title of best man today, but believe me when I tell you, Tanner is the best man there is. The kind deserving of an incredible woman like

Jewel." He swallowed with obvious emotion. "They say you don't marry the person you can live with, you marry the person you can't live without. I'm pretty sure that's true for my brother and Jewel. Here's to the both of you. May you have a long life together filled with happiness and love. To Mr. and Mrs. Tanner Bridwell."

"Hear, hear," people throughout the room echoed. "To the bride and groom."

Several more people gave toasts, including Jewel's father and her maid of honor. Many of the guests were wiping their eyes when it was over. JD, too, felt a tightness in his chest.

Tanner and Jewel had faced and overcome their own set of difficult obstacles, almost not making it to the altar. JD took encouragement from their perseverance and devotion to each other. If he worked hard enough, maybe he, too, could wind up happy with someone special.

Someone like Carly?

Too early to say if she was the one, not when they were working hard to keep their relationship platonic. Heck, they hadn't even kissed. But that didn't stop him from contemplating the possibilities. She was everything he wanted in a wife, best friend, life partner and mother to his children.

If only he were everything she wanted in a husband instead of a man who might suffer from chronic health problems the rest of his life and who had no solid career plan. Imagining a life with her would only lead to disappointment and misery for them both.

Not for the first time he wished they'd met earlier. Then she would have known him before he became a paler image of his former self. When he'd had all the confidence in the world and let nothing scare him.

The cake cutting came next, with the guests laughing and taking pictures when Tanner and Jewel fed each other their pieces. JD was just finishing his cake when the wave of dizziness and disorientation he'd been hoping to avoid today suddenly struck him. The next instant, his stomach turned upside down. If he hadn't been sitting, he'd have crashed to his knees.

He had to get out of here. Now. Before he stole the spotlight from the bride and groom for all the wrong reasons.

Uncertain of his ability to navigate the room without knocking into someone, he approached Daniel, who happened to be standing nearby.

"I hate like heck to cut out early, but I need to go," he said, his voice strained.

"You okay?" Daniel's features knitted with concern.

Sweat poured from JD's temples and ran down the sides of his face. "I'll be fine. Just have to get out of here. Right now!" He closed his eyes and concentrated. "Tell Tanner and Jewel I'm sorry and that I'll see them after the honeymoon."

"I will." Daniel placed an arm on JD's shoulders. "Can I help you out?"

"I'm all right."

"Take it easy, man. Call me if you need anything."

JD slipped out of the parlor and slowly made his way to the foyer, running his hand along the wall to steady himself. Each step was agony. The hardest part, however, was the short walk from the porch to the parking area where he'd left his truck—he'd been forced to stop several times until the dizziness waned. Once he was finally sitting behind the steering wheel, he steadied his breathing and waited for the attack to pass. Just when he began thinking he might have to camp out in his truck overnight, his symptoms receded.

He gave himself another fifteen minutes before driving the half mile down the road to Powell Ranch, hugging the side of the road and his emergency flashers blinking as a precaution. Once at the ranch, he headed straight for his bunkhouse—only to slow down when he spotted Carly's car.

She was here! And if not for his recent attack and reminders of what a lousy boyfriend he'd make, he would have parked and gone in search of her. But Carly deserved much more than he could offer her, and he refused to lead her on only to ultimately end their relationship when the going got tough. And it would get tough. How could it not when she was fresh from an abusive marriage, balancing two jobs along with being a single mother, and his life had been completely upended?

So, instead of stopping, he continued to the bunkhouse, where an exuberant Hombre greeted him. After changing his clothes, he took another dose of his medication with a large glass of water and topped it off with some of the pink stuff for his nausea. By then, Hombre was scratching at the door, eager to go outside after hours of confinement.

JD had every intention of avoiding Carly. She was probably at the maternity pasture or in the round pen. He'd get one of the wranglers to handle the five o'clock feeding.

But when he opened the door, Carly was standing on his stoop, her hand raised.

"Oh! There you are. I was just about to knock."

Rickie squawked hello from his stroller.

"Ah, hi." JD swallowed his surprise.

"Are you busy? If not, I have a favor to ask."

Carly flashed him a thousand-watt smile, and JD's well-laid plans promptly flew out the window.

CHAPTER FIVE

"SORRY. I CAN see I'm interrupting." Carly had taken one look at JD's startled expression and knew she'd chosen a bad time.

"It's fine."

"Now I feel stupid." She stumbled over her words.

Before she could retreat, Hombre squeezed between JD's legs. He immediately went to the stroller and greeted his new best pal, Rickie, with a tail-wagging and hand-licking. Rickie squealed with delight.

"What's up?" JD stepped out onto the bunkhouse porch and closed the door behind him.

"You changed from your wedding clothes."

Really? she thought. That was her best comeback? Why couldn't she just state the reason she'd come looking for him?

Because his reaction to finding her at his door had disconcerted her. She wasn't used to this reserved version of JD.

"Yeah," he said. "I didn't want to get them dirty."

"You looked nice." She smiled again, attempting to smooth over the awkwardness between them.

"You saw me?"

"I saw some pictures."

"When?"

"Online. Sweetheart Ranch's social media page," she explained. "I get notifications when posts are made, just in case I need to respond on behalf of the boutique. Several of the guests took pictures and posted them, tagging the ranch."

"That was fast."

"I'm guessing you didn't have an attack."

"Not during the ceremony. I did later at the reception and cut out early to be on the safe side."

"That's great. Not great you had an attack and had to leave," she amended, "but that you made it through the entire ceremony. I know you were worried. People commenting on the posts said the wedding was beautiful."

"It was really nice. The reception, too. What I saw of it. I got through the toasts and most of the cake cutting. Missed the gift opening and sending off of the newlyweds."

A real shame he had to miss any part of the wedding and reception, and Carly sympathized. How often did she take for granted her ability to go wherever she wanted and do whatever struck her fancy while JD couldn't even drive the short distance to town without meticulously planning every detail of his trip?

She understood his reasons for not wanting to get involved with her or anyone. He no doubt saw himself as a burden. A hindrance. Someone who dragged their partner down rather than lifted up and supported them. A taker rather than a giver. Knowing him, he worried any romantic partner would eventually grow weary of constantly carrying the bulk of the relationship weight.

"I know it must have been hard for you today," she said. "You're a good friend to Tanner."

"He's a good friend to me. I wouldn't have a job if not for him. Holding myself together for his wedding is nothing compared to what I owe him."

Carly liked that JD was loyal to his friends and family. Then again, she liked a lot of things about him. More every day.

Stop thinking about him like that, she reminded herself for possibly the hundredth time.

"I, um, was wondering if you could help me with a problem. That's the reason I came knocking on your door."

"Sure. What do you need?"

They stepped out from under the shade of the bunkhouse porch and into the late-afternoon sunlight, Carly maneuvering the stroller down the one step. She started in the direction of the pasture, acutely aware that JD walked on the other side of the stroller rather than beside her. Hombre trotted along, stopping to investigate periodically as was his habit.

"You know Itchy?" she asked.

"The mini donkey?"

"That's him. He's my latest model. Well, he would be if he weren't being stubborn and not cooperating in the least."

"Donkeys are donkeys, regardless of their size."

"He let me put the charms in his mane, but now he won't move out from under the awning. It's too dark in that corner for me to get any decent pictures."

"Why not use a different donkey?"

"Itchy's the cutest one."

He was also the smallest. His corral mates were identical to him, right down to their gray coloring and distinctive cross markings. The only difference was his diminutive size and rotund belly. He'd make a perfect model for her new line of playful and whimsical charms.

As they neared the corral housing, all four

donkeys, including Itchy, mobbed the gate. They apparently associated JD with being fed. Carly hated disappointing them.

"Hass, hass!" Rickie called and kicked his feet.

"Yes, sweetie. Horses." Technically no, but she wasn't about to correct him. She was too pleased he'd mastered a new word.

"Don, don, don!"

"He can say donkey now?" JD's brows shot up. "I'm impressed."

"No." She sighed. "He means down. Our latest new word as of yesterday. Ever since he learned to walk, he hates being confined in any way, including his stroller, playpen and being held. He's turned into a baby on the move."

Carly had no choice today other than restraining him. She couldn't let him wander loose, not with so many dangers lurking about. Even a miniature donkey like Itchy could easily bowl Rickie over and cause an injury with his sharp hooves. Then there were the countless places where tiny fingers could get pinched, the ragged edges that punctured skin and the protruding objects that sensitive heads might bump into.

Rickie started to wail. The next instant, Itchy let loose with a deafening bray. He was joined by one of the other donkeys.

Carly rocked the stroller, resisting the urge to cover her ears. "Itchy doesn't seem to have a problem coming out from under the awning now."

When Rickie continued wailing, JD removed his cowboy hat and plunked it on the boy's head as if it was the most natural thing in the world. Carly's insides melted before she could renew her resolve not to let JD affect her.

"Donkeys have unique personalities." He paid no notice of her and, unlatching the gate, entered the corral. Hombre went, too, but then quickly wandered off in search of adventure. "You have to know what motivates them."

"Like with young foals." Carly stationed Rickie's stroller in an out-of-the-way patch of shade that was also close enough for her to keep an eye on him. She then slipped through the corral gate.

"Sort of. They both have strong survival instincts and see everything, and I mean *everything*, as a threat. That includes jewelry hanging from their mane and a cell phone taking pictures. Itchy, especially. He's small and almost everything is bigger than him. Can be pretty intimidating."

If only Rickie had strong survival instincts like Itchy. Then maybe Carly wouldn't have to worry so much about him getting hurt or constantly chase after him.

"Are you going to employ your special horse-whispering skills like with the foal?"

He removed a halter from the post where it hung. "Not this time. And calling me a horse whisperer is a stretch."

Carly would disagree. He had the voice for it.

She expected him to put the halter on Itchy and was about to protest—halters tended to distract from her jewelry—but then he slipped it onto one of the larger donkeys.

"I'm going to lead them ahead," he told Carly. "You let me know when Itchy's in the right spot."

"What if he doesn't want to go?" Carly glanced over at Rickie. He'd fallen asleep with JD's hat clutched to his chest. He'd already taken a nap, and she fretted a second one might prevent him from going to sleep at his normal bedtime tonight. But she chose not to wake him, needing the short respite in order to take her pictures.

"He will." JD buckled the halter, having some difficulty because the little fellow kept pushing at JD's arm in a bid for attention. "Donkeys are instinctively herd animals, even ones Itchy's size. He won't like being left behind. None of them will."

He sounded sure.

"Where do you have in mind?"

"Over there." She indicated a sunny corner of the corral.

He started in that direction. *"Vamos, chicos."*

As predicted, the three remaining donkeys meandered after JD and their cohort, long ears bouncing and stubby tails swishing with each step. The gold and silver charms in Itchy's mane caught the sunlight and reflected it back in bright, glittering slivers. Carly had been right to insist on taking pictures out in the open. They should turn out well.

Suddenly, Hombre emerged from beneath a flatbed trailer left outside the corral. He proudly carried an old worn glove he'd found somewhere in his explorations. When JD commanded him to drop the glove, Hombre refused and trotted off. No one was getting his prize.

JD brought the donkeys to a halt. "Right about here?"

"Perfect."

Carly removed her phone from her pocket and started snapping away. Itchy cooperated by standing still and far enough away from his corral mates that they weren't in any of the shots. After a few moments, Carly scrolled through the pictures, deciding to crouch and try a front-on angle rather than from above.

Itchy ignored her. When a slight breeze came from nowhere and lifted his mane and tail, Carly was able to get the exact shots she'd been hoping for.

"You'll be the star of my website," she told the mini.

He looked away, making his opinion known.

She pushed to her feet and pocketed her phone, her gaze traveling to where Rickie continued to snooze in the stroller. Though all appeared well, she was anxious to check on him.

"You done?" JD asked. He'd waited patiently the entire time. Also silently. Any other day they'd have been chatting.

"I was hoping to get a shot of Itchy in front of the ranch office by the bougainvillea bushes. They're in full bloom, and I thought the blossoms would add a nice touch of color. But that was before I realized how hard it is to lead a donkey who doesn't want to be led."

"I'll take him for you."

"Really? You sure? I hate to impose."

"I don't mind."

They walked to the corral gate in relative silence. More unusual behavior for them. She decided his funky mood must be a result of the wedding and his attack. That would make sense. He might resent being forced to leave early.

Unless there was another reason. One that

had to do with her. Their relationship had altered lately, becoming less platonic. He could be withdrawing as a result and attempting to reset them back to the way they had been, something she understood.

At the gate, he removed the halter from the larger donkey and hung it on the post. He then grabbed a smaller halter and placed it on Itchy.

"Stand guard," he told her. "Make sure the others don't get out."

Carly blocked the three larger donkeys, who didn't like that Itchy got to leave while they were made to stay. Itchy wasn't all that keen on leaving them, either, so JD had to pull him along through the gate. But once outside the corral, his demeanor changed, and he trotted ahead. Hombre appeared from nowhere to tag along, the glove still clutched in his mouth.

A quick peek at Rickie assured Carly all was well—he hadn't awakened from his nap. At the ranch office, Carly took a couple dozen more shots of Itchy, who nibbled on the bougainvillea blossoms. Hombre made Carly laugh by trying to give a still-sleeping Rickie the glove and then waiting for him to throw it. She couldn't resist and took several pictures of the pair.

"I'll send you some," she said and texted JD the best two.

"Thanks. My mother will like seeing them."

The strange, awkward silence from earlier resumed. Carly wished she knew what had happened between the last time they'd talked and today and if she had reason to worry.

She started to ask, only to hesitate when he said to Itchy, "Let's go, *amigo.* I'd better get you back before feeding time."

Feeding time wasn't for another forty-five minutes. He was making an excuse.

"I suppose we should get going, too."

Defeat set in when he didn't offer to walk her to her car and help with Rickie's stroller like usual.

"See you later," he said.

She didn't move, not quite ready to surrender. Something had triggered this sudden mood change in JD, and Carly refused to leave without first trying to discover what.

"We'll go with you," she blurted and pushed the stroller ahead, her hopes rising when JD nodded resignedly.

"DID I TELL you Evelyn called me yesterday?" Carly attempted to fill the awkward silence between her and JD with small talk. "She and Patrick Sr. asked to visit and offered to take Rickie to the park. I vetoed that idea but told her we were free any evening this week."

"That's nice of you."

JD led Itchy while Carly pushed a sleeping Rickie in the stroller. Same as before, he'd put Itchy between them. His message couldn't have been clearer, and the loss of their former easy and natural closeness hit her hard. What had happened?

"I'm doing it for Rickie," she said. "I hardly knew any of my grandparents and missed out on a lot. Other people had big gatherings during the holidays, but I only had my immediate family. It was kind of sad. Rickie has a whole family on Pat's side. Aunts and uncles. Cousins. He should have the chance to get to know them. As long as Pat's not there."

"Have your mother and Evelyn started talking since the horse show?"

"Mom hasn't said. That's no guarantee they aren't in contact. I could ask her but right now ignorance is bliss."

They passed the arena on their return trip to the donkeys' corral, garnering the stares of several riders and spectators standing along the fence. Carly supposed a woman pushing a stroller, a man leading a donkey and a dog trotting along beside them made for an interesting sight.

Another silence descended, and Carly struggled to keep the conversation going. "You were going to tell me more about Hombre's agility classes."

"We've been working on our homework every morning and evening." He glanced backward at the dog, who trailed behind Itchy. Every few seconds he'd dart in, only to stop short of nipping the mini's hooves.

"You have homework? Really? Like what?"

"Basic commands. He's pretty much mastered Sit and Lie Down, but Stay, Come and Leave It are lost on him."

"He'll improve. He's smart."

"He likes jumping onto crates and the old bench behind the horse barn."

"Is that part of your homework?"

Finally, he smiled. A small breakthrough but Carly would take it.

"We're prepping for the bridge and the seesaw obstacles," he explained. "I will say one thing. He's been less destructive lately. If the agility training curbs his chewing, it'll be well worth my time and money."

She released a contented sigh. The conversation was going well, even if they weren't discussing anything deep or meaningful. With luck, she could build up to asking him what had happened today to cause his change in mood, and he'd tell her rather than clamming up like before. She just needed to wait for the right moment. Or create one.

"Maybe Rickie and I could come watch you and Hombre on Wednesday."

"Maybe." JD's smile instantly faded. "Let's see how things go."

Uh-oh. She'd made a mistake. Gone too far. She opened her mouth to change the subject, only to stop herself.

Enough was enough. They weren't teenagers who danced around each other. They were grown-ups.

"Are you made at me, JD? You've been acting…different today."

"No."

"You can be honest with me. We're friends."

"Are we?"

His question startled her. "Of course."

His dark eyes sought hers and held. "Or are we something else? I admit, I've been confused lately."

"My fault. I've given you the wrong impression. Flirted even though we agreed to keep things platonic."

"I'm equally to blame. More so, in fact. You're still recovering from your divorce and not ready for a new relationship. I had no business flirting back and encouraging you."

"I am ready," she insisted.

"You think you are. You want to be. But what Pat put you through, that takes times to recover from."

"I've made huge strides since moving to Mustang Valley." Carly went out on a limb. As Becca often said, no risk, no reward. "Since the first day we met, I've thought we're two people right for each other but that the timing was wrong."

"I agree with you on that."

"Except what if we're wrong? What if fate or a higher power is actually putting us together and giving us feelings for each other so that we act on them? Now, not later?"

In the few seconds he contemplated her words, Carly's hopes soared, only to plummet.

"I won't lie to you. I have feelings for you, Carly. Strong ones. And while you may think you're ready to start dating again, I'm not. The wedding today showed me just how far from ready I am."

"Okay, you had an attack. But you're doing well. Your coping techniques are really helping."

"I had to leave early and could barely drive myself the short distance home. What if we'd gone to the wedding together and I had the attack?"

"I'd have left with you."

"And missed out. Why should you be forced to sacrifice on account of me?"

"It was just a wedding."

"You aren't listening to me. Meniere's Disease hasn't just taken over my life—it's altered it entirely for the worse. It's forced me to move away from my family, give up my rodeo career, take what amounts to a pity job I only got because of my friend, and quit doing things other people take for granted—like traveling or going to a movie or even riding in an elevator—because they may trigger an attack. If we were to go on a date, I couldn't drive."

"I don't mind."

The rigid set of his mouth returned. "I refuse to be a responsibility you're forced to bear, Carly, and believe me, I'd be one. Make no mistake."

"Other couples navigate health problems. We can, too."

"Tell me, how would your family and friends feel about you dating a washed-up bull rider who needs constant babysitting?"

"You're not washed up and don't need babysitting."

"I'm scared to death to hold Rickie because I might drop him. And what about when he's older? You want a man in your life who might not be able to play sports with him or take him on rides at the amusement park or go on his Boy Scout camping trip because what if I spend half the trip flat on my back?" JD let out a low groan of frustration. "It'd be different if we'd been dating for a while and then I got sick. But no way am I starting out a relationship with this kind of obstacle to overcome. You'd eventually resent me, and I can't live with that."

Desperation clawed at her. "You'll get better."

"I pray that's true. But until I improve, we can only be friends. Anything else isn't fair to either of us."

He was right. One hundred percent. That didn't ease her pain. Carly wanted more from JD than friendship. She hadn't been sure before today. Her sense of profound loss and despair when he'd withdrawn had forced her to admit what she'd been denying for weeks.

The emotional highs and lows of the day had taken a toll on her, and she felt empty inside. "I wish you didn't make so much sense."

"Me, too."

For one crazy second, she imagined throwing her arms around him and saying she didn't care about being sensible, just to see if he'd kiss her or push her away. She resisted. Why set herself up for even more pain?

Releasing the brake on the stroller, she turned it in the direction of the parking area and her car. She'd put herself out there, and he'd rejected her. Saying more wouldn't make a difference. His mind was set.

"I'd better go."

"Carly, wait."

If he intended to apologize, he didn't get the chance. All at once, a group of about twenty people rounded the corner of the horse barn.

Two of them sat in motorized wheelchairs, one used a pair of elbow crutches and three individuals wore matching polo shirts with the words Harmony House and a logo printed on the front pocket. JD's boss, Ethan, and his wife were also among the group, and hellos were exchanged.

Carly immediately recognized this as a tour of the ranch. She'd seen a similar group of special-needs adults here once before, and Becca had told her the ranch regularly participated in various outreach programs. Last winter, Becca volunteered herself and her horse for a vets-with-PTSD program. She'd raved about the positive results with the men and women and the satisfaction she'd gotten from helping.

"Sorry, boss." JD shortened Itchy's lead rope and pulled the mini closer. "I didn't realize there was a tour scheduled today."

"It was last minute. I figured you were busy with the wedding or I'd have told you. How'd it go, by the way?"

"Good. I—"

"Look, a pony!" one of the men said, interrupting JD and pointing to Itchy.

No one corrected the man.

"He's so cute." A young woman with Down syndrome broke away from the group and hurried toward them, her arms extended.

Carly wasn't sure if the woman was referring to Rickie or Itchy. As it turned out, she was wrong on both counts.

The woman dropped to her knees and called, "Here, doggy, doggy," in a thick voice.

"Wait, Amy. Be careful." The uniformed man rushed to intervene.

Hombre was faster and approached the woman without the least hesitation, his tail wagging at high speed.

"Hombre, no!" JD's quick movements startled Itchy. The mini donkey jerked and turned sideways, forcing JD to stumble to a stop or else risk being run over. "Leave It."

The commands fell on deaf dog ears. Hombre and the woman were locked together so tight, a crowbar couldn't have separated them. When he licked her face, she laughed uproariously.

JD waited, and Carly understood his hesitation. This was a large group of mostly strangers. Though normally wonderful with people, Hombre might become overwhelmed—or startled or frightened—and become aggressive.

"You're a good doggy woggy," the young woman said. "I love you."

The uniformed man placed a hand on her shoulder. "Amy, you shouldn't approach unfamiliar dogs. It's dangerous. What if they bite you?" His gaze traveled from JD to Carly. "We have a dog at the residence, and she doesn't understand they aren't all friendly."

"Ethan, you mind?" JD held up the lead rope.

"Sure thing." His boss circled the group and took charge of Itchy, freeing up JD to supervise Hombre.

"He's still a puppy and likes everyone." His casual response belied a tension Carly recognized, having seen it before.

By now, the dog and Amy were best buddies. If she stopped petting him for even one second, he'd paw her until she resumed. Amy found his antics highly amusing and began purposefully not petting him. Hombre patiently indulged her.

"Oh, I have to video this." A uniformed woman took a phone out of her fanny pack and began filming. "Amy's parents will be thrilled."

After a few moments, the uniformed man took hold of Amy's arm and, gently tugging her to her feet, propelled her back to the group. "I think that's enough for now, Amy. These folks need to get on with their business."

His efforts were in vain. Hombre refused to leave his adoring fan.

"Hombre, Come," JD commanded. When the dog ignored him, JD started forward, his mouth set in a rigid line.

Uh-oh, thought Carly. Poor Hombre was in serious trouble.

Before JD could reach him, the dog invaded the group and was welcomed like a long-missing relative. Undeterred, he squeezed in between the residents.

"Come on, boy."

"Please," the residents begged in unison. "Can he stay?"

"You'd think they didn't see a dog every single day," the uniformed man remarked. He seemed to have given up and resigned himself to watching.

Carly, too. Moved by what she saw, she leaned down and placed a hand on her sleeping son. Connections of all kinds were truly a marvel, be they between people or even people and animals.

A few minutes later, the uniformed man announced they needed to return to Harmony Home in time for supper. Ethan and his wife bid farewell to the group and offered to return Itchy to the donkey corral. JD pried Hombre loose from his new second family, much to their dismay. His promise that they could play with the dog again the next time they were at Powell Ranch was met with a chorus of "When? When?"

Amy wanted to give JD a hug. He obliged her and wrapped his arms around her short frame, holding her close and patting her back.

Everyone in the group waved as they departed for their vans in the parking area.

Carly and JD remained where they were, the effects of what they'd witnessed lingering.

"Hombre was pretty amazing," she said.

"He's full of surprises."

If not for her uncertainty of his response, she might have followed Amy's lead and given JD a hug. Hadn't she been thinking along those same lines right before they'd encountered the tour?

Oh, what the heck. What was the worst that could happen? He'd push her away?

She skirted the stroller to where he stood. "Goodbye, JD."

"About before, I'm sorry. I only meant to—"

She didn't give him a chance to finish before

looping her arms around his neck. “No talking. I don’t want to argue, not after what just happened. I feel too good to ruin it.”

He resisted for only a few seconds, his muscles stiff. Then, releasing a low groan—of satisfaction or resignation, Carly wasn’t sure—he drew her close and rested his chin on her head. She closed her eyes and slowed her breathing to match his, wishing this were the first of many such hugs instead of potentially a one and only.

They stayed like that for several long moments, immersed in the kind of comfort and contentment that only came from holding someone special. Carly hadn’t pressed her cheek to a man’s chest since long before her divorce. She did so now, inhaling the heady masculine scent of JD and surrendering to the sense of well-being his strong arms provided. Neither of them appeared in a hurry to break apart, though eventually they did, having no choice.

It was only a hug, she told herself later as she drove a still-sleeping Rickie home. Except it had been much more. She knew it deep in her very core, and she suspected JD did, too.

Which begged the question, what now? Did Carly back down or, armed with the newfound understanding that she wanted more than friendship, fight for him? For them?

CHAPTER SIX

JD CLIPPED THE leash to Hombre's collar before climbing out of his truck. Park rules aside, the dog would lead him on a wild-goose chase if left unrestrained. Assuming they even reached the area where the dog agility classes were held, Hombre would go nuts, insisting on playing with the other dogs and investigating every little piece of trash or crawling insect.

Shutting the truck door behind them, JD set out toward the park entrance, commanding Hombre to heel. The dog obeyed only because JD maintained a tight hold on the leash.

This particular "homework assignment" hadn't come from the instructor. JD had decided on his own to add to Hombre's training after he went rogue with the tour group from Harmony House.

Granted, the dog had made several new friends, but JD couldn't allow him to go off on his own anytime he felt like it or just because someone called him. Too much potential for danger. A few years ago, his mother's little spaniel had been dognapped. She'd loved people and gone to anyone who spoke nicely to her.

With each step, JD's anxiety grew. Would Carly be here tonight? He'd tried to discourage her last Saturday when she'd mentioned it, and then they'd argued. When he would have continued their discussion after the tour ended, she'd wrapped her arms around him and promptly left for home. As a result, he'd existed in a state of confusion, elation and regret for the last four days.

He shouldn't have let her hug him. At the very least, he should have ended it sooner. Not stood there and held her, encouraged her.

Losing himself in her warm embrace had been easy. More than that, it had felt good. Right. Natural. He'd had a rough day, between his attack at the wedding and their falling-out afterward at the ranch. Then, with one simple hug, she'd broken down his barriers, given him the comfort he needed and restored him to the man he'd been before his life took a drastic turn.

But there were consequences. In hindsight, he should have manufactured some excuse to explain his foul mood and avoided the truth. Then he wouldn't have made the already difficult path they were treading all the more difficult.

Were circumstances different, he'd have asked Carly out on a date when they first met. She stirred feelings in him no woman ever had before, and he could easily imagine himself falling in love with her.

Who was he fooling? There was no imagining about it. JD stood at the edge, a mere step away from the precipice.

Except, for the moment, his future remained in limbo. More than that, Carly hadn't yet recovered from Pat's abuse, regardless of her claim to the contrary. JD could see the aftereffects: her difficulty relinquishing even the tiniest control, her overprotectiveness and her distrust of her former in-laws.

All the wishing and wanting in the world wouldn't change that. Healing required time and patience and no other complications to hinder the process.

They hadn't talked since Saturday and had exchanged only a few casual texts. The reprieve was for the best. If JD and Carly had continued on their current course of flirting, one or both of them would have ended up hurt and unhappy—which was the last thing they needed on top of everything else.

Inside the park, he and Hombre made their

way toward the west corner and the fenced-off dog area where the agility classes were held. Even from this distance, JD could see the colorful obstacles and several of his classmates milling about with their dogs.

"*Vamos, amigo.* We don't want to be late."

Hombre eagerly trotted alongside JD. A mild evening breeze warmed his bare arms and legs, an uncommon sensation for him. He seldom wore cargo shorts or athletic shoes. He'd also swapped his cowboy hat for a ball cap, leaving him feeling like a fish out of water. But he'd learned during last week's class that casual clothes were better suited for running backward and waving his arms than his usual attire of jeans and Western shirts. Not to mention, athletic shoes didn't slip and slide in the long grass like boots.

Cutting across a wide-open area, he and Hombre passed a group of five young boys. They'd been tossing a football back and forth when a disagreement suddenly erupted between two of them. It quickly escalated from shouting to a shoving match. The shorter of the two boys landed hard on his hind end, only to rise up and charge the taller boy.

Hombre instantly lost control, barking at the boys and pulling so hard on the leash he almost got loose.

"No, Hombre. Leave It."

The dog refused to listen and twisted to and fro, bouncing on his front paws. The three boys who weren't fighting glanced over, only to return their attention to their pals. A barking dog was far less interesting than a fistfight.

JD stopped for a moment and considered breaking up the fight. If nothing else, yelling at the boys to stop. The next second, a man came running toward them, his face red and his features knotted in anger.

"What's going on?" he shouted.

Deciding the man must be someone's father, JD tugged on Hombre's leash and dragged him away.

"Don't like it when people fight, do you, boy?" He reached down and gave the dog a reassuring pet.

As if in answer, Hombre woofed softly. He'd behaved similarly once before, barking angrily when two men bidding on the same horse at the ranch's semiannual stud auction had gotten in a heated debate that nearly came to blows.

Funny how the dog reacted differently to various situations. He seemed to possess an instinctive ability to read moods. He comforted JD during his attacks, played gently with Rickie, showed patience with Amy and the other special-needs adults, and barked angrily during loud physical altercations.

If only JD could curtail Hombre's less desirable tendencies, like his short attention span and chewing fixation.

They covered the remaining distance to the agility class quickly. JD greeted the other dog owners while Hombre sniffed noses and tails with his classmates. They found a place on the outskirts of the circle where there'd be fewer distractions for Hombre and a clear view of their surroundings for JD. But, per usual, Hombre had a hard time staying focused. He preferred romping with the dog nearest him rather than sitting still. When JD corrected him, he pulled on the leash, twisted and yipped.

Because there were two new students, the instructor—a perky, fit middle-aged woman wearing a T-shirt featuring her company logo—gave a short speech.

"Dog agility isn't just about competing in trials. Even if you go no further than these classes, both you and your dog will build confidence and trust in each other to last a lifetime. More than that, you'll have a lot of fun and, here's a big plus, get into shape."

She wasn't kidding. JD had been surprised at the amount of running required for the owners, not just the dogs.

"Our course today consists of the tunnel and jump from last week," the instructor said. "Plus six weave poles. Each week, we'll add more challenges. Ramps. Seesaws. Additional jumps arranged in patterns."

She went to each obstacle, describing it in further detail. Glued to her heels was her dog and star agility competitor, Flash, an energetic and remarkably obedient border collie. Maybe there was hope for Hombre after all.

"Who wants to go first?" she asked.

A young woman with a comical-looking short-legged terrier volunteered, and the instructor adjusted the jump to a lower height. The remaining owners and dogs waited on the sidelines, watching and learning. Though the humans were doing most of the learning. The dogs either, like Hombre, let their attention wander or even snoozed.

The terrier did well. Following his owner's commands, he cleared the jump, zoomed through the tunnel and zigzagged through the weave poles. Then again, the pair had taken the class before.

"Show-off," JD muttered under his voice.

Hombre appeared unimpressed.

At the end of the course, the terrier's owner rewarded him with a treat. JD also had a pocket filled with kibbles.

Eventually, it was their turn, and JD removed the squeaky ball he used to get Hombre's attention. He also used the toy to give direction and as an incentive. Hombre loved chasing the ball when he finished an obstacle.

They sat about ten feet in front of the jump, waiting for the instructor's go-ahead.

"You need a running start," she told JD. "Then, as soon as he's over, walk him back to the starting point."

Squeaking the ball, JD jogged toward the jump. Hombre immediately hopped up from his sitting position and followed JD—around the jump rather than over it.

"You cut left too soon," the instructor said. "Try again."

The second time, Hombre sailed over the jump but knocked down the rail.

"Attaboy." JD tossed him a kibble, and they walked back to the starting point. What mattered was that Hombre had completed the jump. Sufficient height could come later.

After three more successful attempts, the instructor upped the difficulty. "Now instead of returning to the starting point, I want you to pivot and lead Hombre back over the jump in the opposite direction." She demonstrated with Flash.

Hombre didn't understand at first. Frankly,

neither did JD, and the instructor had to step in and show him how to cue Hombre. The next time, they did better, though Hombre knocked down the fence rail again. Four attempts later, and they were pros.

"Your dog is a natural," the instructor told JD.

"Too bad his owner isn't."

"Keep practicing. You'll improve."

JD and Hombre returned to their place on the sidelines to wait for their next challenge: the tunnel. All at once, Hombre spun and started barking, a little like earlier only more excitedly. If not for JD having wound the leash around his hand, the dog would have bolted. What was it? Another fight? A strange dog? Just as abruptly, the barking became an exuberant, high-pitched yelp.

JD glanced over his shoulder to see Carly approaching, pushing Rickie in his stroller.

His pulse spiked. She'd come! Despite their argument.

"I get it, boy," he told the dog. "I'm pretty excited, too."

The next second, he cautioned himself to keep a level head. Rickie liked the park. She'd probably brought him to play and just stopped by for a quick hello.

But, no. Rather than wave and leave, she

pointed to a spot on the ground, indicating that she would wait for him there. After that, concentrating on class became an exercise in futility for JD. Hard to believe, but Hombre actually paid better attention than him.

"A LOT OF dogs dislike the tunnel," the instructor explained. "They can't see through to the other end, and that intimidates them. Don't be discouraged. I promise you, I've yet to meet a dog who didn't eventually learn."

JD listened as the instructor wrapped up the class. He'd managed to stay focused well enough that she hadn't called him out, but only just barely. His glance had continually strayed to where Carly sat on the grass a short distance away, the pull she exuded too irresistible to resist.

On several occasions, he noticed her taking pictures of him and Hombre with her phone. Once, she stood and moved a little closer, holding her phone in front of her and staring at the screen. It took a second for him to realize she was filming him. His ability to concentrate deteriorated still further.

"Just look at Hombre."

Hearing his dog's name, JD's attention snapped back to the instructor.

"He refused to go through the tunnel at first,

but by the end of class tonight he had the best time of all the dogs."

All the students looked JD's way. He smiled and patted Hombre's head.

"Continue practicing your basic commands this week," the instructor continued, "especially Stay and Come. I'll see you next Wednesday. We'll be adding a new pattern to our training."

The group of owners and dogs dispersed, going their separate ways. JD headed to where Carly sat on the ground next to Rickie's stroller, Hombre pulling hard on the leash and panting. When she started to rise, JD put out his hand and helped her up.

Electricity exploded from where their palms touched and arrowed straight to his heart. She must have felt the shock, too, because when she met his gaze, he saw an echo of that electricity flit across her features.

She spoke first, a soft smile on her lips. "Hi there."

JD's brain had turned to mush, and he had to remind himself to answer her. "You're here."

"I am." She brushed bits of dried grass from her shorts. "You mind?"

Was she kidding? "I'm glad."

"Hi, hi, hi," Rickie shouted from the stroller and waved his arms.

"Hey, Rico. Another new word?" he asked Carly.

"And I actually understand this one."

"Pretty soon he'll be having real conversations with you."

"I'm not sure whether I'm anticipating that day or dreading it."

Hombre had taken up residence on the other side of the stroller. Placing his head on the bar, he licked Rickie's fingers. As expected, the boy burst into laughter and grabbed Hombre's ears.

Carly, meanwhile, gave JD a long once-over. "I can't recall ever seeing you in shorts and sneakers."

"I don't normally like to show off my chicken legs."

"You don't have chicken legs." Her eyes twinkled. "Far from it."

Was she flirting with him again? Her remark could be taken several ways. When JD next looked, however, the twinkle had disappeared, and he decided he must have been mistaken.

"Did I see you taking pictures and videos?" he asked.

"Hope you don't mind. I'll send them to you."

"My mother will like seeing me in action, especially doing something other than bull riding."

"Has she met Hombre?"

"Not since I first got him."

Carly touched his bare arm and then pointed as they left the dog park. "You care if we take Rickie to the playground? He could use a break from his stroller."

JD tried not to focus on the spot where her fingers had briefly brushed his skin. "Lead the way."

Hombre insisted on walking beside the stroller and would have nipped at the wheels if not for JD's tight hold on the leash.

"Evelyn and Patrick Sr. came by for a visit on Monday," she commented when she and JD settled on a bench near the edge of the playground. Rickie frolicked with Hombre on the grass at their feet.

"How'd that go?"

"Good for the most part. They brought some gifts for Rickie. A toy dump truck and a wagon, both of which he loves. Also some clothes, which he's less interested in." She gave JD a noncommittal shrug. "Flowers for me."

"They're making an effort."

"They are."

"You don't sound convinced."

She sighed. "I wish I could take their gestures at face value and not look for ulterior motives. And I might have been able to do that if they'd just played with Rickie and not brought up Pat."

"Are you really surprised?" JD wasn't. He'd have been surprised if they hadn't mentioned her ex-husband.

"Truthfully, yes. I told Evelyn when we agreed on the visit that there was to be no talking about Pat."

If she and JD were dating, he'd have used the moment to drape an arm across her shoulders. But they weren't dating. And he, not she, had been the one to veto that idea. Which left him having to settle for the platonic comradery they'd almost lost.

"Apparently he's quit drinking and been going to AA meetings," she continued. "Evelyn told me he earned his six-month sober chip a couple weeks ago."

JD nodded. "I'm not defending him, but that is progress."

"It is. Pat's temper and violent tendencies always worsened when he drank."

"Alcohol does that to some people. I've known a few guys on the circuit with that problem. Easygoing, happy-go-lucky until they got a few beers in them."

"I guess Pat has also managed to hold down this last job. Evelyn let drop that he could contribute financially to Rickie's upbringing."

"I thought he didn't have to make child-support payments in exchange for abdicating his parental rights."

"Exactly!" Carly reached down to stop Rickie from eating grass. "If I were to take any money from him, I might jeopardize our custody agreement."

"Did you tell Evelyn that?"

"She knows already. What I did say was I'm doing fine financially and don't need Pat's assistance."

"You think she was serious or just fishing?"

Carly frowned thoughtfully. "Hard to tell. She could be proud of Pat's accomplishments, letting me know he's changed, or trying to change. Then again, she might be laying the groundwork for Pat attempting to renegotiate custody."

"Would he?"

"Doubtful. I think it's much more likely she's hoping I'll change my mind and allow Pat to visit Rickie. Which I won't."

"Are they seeing Rickie again?"

"Next week. I might, *might*, let them take him to the park for an hour." She shoved her hair back from her face. "I'm such a pushover. But they really were sweet with him. Especially Patrick Sr. He couldn't stop laughing when Rickie pulled on his beard."

"He seemed like a decent guy when I met him at WestWorld."

"Oh, he is," Carly readily agreed. "Very laid-back. Evelyn's the one who calls the shots in their marriage, for sure."

"Some men like a bossy woman."

"Not you, I suppose."

"Depends on the woman." JD let a smile creep into his voice. "I'm not against taking a little direction."

"Why do I doubt that?" Carly scoffed.

"Well, if the woman happens to be right."

"Ha, ha, ha," she teased. "I'm not fooled. For all your laid-back charm, you can be very stubborn."

"You think I'm charming?" The question was out before he could stop himself. Now who was the one flirting? "You don't have to answer that," he said before she could.

"JD." She sighed softly. "I know we—"

"No."

It didn't matter what she intended to say. He'd been the one to put on the brakes to any romantic relationship and for good reason. Now wasn't the time to return to dangerous waters.

She looked away. "All right."

For the last five minutes, Rickie and Hombre had been engaged in a game of tug-of-war with a toy key ring. Suddenly, Rickie lost the battle. He fell forward and landed on his hands and knees. Though unhurt, he started to cry, refusing to stop even when Hombre licked his face.

Carly pushed off the bench and reached for him, swinging him up in the air and down onto her hip. "I think one of us is getting tired."

"I should get Hombre home, too. He's put in a long day."

"He's an awful good babysitter."

"And, apparently, not bad at dog agility."

"I saw. You going to enter him in competitions?" Carly settled Rickie in his stroller and adjusted the shade.

"I seriously doubt it."

"What about getting him certified as a therapy dog? He was great the other day with the Harmony House residents."

"I doubt he'd pass the tests. He doesn't always listen. On the way to class tonight, he went wild when these two boys got into a fight. The same thing happened before at a stud auction when two of the bidders argued."

"Really?" She studied Hombre. "I wouldn't have guessed him to have an aggressive bone in his body."

"Fighting of any kind upsets him."

Rickie's crying had lessened to a whine. Carly reached into the diaper bag for a bottle of juice. That did the trick, and he drank noisily, his eyes moist with tears.

Together, they began walking toward the parking area. At a fork in the walkway, Carly pointed east.

"I'm over there."

Figures, thought JD. "I'm in that lot."

"Thanks for going to the playground with us. We had a good time."

That she included Rickie in her statement, making it less personal, wasn't lost on JD.

"Me, too. Maybe you can come watch another class."

"We just might."

Rickie chose that moment to toss his empty bottle onto the ground. JD reached down for it at the same time Hombre dove in.

"Leave It."

For once, Hombre obeyed. As JD straightened, the bill of his ball cap clipped Carly's chin.

"Sorry," he said. "You okay?"

"I'll live." She rubbed her chin.

JD watched, captivated by her slim fingers and full lips.

After a moment, when neither of them had moved, she leaned in closer.

"Carly." As much as he wanted to kiss her, and there was nothing JD wanted more, he couldn't let himself. Only trouble and confusion would come of it. "We'd better..."

"You're right." She drew back. Breathed deeply. "Bad idea."

"If things were different..." Again, he let his sentence trail off.

"But they're not."

"No."

They continued to stand there as if trapped. Which maybe they were by some unseen spell.

"Need help loading Rickie's stroller?" he finally asked.

"We're fine. Thanks."

"See you later, then."

"Okay."

This was getting ridiculous. JD forced himself to turn away. Carly stopped him with a hand on his arm.

"What if it wasn't such a bad idea?"

"Except it is."

"Do you know that for a fact? Seems to me you're just making assumptions based on the worst-case scenario."

He almost laughed. "Are you actually arguing with me about whether we should kiss or not?"

"I'm presenting a different perspective."

The electricity from earlier returned. JD didn't need to touch her to feel it.

Thread by thread, his control slipped away. It snapped completely when she floated into his arms.

"I wish I could resist you, Carly Leighton," he whispered against her lips.

"Do you?"

She knew him better than he knew himself.

The next instant, their mouths met, and their hold on each other tightened. For something he'd insisted was a mistake, nothing had ever felt better, and he savored her sweet deliciousness as he let himself get lost in their kiss.

Seconds passed. Like him, she didn't seem in any kind of a hurry. He understood. They would only ever have one first kiss. Best to make it last.

A tug on JD's hand returned him to reality. Leave it to Hombre to remind him that maybe JD should quit now before things went too far.

Slowly, he broke away, his thumb remaining to caress Carly's cheek. The mild disorientation unbalancing him had nothing to do with his Meniere's Disease. It was all Carly's doing.

"Sorry," he murmured.

"Hardly your fault. In fact, I'm pretty sure I kissed you. And it was…" She sighed.

"Yeah."

"You're not going to ruin the moment by

telling me nothing's changed, and that you still aren't ready for a relationship?"

"Not tonight."

"Good. Let's give ourselves one night off from worrying about what we should and shouldn't do."

He might have said more, except Rickie let out a loud squawk.

"I'd better go." Carly reached for the stroller handle. "Night, JD."

He didn't stop her or dispute her. What would one night hurt?

Eventually, he set out toward the parking lot. He'd just reached his truck when his phone buzzed. Pulling it from his pocket, he read the text message from Carly.

Okay, you're right. We probably shouldn't have kissed. But that doesn't mean I'm going to forget it happened. Not ever ☺

Neither was he.

CHAPTER SEVEN

DURING THE PAST forty-five minutes, Carly had sorted all her screws by size, her various wires and leather strings by length, and her charms by design. She'd also arranged her bead bins by color and cleaned her paintbrushes.

What she hadn't done was work on any jewelry, her entire purpose for letting Evelyn and Patrick Sr. take Rickie to the park for an early-evening playdate. Unable to concentrate, Carly had fussed and fidgeted and paced and busied herself with mindless tasks.

Evelyn and Patrick Sr. had promised they'd return in an hour, well before dark, and Carly was counting the seconds. She'd reminded herself over and over she had nothing to worry about. The first two supervised visits with "Grammie and Gramps" had gone well—lunch at WestWorld and then another visit three days ago. Carly had been a little surprised when Evelyn called and requested yet a third visit today instead of next week as they'd initially discussed. But since she'd had no other plans, and was determined to keep her promise, she'd relented.

Carly had felt calm and composed right up until she put Rickie in the back seat of her former in-laws' car. In that moment, separation anxiety had kicked in and continually worsened. Chewing on a thumbnail, she checked the workroom wall clock for the umpteenth time. Ten minutes until they returned.

"Enough already," she chided herself, only to fumble and drop a small hook onto the floor. It promptly disappeared into the carpet weave. Groaning, she got down on her hands and knees, combing the carpet until she found it. Rickie had a tendency to put small objects into his mouth, and this one could be a choking hazard.

When her phone rang from the charging station on the shelf, she dove for it with both hands extended. Had something happened to Rickie? Was he hurt? Were Evelyn and Patrick Sr. going to be late? What would Carly say to them if that were the case?

She released a long breath upon seeing Becca's picture on her phone display and answered with a bright, if forced, "Hi, you. What's going on?"

"Just thought I'd check in. Figured you'd be climbing the walls about now."

"And you'd be right."

Carly had phoned Becca during her lunch break to tell her about the visit. Becca had commended Carly for being so accommodating to her former in-laws and admitted she'd be unable to do the same in Carly's shoes.

"When are they due back with Rickie?" she asked.

"Ten more minutes." Eight, actually, but who was counting?

"Let me take your mind off them."

"How are you going to do that?"

"Let's talk about JD."

Carly rolled her eyes at her friend's solution. Discussing JD wouldn't alleviate her anxieties—it would likely increase them. "How is that going to make me less anxious?"

"It's not. But you'll have a different reason for pacing the floor."

Her friend was right.

"Have you spoken to him since last night?" Becca asked.

"No."

Of course, Carly had spilled to Becca about the kiss she and JD shared. Becca had been thrilled.

"He didn't respond to your text?"

"I shouldn't have sent it." Carly had mentally kicked herself afterward.

"Nonsense."

She imagined her friend's dismissive scowl. "We agreed that neither of us is in the right place for a relationship."

"Hmm. The way it sounded to me, he said he wasn't in the right place and you went along. Not the same thing."

A technicality. Carly wasn't about to split hairs. "I refuse to pressure him if he's not ready."

"Are you sure he isn't? You didn't think you were ready, either, and now look at you. You're flirting with him and sending romantic texts."

"It's only been a little over a year since Pat and I divorced, and the two years leading up to it were horrendous. What if JD and I start dating and I find out I'm carrying all this emotional baggage I didn't know I had?"

"You and Pat separated long before you divorced. Besides, you were good and done with him the night he shoved you into that wall."

Becca had a point.

"When am I finally going to get to meet JD?" she asked.

"You've seen him plenty at the ranch."

"Seen him. Said hello when we crossed paths. We haven't been officially introduced."

Carly chuckled. "You could go up to him anytime you want."

"What I want is for you to introduce us. That way I'll look less like the best friend shaking down the potential boyfriend."

"You wouldn't!"

"I'm thinking you could arrange another photo shoot this weekend, get him to help you with the foal, and I'll just casually meander over."

Carly snorted. "He'll see right through that."

"What if he does? He'll realize you're seriously interested in him."

"I repeat. I'm not seriously interested."

"Liar."

Becca was right again. Not that Carly had intentionally been leading JD on. Flirting with him had occurred naturally. They did have this amazing connection after all.

"Which is why I need to quit with the conflicting signals," Carly reiterated. "Before I make a fool of myself and ruin our really nice and important-to-me friendship."

Her gaze landed on the wall clock. What? Sixty-three minutes since Evelyn and Patrick Sr. had left with Rickie! Becca was right. Talking about JD had momentarily distracted Carly.

She wandered from the workroom to the living room while Becca rambled on about an irritating coworker at the real estate office where she worked. Peering through the shutter slats, Carly's stomach tightened at the sight of the empty driveway. Was it too soon to call Evelyn and ask if they were heading home?

Yes. Probably. Five more minutes. Then she'd call.

All at once, Carly spied a flash of movement through the shutter slats. Not caring if she was seen, she flipped them open. Evelyn and Patrick Sr.'s Honda sedan rolled slowly into the driveway. Carly closed her eyes and whispered a soft "Thank you."

"What's that?" Becca asked.

"I've got to go. Rickie's home."

"Oh, good."

Becca might have kept their conversation lighthearted, but the enormous relief in her voice couldn't be denied. She'd been as worried as Carly, whose heart swelled with love for her friend.

"I'll talk to you later." She disconnected the call and opened the front door. Since waiting inside was impossible, Carly's feet walked her outside with a mind of their own.

Evelyn and Patrick Sr. were just getting out of the car when Carly reached them. Both wore huge smiles.

"How'd it go?" she asked, resisting the urge

to open the rear passenger door and confirm for herself that Rickie was safe and sound.

"He was an angel," Evelyn gushed. "Just perfect."

"He sure likes to play in the sand," Patrick Sr. added. "Refused to leave the park without taking a bucketful with him. Got my freshly cleaned car pretty dirty."

Earlier, they'd shown Carly the toy pail and shovel they'd bought for Rickie. They'd been so pleased, she hadn't mentioned he already had a whole collection of sandbox toys.

"Probably going to need a bath." Carly tapped her foot, resisting the urge to hurry them.

"Boys will be boys." Evelyn finally opened the car door.

Carly wasn't certain boys were the only babies who got dirty. Some of the little girls at Rickie's day care gave the boys a run for their money.

Evelyn leaned into the car and attempted to lift Rickie from his seat. Maybe because he'd spotted Carly over his grandmother's shoulder, or he'd worn himself out playing, but he started to cry and kick in protest.

"What happened to our little angel?" Evelyn cooed.

"He can get cranky this time of day." Carly stepped in. "Here. Let me take him."

Evelyn obliged, retreating to allow Carly access. As she was lifting him from the car seat, a bit of paper on the car's floor caught her attention. Recognizing the familiar color and logo, she instantly froze. It was Pat's favorite brand of gum and one he'd frequently chewed near the end of their marriage to mask the smell of alcohol on his breath.

Had Pat been sitting in the back seat of his parents' car? With Rickie?

Instinctively clutching her son tighter, she reached down and plucked the gum wrapper off the floor. Though impossible, she swore the paper burned her fingers.

Turning, she held it up to Evelyn and demanded, "Was Pat in the car with you?"

Evelyn jerked as if doused with cold water. "What are you talking about?"

"Pat chews this gum. Did you violate the terms of our custody agreement?"

"Of course not!"

By now, Patrick Sr. had joined them. "Wait just a minute, Carly. No need to get riled."

"That's from a couple weeks ago." Evelyn drew herself up to her full five feet. "I told you, we took Pat to his AA meeting to receive his six-month sobriety chip."

Carly's anger and bluster deserted her in a swift rush. Regret and shame rushed in to fill the empty space.

"I'm sorry." Feeling her face flush, she stuffed the gum wrapper in her shorts pocket. "I jumped to the wrong conclusion."

"Yes, you did," Evelyn concurred, stiff-lipped.

"No harm done," Patrick Sr. said gently.

But Carly could see the hurt on her former in-laws' faces. She'd allowed her acute anxieties to get the best of her, and instead of simply asking, she'd launched into an attack. She might not have always gotten along with Evelyn and Patrick Sr., but they weren't dishonest people.

"Let me get the car seat for you," Patrick Sr. offered. They'd borrowed Carly's for the trip to the park.

Once they were inside, they said their goodbyes. Rickie had stopped fussing enough to tolerate hugs from both grandparents and kisses from Evelyn.

"See you soon, my angel." She brushed his hair from his damp face.

"Thank you again," Carly said, seeing them to the door. "Call me this weekend."

They waved to Rickie, and he waved back.

Carly smiled brightly, hoping to recover some of the ground with them she'd lost.

Closing the door, she carried Rickie to the hall bathroom. "Let's get you cleaned up and ready for bed."

While she bathed Rickie, dressed him in his pajamas and fed him his bedtime bottle, she mentally justified her actions. She'd had every right to ask about the gum wrapper. Her first duty was to protect her son.

She'd handled the situation poorly, however. Vowing to do better, she put a sleepy Rickie to bed. Standing over the crib, she watched until he drifted off. On impulse, she removed the gum wrapper from her pocket and studied the logo in the night-light's soft illumination. Pat had been sober for six months according to Evelyn. Yet he must still be chewing gum. Old habits, Carly supposed.

It was then she remembered Patrick Sr. mentioning the sand and his car being freshly cleaned. Had the gum wrapper been missed? The only other explanation was that Evelyn and Patrick Sr. had lied to Carly about Pat being in the car.

The chill from earlier returned, and Carly hugged herself. She had no proof one way or the other, but the inconsistencies in her former in-laws' story couldn't be denied. The question facing her now was—did she confront them or let the matter go?

JD STOOD IN the maternity pasture and mentally counted—not mares and foals, but rather days. Eleven of them since his last attack at the wedding. No dizzy spells. No uneasy stomach. No aural fullness. This had to be a record for sure. He knew better than to think he'd been cured. But a remission? Maybe. A lessening of symptoms due to careful management and coping techniques? Definitely.

As he bent to inspect the bay's right front hoof—something was causing her to limp—he considered the ramifications of what this newfound freedom could mean for him.

He'd be able to take an elevator. Peer out a second-story window. Walk down a flight of stairs. Attend social events without being forced to leave early. Fly in a plane. Ride in a boat. Drive more frequently and for longer distances. Look for a new job.

Ride a horse again. God, how he missed that.

Rodeoing still remained out of the question, for the immediate future, anyway. But he could go to the movies and two-step with a pretty woman in the Poco Dinero Bar and Grill on a Saturday night. A pretty woman like Carly.

Dating. Could he? Too soon to say yes. Yet the possibility existed, when a week ago he'd almost given up.

The prospect of holding Carly close as they glided across the dance floor exhilarated him more than the prospect of climbing on a horse. The last thing he wanted was for her to have to drive him home from their date as he slumped in the seat, gripping the handhold and praying he didn't vomit.

Eleven days, he reminded himself as he straightened and let the mare's hoof drop. Dwell on the positive, not the negative. Maybe if he went a full two weeks, he'd ask Carly out.

His phone rang, and, seeing his boss's name, he answered quickly. "Yeah, Ethan."

"How's Dolly?"

JD studied the mare. She hadn't moved. "I'm not seeing any obvious cause for concern. No thrush or abscess or cracked hoof. My guess is she stepped wrong and pulled a muscle."

"Should we call the vet?"

Ethan Powell took an interest in every horse on the ranch regardless of who owned it.

"I'd give her another day." JD patted the mare's rump.

"The owner's worried. She's a proven breeder, and he has a potential buyer coming out to see her this weekend."

JD evaluated the mare again. "Up to you."

"What would you do if she were your horse?"

"Dose her with some bute and assess her again in the morning." The equine anti-inflammatory worked a lot like aspirin in people and usually provided fast relief.

"Try it. And keep me posted."

"Will do."

The instant JD started for the gate, Hombre scurried out from beneath the water trough where he'd been hiding to evade the heat. The two of them went to the supply room located in the horse barn. With anywhere from sixty to eighty horses in residence at any given time, common medications and remedies were kept on hand. JD returned to the maternity pasture with a tube of bute and a halter. Dolly wasn't thrilled about taking the pasty substance, but she eventually complied, smacking her lips and rolling her tongue much like Rickie did when he ate refried beans.

Removing the halter, JD sent Dolly off to join the others. One of the friendlier mares followed him to the gate, Hombre trotting along beside them. Too curious for her own good, the mare frequently pestered the hands when they graded the pasture or unloaded feed. JD thought it a shame she was stuck in here when she obviously wanted to be ridden. But, then, she belonged to someone else, and any decisions regarding her care and exercise weren't his to make.

"Lo siento, chica." He rubbed her soft nose when she hung her head over his shoulder. "You can't come with me."

She refused to take no for an answer and tried to muscle her way with him through the gate.

"I'd ride you if I could."

Her woeful expression seemed to ask, *Why not?*

Why not, indeed? JD had been feeling great for eleven straight days. Wasn't it about time he tried? And if he succeeded, just think of the possibilities. He and Carly dancing came instantly to mind.

"All right. You've convinced me, girl. Let's give it a try."

He slipped the halter onto the mare's sleek head. She wasn't particularly tall, a plus for him. Once he'd buckled the halter, he gathered up the lead rope in his left hand and, bracing both palms on her back, hoisted himself up. His right leg slid easily over her back, and he gingerly raised himself to a sitting position.

"That wasn't so bad." His mouth expanded into a broad grin.

A green broke horse wouldn't have responded to mere leg cues and tugging on a lead rope, but this mare was well trained in addition to having a docile nature. At JD's prompting, she walked across the pasture toward the other side and away from the other horses and foals. Her tail swished and head bobbed in rhythm with each step.

Halfway to the other side of the field, JD pushed her into a slow trot. Hombre kept pace with them, yipping excitedly as if to cheer JD on. At the fence, he pulled the mare to a stop and conducted a thorough check of his symptoms.

There were none, and exhilaration coursed through him as they started out again. He wanted to laugh. To shout to the sky. Meniere's Disease wasn't going to defeat him.

The mare must have sensed his mood, for she gave a little hop with her back legs and broke into an easy canter. JD adjusted his weight, settling in to match her gait. In the center of the pasture, he turned her and executed a wide circle. He might have been flying. Not even riding the biggest, toughest bull compared to this feeling.

JD whooped and raised his free hand. With this one small ride, he'd reclaimed a big piece of the life he'd lost.

One minute later, a wave of dizziness hit him like a punch to the face and sent his head reeling. Scenery blurred and then vanished, sucked up by a giant invisible hose. His stomach constricted and collided with his lungs, cutting off his breathing. JD didn't even notice he'd tumbled from the mare until he hit the ground with enough force to rattle his bones.

He lay there, eyes squeezed shut, the hot summer sun beating down on him, unable to move for fear of losing his lunch. Behind him—or maybe it was to his side—Hombre barked relentlessly in his ear. The loud, sharp sound threatened to split JD's skull wide-open.

"Quiet, boy."

The dog lay down beside him and licked his face. Cracking open one eye, JD saw the mare standing ten or twelve feet away, her head hung low and the lead rope dragging in the dirt.

He tried to focus, his hand stroking Hombre's head. "I'm okay, boy."

Was he? God, what an idiot. He deserved this for thinking a short spell with no attacks meant he'd conquered his affliction.

Another wave of dizziness and nausea struck him, though this one was less severe. Hombre whined in response, the sound piercing.

Rolling over onto his stomach, JD decided that nothing but his pride was injured. He tried to move, and the earth beneath him rolled and churned like the sea during a storm. Rather than pass out, he rested his head on his stacked arms and waited for the worst of the attack to pass. Within seconds, his aching head began to heat, and sweat poured down his face. Where was his hat? He didn't bother looking around.

JD remained where he was, time losing all meaning. Hombre eventually quit whining and rested his head on JD's back, the contact soothing. At least, thought JD, he wasn't entirely alone. Then again, he should be grateful none of the other ranch hands had witnessed his debacle. He'd have been the brunt of their jokes for weeks.

Amazing how one could go from being on top of the world to literally lying in a crumpled heap at the very bottom.

"JD! Are you all right?" a voice called from a great distance away.

It sounded like Carly. No, impossible. His mind must be playing tricks on him.

But then she called again, and he groaned. Of all the people to find him, why her? Could his luck get any worse?

He tried rising up on his arms and discovered he was able to without feeling like he'd been shoved out of a plane at ten thousand feet. Little by little, he inched to a sitting position, the huge gulps of air he swallowed going a long way in restoring his battered system. What he'd give for a glass of water.

"JD! Are you okay?" Carly suddenly materialized. And then she was on her knees in front of him, her cool, silky hands cradling his cheeks. "Did you have an attack?"

Like that, he changed his mind, glad she'd found him. His damaged pride was a small price to pay for the instant healing and comfort she rendered with a mere touch.

CHAPTER EIGHT

JD SEARCHED HIS MEMORY. The last time anyone had helped him up after a fall was five months ago at the La Fiesta de los Vaqueros Rodeo. Only that guy had been a comically costumed bullfighter and JD had been tossed twenty feet through the air from the back of a big ugly bruiser named Captain Jack.

The man hadn't smelled like fresh flowers nor been soft to hold like Carly. Neither had he fit nicely into the crook of JD's arm and gazed at him with jade green eyes filled with concern and, no denying it, affection.

Damaged ego aside, there were definite advantages to Carly finding him lying in a crumpled heap in the middle of the maternity pasture.

The next instant, he reminded himself she was off-limits. He had no business enjoying the benefits of their very close proximity. Except he did enjoy them. A lot.

What the heck. He'd allow himself this one

small indulgence. Just from here to the pasture fence. Later, he'd kick himself in the hind end.

"You sure you're okay?" She tightened her hold on his waist. If not, he might have staggered.

"I'll live."

"Tell me you weren't riding that horse!"

"For about five minutes. Until I fell off."

"Why would you do that?"

"I've been feeling good lately."

"And that was an excuse to push yourself?"

No, the excuse had been Carly and wishing for what they couldn't have.

What he said, however, was, "I didn't get hurt."

His remark earned him an exaggerated eye roll and head shake. "Come on."

At the fence, he said, "Wait. I need the halter."

"Don't move." She gave him a stay-put look. "I'll get it."

"Yes, ma'am."

Carly slipped away and hurried off toward the mare. He hugged the top railing to avoid swaying. What an idiot he'd been, thinking of them dancing. He could barely stand on his own two feet.

Hombre went with her. JD didn't call after the dog. He'd rather go with Carly, too.

The thought reminded him of agility class

tonight. How would he manage? While feeling better, he wasn't yet ready to get behind the wheel, much less run an obstacle course.

JD groaned under his breath. He hated that his condition affected every single aspect of his life. Though, today, he had only himself to blame. He shouldn't have tried riding.

On the upside, he'd gotten the chance to hold Carly. That alone was worth a little suffering.

"Can I get you something?" she asked, returning with the halter. "Water? Your medicine?"

What he needed was a chair, but he refused to admit it and settled for leaning his back against the pasture fence.

"You mind hanging the halter on the post with the others?" He gingerly hitched his chin toward the gate. Good, no wave of nausea. It was then he noticed the absence of a stroller. "Wait. Where's Rico?"

Hombre must have also noticed, for he scouted the area, nose to the ground as if searching.

"With Evelyn and Patrick Sr. They took him to the Little Tykes Gymboree."

"What's that?"

"An indoor playground for kids five and under. The place has a toddler area with slides and tunnels and ball pits. Now that Rickie's walking, he can finally go." Her features slowly fell, and her posture deflated. "I'm sure he's having a great time."

Without her. JD could see in her eyes that she desperately wanted to be with her son.

"I'm impressed," he said.

"With what?"

"You letting Evelyn and Patrick Sr. take Rickie. Where is this gymboree place?"

"Rio Verde. Nine-point-three miles from here. Not that I google-mapped it or anything." She smiled guiltily. "They promised to have him back by seven tonight sharp."

"Three whole hours? Wow."

"Don't remind me." She heaved a long sigh. "They're supposed to check in every hour. Yes, it's overkill. I really don't care. My way or the highway."

"Have they? Checked in?"

"Evelyn sent me a text five minutes ago and included a picture of Rickie sitting on a teeter-totter with another boy about his age. I suppose I can relax for a little while. They weren't in an accident on the drive there."

"Poking fun at yourself. You're making progress."

She shrugged. "I really do want Rickie to have a relationship with both sets of grandparents. If I were to deny him, he might resent me someday. I couldn't live with that."

"Sure you're not trying to convince yourself more than me?"

"Honestly? I'm not sure at all."

"That's my girl." Feeling better, he started walking, holding on to the fence for balance. The sun beat down on him, making him wish he'd cared less about looking like a loser and accepted that water Carly offered.

She strolled along beside him. "If they'd asked me last week, I probably wouldn't have let them take Rickie. But I felt bad after what happened."

"Uh-oh." He stopped, assessing his condition before continuing. "Tell me."

"Let's get out of here first."

They exited the pasture, JD growing stronger with each step. "You mind if we stop at the bunkhouse? I should take my meds and sit down for a bit. I don't want to relapse during Hombre's class tonight."

"You still planning on going?"

"I don't need to leave for another twenty minutes. I'll decide then."

"But you had an attack."

"Because I rode the mare. Trust me, I won't be making that mistake again." Next time, he'd be better prepared. Take his meds before instead of after, for starters.

"Come on." Carly took hold of his arm.

JD liked the sensation of her fingers pressing into his arm and her cheek brushing his shoulder. Much as he shouldn't go there, he ran headlong, his mind conjuring up pictures of him and Carly gliding across that dance floor.

Inside the bunkhouse, she plopped down on the couch, Hombre at her feet. JD drained an entire bottle of water with his pill and then grabbed an ice pack from the freezer, which he placed on the back of his neck. Like the squishy ball, ice packs were a self-discovered treatment that sometimes lessened his symptoms.

He joined Carly on the couch, bringing an extra bottled water for her. Once Hombre realized there'd be no food forthcoming, he circled twice, lay down and promptly fell asleep.

"All right." JD passed Carly the bottle. "What happened the other day?"

"I made a big deal out of nothing. Jumped to conclusions. I didn't tell you because... because I was embarrassed." She unscrewed the lid on the bottle and took a sip. "When Evelyn and Patrick Sr. got back from the park, Rickie was cranky and wouldn't let Evelyn lift him out of the car seat. So I did. And I spotted a gum wrapper on the floor. From the kind of gum Pat chews. I accused Evelyn and Patrick Sr. of letting Pat see Rickie."

"That's not an unreasonable leap to make."

"According to Evelyn, yes, it was. She and Patrick Sr. were pretty upset and angry with me."

"Let me guess. You felt guilty about wrongfully accusing them of something they didn't do and, to compensate, said they could take Rickie to the indoor gymboree."

"No. Maybe." She frowned. "When you put it that way, I'm feeling taken advantage of."

"You said yourself, Evelyn is a manipulator."

"I should've known better."

"Look. More than likely, the gum wrapper was from a different day when Pat was in the car with them."

"Except they claimed they hadn't seen him recently, and Patrick Sr. mentioned just having the car freshly cleaned."

"Huh…" JD scratched his chin.

"Yeah. That's what I say."

"I get why you're concerned. It's understandable. But, and I can't believe I'm siding with Evelyn and Patrick Sr. on this, a gum wrapper isn't hard evidence."

"It's not," Carly agreed. "Which is why I let them take Rickie today." She huffed and sank farther into the couch. "Doesn't matter now. They have Rickie, and I came to the ranch rather than go slowly insane alone in the house." At that moment, her phone dinged. Sitting bolt upright, she pulled it from her pocket and swiped the display. "It's another picture of Rickie. He's in the ball pit." Smiling, she turned her phone to show JD.

"He seems okay. Conscious. In one piece. No obvious injuries."

"Should I demand to talk to him? Just kidding!" she hurriedly added.

Only, she wasn't. Her anxious demeanor spoke volumes. JD wished he could stay and keep her company. Unfortunately, he needed to head out soon. Unless…

"Hey, why don't I cancel tonight."

She sprang up from the couch. "Hombre's agility class. Oh, my gosh. I totally forgot."

He also stood, glad to find his legs strong, his head clear and his balance stable. "I don't have to go."

"Of course you do. Are you better? Can you drive safely?"

"The park isn't far. Two-point-three miles. Not that I've google-mapped it or anything."

"I'll go, too. We can use my car."

"You're busy."

"Trust me, I need a distraction. You'd be doing me a favor."

He'd already spent more time with her than was wise. Any more would be tempting fate. What so-called friend fixated on how nice the other person smelled and how soft the caresses of their fingers felt?

The silent lecture JD gave himself turned out to be a complete waste of time. "Sure. Let me get Hombre's leash."

Carly bounded out the door ahead of them.

At the park, Hombre sniffed noses and the less polite body parts of his dog classmates before focusing his attention on the weave poles. JD couldn't believe how fast Hombre mastered the difficult trick. Granted, he made some mistakes, knocking a few poles over and breaking the pattern. But overall, he performed well, earning the instructor's praise.

Carly clapped from the sidelines, distracting JD far more than she did Hombre.

"If he continues improving," the instructor told JD at the end of class, "you'll be able to enter him in competitions soon."

He smiled and muttered an appropriate response. Here he was, desperately wanting nothing more than to return to competition. Except he'd been thinking of bull and bronc riding, not dog agility trials. If he had a better sense of humor, he'd laugh at the irony.

Carly raved about Hombre during the entire drive back to Powell Ranch. She'd taken another video of JD and Hombre and sent it to JD's phone.

While JD watched it, he asked, "You hear from Evelyn again?"

"She sent another text and picture right before class was over. They should be home about the time I get there. Maybe even a couple minutes ahead of me." She swung her car into the ranch driveway. "I texted back that I'd be right along and for them to go in the backyard if they didn't want to wait in the car."

In front of the bunkhouse, JD opened the passenger door and got out. "Thanks again for going with me. And driving."

"Thanks for letting me tag along and putting up with my mild neurosis." She reached into the back seat and petted Hombre before JD let him out.

He came around to her side, and she rolled down her window. "Still feeling good?"

"Like I never had an attack."

That his spells could literally knock him to his knees and then vanish completely never ceased to amaze him. Apparently, it wasn't the same for everyone. His doctor said JD was one of the lucky people.

"Okay. I'll see you later, then." Carly didn't hide her eagerness to leave.

He wouldn't delay her. "Good night."

A microsecond after he stepped back, she threw the car in Reverse and drove off. Not that he'd been expecting a repeat of their previous kiss. Imagining it. Wanting it. But not expecting it.

"Let's go, boy."

He and Hombre set out on their nightly ritual, an inspection of the grounds that included the horse barn, outdoor stalls and pastures. JD didn't like retiring for the evening without first assuring himself that everything was secure and peaceful and in order.

Hombre behaved well. No chasing livestock or running off. The agility classes were really helping with his behavior issues.

No sooner had JD kicked off his boots and settled on the bunkhouse couch, TV remote in his hand, when his phone dinged. Grabbing it, he read the message from Carly.

They're late and not answering my calls.

He groaned, feeling her frustration and desperation. Evelyn and Patrick Sr. hadn't returned with Rickie. Poor Carly must be frantic. He texted back.

You need me to come over?

Okay for now. Let you know. Thanks. ☹

He considered going anyway but chose to wait. Her former in-laws hadn't much liked finding him with Carly and Rickie at West-World, and he didn't want to be the cause of more problems for her. She had plenty already.

Waiting to hear back from her was akin to slow torture and concentrating on the TV an exercise in futility.

CARLY GAVE EVELYN and Patrick Sr. exactly twenty minutes before calling them. That seemed a reasonable amount of time to wait before panicking. They could have encountered a traffic delay, momentarily lost track of time, been waylaid because of Rickie being fussy or uncooperative.

When Evelyn didn't answer her phone, Carly started calling every ten minutes. Four phone calls in total. They were now almost an hour late!

Organizing and tidying, her usual method for releasing pent-up frustration and worry, had no effect whatsoever. Carly paced the floor, adrenaline pouring into her system. Every few minutes, she peered out the living room window, straining to see if a car had pulled into her driveway.

After the second unanswered phone call, she'd contacted her new horse jewelry client and rescheduled their 8:00 p.m. video chat, apologizing profusely and saying she had a family emergency. Even if Evelyn and Patrick Sr. brought Rickie home within the next few minutes, Carly couldn't possibly get him changed and put to bed in time for the chat. That, and she'd be an emotional wreck. Not the best time to win over a potential new client.

Five more minutes passed. She began thumbing through her phone for the number to the nearest hospital. Should she call the police first? How long until the authorities issued an Amber Alert? She knew the make and model of Evelyn and Patrick Sr.'s car but not their license plate number.

Oh, for heaven's sake. What was she thinking? Evelyn and Patrick Sr. hadn't abducted Rickie. Carly attempted to quiet her erratic thoughts. They served no purpose other than to escalate her anxiety through the roof. Surely Rickie would be home soon, and there'd be a reasonable explanation.

There had *better* be a reasonable explanation. If not, heads would roll. Once Carly was assured of Rickie's well-being.

JD had volunteered to come over when she'd texted him earlier. Though sweet of him, she'd declined. Now she was debating texting him back and admitting she'd changed her mind. If something had happened to Rickie, no way could she bear being alone. Neither would she be in any shape to drive herself to the hospital or the scene of an accident if, God forbid, something bad had happened.

Stop that, she chided herself. *Now*. She hadn't gotten this upset that time her parents were late returning Rickie.

But the differences were 1) her parents had called to let her know, 2) they hadn't turned their backs on her for a full year and, perhaps most important, 3) she hadn't recently found one of Pat's gum wrappers on the floor of their car and been given an explanation full of holes.

When her phone suddenly rang, she jerked and let out a small gasp. Seeing Evelyn's number on the display, her limbs melted and she reached for the kitchen counter in order to steady herself. With trembling fingers, she placed the phone to her ear.

"Hello! Evelyn. Where are you? Is Rickie okay?"

"You sound out of breath." Her former mother-in-law spoke as if she were sitting in the sunshine sipping tea, not a care in the world.

"You're late."

"A little. Hope you don't mind."

Carly ignored the lack of an apology. "Why didn't you answer my calls? You were supposed to have Rickie home an hour ago."

"Little Patrick was hungry. We stopped at that fast-food restaurant on the corner of Sage Brush and Los Gatos Way. You know the place. He's such a good eater. Just loves french fries. He ate the whole bag."

"I packed snacks." Carly's relief was quickly fading, replaced by anger.

"Oh, that's right. I forgot to look," Evelyn singsonged in her sipping-tea voice.

"I was worried. Why didn't you call? Or answer *my* calls?"

"My battery died right after I sent you that last picture. I used the car charger on the way here. By the way, I might lose you. I only have ten percent power."

"What about Patrick Sr.'s phone? I tried him, too."

Evelyn gave a dismissive snort. "He can't hear a thing. I keep telling him to see a specialist."

Carly silently counted to five, breathing deeply and allowing the air to fill her lungs completely. Rickie was fine. He'd be home soon. No sense working herself up into a frenzy. Evelyn's excuses were reasonable, if a little too convenient and cavalier.

Except she'd promised Carly to stay in contact, which she'd done until six thirty. Then, suddenly, radio silence. Who cared if Carly's demands were a bit over the top? Evelyn had agreed to them. She could have used Patrick Sr.'s phone. Or called in the car while her phone was charging.

Here was a thought. She could have brought Rickie home on time.

Carly's mind went to a dark place. She imagined Evelyn purposely keeping Rickie away longer than agreed on. Instead of asking Carly—and risking no for an answer—she'd shut off her phone and done exactly as she pleased.

The next second, Carly scolded herself. The situation was probably just how Evelyn described it. Rickie had been hungry, Evelyn had forgotten about the snacks, they'd stopped at the fast-food restaurant on the way home and Evelyn's phone battery had died.

"How long until you're here?" she asked.

"We're not quite done eating. And Rickie's having such fun."

Not done yet? Was she kidding? What little remained of Carly's patience instantly evaporated. "When exactly?" she demanded.

"Another thirty minutes or so," Evelyn offered in her sunshine-and-tea voice.

Considerably past Rickie's bedtime. Carly fumed but instead of yelling said, "I'll see you then," her tone crisp.

As soon as she disconnected, she texted JD, letting him know Rickie would be home soon. He texted back, saying he was glad and included a smiley face.

Funny, Becca had always been Carly's favorite go-to person next to her parents. The first one she contacted to share news or bemoan an injustice or, like tonight, vent. Now, it seemed, JD had taken her place.

Because they were friends. *Just* friends. Fantastic kiss aside, their relationship status hadn't changed. Which was for the best. Because neither of them was ready for more.

Maybe if Carly kept telling herself that over and over, she'd eventually come to believe it.

The next thirty minutes dragged. Carly's mind traveled a few more times to the dark place before she hurriedly crawled her way out. She shouldn't make a bigger deal of this than was warranted.

Evelyn was used to being in charge. Not that

Patrick Sr. was weak, but, between the two of them, she had the stronger personality and typically called all the shots. More than once, Carly had wondered how the dynamics of their relationship had affected Pat. He wasn't a victim of either verbal or physical abuse, nor had he grown up in a toxic home environment. If he'd been bullied as a child, no one had ever mentioned it.

Yet, something caused him to become abusive when he drank. That nature-versus-nurture question again.

Hopefully, his AA meetings would help. The chances were good if, and only if, he put in the work.

Carly shouldn't have been surprised that Evelyn and Patrick Sr. were late for a second time tonight. They pulled into her driveway precisely thirty-seven minutes after their phone call, at the same moment Carly was dialing their number. She hung up and went outside to greet them, plastering a smile on her face for Rickie's sake.

It proved unnecessary. He'd fallen asleep in his car seat, no doubt exhausted. In a repeat of the other day when Evelyn and Patrick Sr. had taken him to the park, Carly lifted Rickie from the car while Evelyn hovered behind her and, yes, Carly looked for a gum wrapper. There wasn't one.

Carrying Rickie inside, she barely listened as Evelyn prattled on about how much fun they'd had and what a little angel Rickie was. Patrick Sr. brought up the rear, setting the car seat on the floor just inside the front door.

"Sorry we're late," he murmured.

"Thank you." Carly nodded stiffly. At least *he* had the decency to apologize. "Be right back."

She left her former in-laws to cool their heels in the living room while she took Rickie to his room and laid him in his crib. She'd change his diaper and dress him in pajamas after Evelyn and Patrick Sr. left.

Only she didn't move. Standing at the crib, she lightly rested her hand on Rickie's back and watched him sleep. The sight soothed her frazzled nerves and allowed her to gather her thoughts before the coming confrontation.

Evelyn and Patrick Sr. were perched on the couch when Carly entered the living room, their spines straightening the instant they saw her.

She didn't sit. "Thank you again for taking Rickie to the toddler gymboree," she said. "I'm sure he enjoyed it."

Patrick Sr. spoke first, a rare occurrence for

him. "Thank you for letting us take him. We promise we won't be late again."

"I understand delays and changes in plans occur. But it's imperative you call me when they do."

"Of course. Absolutely."

Evelyn shot him a look before addressing Carly. "We were only trying to help you."

"How's that? By upsetting me and causing me needless worry?"

"You're juggling a lot. A full-time job at the wedding boutique, your jewelry side business and being a single mother. We wanted to give you a break. Free up your evening. You said you had a video chat scheduled. How did that go? Better with no crying baby in the background, I bet."

"Actually, I canceled. I was too upset about Rickie being late and having no idea where you were to talk to the client."

"I... We honestly had no idea. We assumed you were busy and wouldn't notice."

Patrick Sr. stared at the floor and not at Carly. Obviously, *he'd* had an idea.

Suddenly overcome with exhaustion, she started for the door. "I don't mean to chase you away, but it's getting late."

Patrick Sr. pushed up from the couch, still not looking at Carly. "We really are sorry."

His lack of direct eye contact made Carly think he was apologizing for more than being late. But what?

At the door, Evelyn paused. “We’d like to see Rickie again. What about Monday?”

Why all the sudden visits? Carly was too tired to ask and in no mood for an argument.

“Let’s talk tomorrow. I need to check my calendar.”

She might pull “an Evelyn” and not answer her phone. No, that would be mean and not like her. Besides, Carly still didn’t know for sure that Evelyn had purposely avoided her calls.

Evelyn didn’t budge. “Little Patrick needs a strong male role model in his life. His grandfather can provide that.”

“He has a strong role model. My dad.”

“Yes. Of course. I wasn’t implying…” She cleared her throat. “Now he can have two.”

Carly swore she heard, *And a father if you’d let Pat see him*, tagged on the end.

She really needed to stop slipping into that dark place. If she weren’t careful, she’d get stuck there for good.

“I’m very glad Rickie’s getting to know you both,” she said. “And you’ll have plenty of chances to spend time with him. I promise.”

“Let us help you, Carly.”

The pleading in her former mother-in-law’s

voice pierced her defenses. Maybe Evelyn and Patrick Sr. were simply two lonely people desperate to fill the empty spaces in their lives. And Carly *was* juggling a lot.

"I will. And I appreciate all you've done."

"It would be different if you had a man in your life. Someone who loved little Patrick."

Again, Carly imagined she heard, *Like his father*, added on the end. What was the matter with her?

As soon as Evelyn and Patrick Sr. stepped outside, Carly shut the door and let a long sigh escape.

On the way to Rickie's room, she noticed her phone on the table, the blinking blue light alerting her to an unread text message. Seeing JD's name, a smile blossomed on her face. She had assumed he'd be in bed by now, needing to rise most mornings at the crack of dawn.

Hope Rico made it home okay. Just thinking of you. Good night.

She pondered the text. Surely he'd meant the word *you* as plural. Like in *you and Rico*. She texted back a response.

He did. He's fine. I'm fine, too. Thanks for thinking of

Her fingers stilled. Which should she type? *Us* or *me*?

Quickly, she added me and hit Send.

This time, Carly's mind went to a very happy place. One where she and JD surrendered to their mutual attraction with no reservations. And she didn't crawl out right away. Rather, she stayed quite a long while and thoroughly enjoyed herself.

CHAPTER NINE

ETHAN POWELL POKED his head out the ranch office door just as JD was passing by. "Hey, pal. You got a second?"

"Sure thing."

"Tie her up in the shade and come on in."

JD had been leading the mare with the limp around the grounds to determine if she'd improved or worsened. The same mare he'd been checking on when he stupidly decided a bareback ride on her pasture mate was a good idea.

Was that only yesterday? So much had transpired since then. Carly finding him facedown in the middle of the pasture. Them going together to Hombre's dog agility class. Her former in-laws being late bringing Rickie home. Her texting him in a panic. He hadn't been able to sleep until learning Rickie was home, safe and sound.

Thx for thinking of me, she'd written. When wasn't he? Try as he might to resist, Carly had taken up permanent residence on the fringes of his mind, frequently moving to the forefront. Like now.

Wrapping the mare's lead rope around the hitching post and tying a secure knot, he gave her a pat before climbing the three short porch steps and crossing to the door. Hombre danced ahead of him, tail wagging. JD let himself into the small and, thankfully, air-conditioned office. Though it wasn't yet ten in the morning, the temperature had already risen to the low nineties. Triple digits by this afternoon were not only predicted but inevitable.

"Que pasa, patron?" JD removed his cowboy hat and claimed one of the two available seats, savoring the welcome sensation of cool air on his sweat-dampened hair. Hombre settled at his feet, panting heavily.

Ethan looked out of place behind the scarred metal desk. The rugged former bull rider and now horse trainer was more suited to straddling a saddle than an office chair. "I need you to run a half dozen of our calmest trail horses over to Sweetheart Ranch today by four. They have a sunset ride and cookout for one of their wedding parties."

"No problem. What time will they be done?"

"Leave the truck and trailer there. I'll pick up the horses on my way home from the community meeting tonight. It should finish about the same time as the trail ride, and I'm going right by there."

"Mind if I take one of the ATVs with me to ride back?" JD asked.

"Good idea. Or—" Ethan grinned "—you could use needing a ride as an excuse."

"For what?" JD had his suspicions but played dumb.

"To ask for a lift. From Carly. I heard you two have been making regular trips to the park."

"We're friends."

"Very good friends, from all accounts."

Ethan had a point. Did friends hug and kiss? Call each other gorgeous? Flirt? It seemed JD and Carly were continually moving and readjusting their boundaries. JD more than Carly.

"Not what I *saw*, either." Ethan propped his elbows on the desk. "Friends don't argue like you two did."

The tour. When JD and Carly had run into the group of special needs adults from Harmony House.

"We had a disagreement," he admitted. "That's over now."

His boss nodded thoughtfully. "Which would explain you two kissing."

Great. Someone had seen them and spilled the beans. JD clenched his teeth, wondering who.

Ethan apparently read his mind, because he answered, "My wife was at the park with the kids."

Why hadn't he looked around first? Easy. He'd been too captivated by Carly. A piano could have fallen from the sky and he wouldn't have noticed. At least they hadn't repeated their mistake last night after agility class.

"We agreed that wouldn't happen again."

Ethan's grin widened. "For two people who are supposedly just friends, you and Carly are doing a lot of arguing and kissing. Sounds to me like you're a couple."

It did to JD, too. "We like each other."

"A lot, apparently."

"If not for my health problems and her recent divorce, yeah, we'd probably be...a couple." Okay, he'd used Ethan's word. "But we *are* dealing with those things."

"Hey, pal. I didn't mean to pry."

JD lowered his voice, not realizing he'd raised it. "She needs a friend more than she needs someone complicating her life." He explained what was going on with her former in-laws and them being late bringing Rickie home last night.

"Poor gal. She must have been a wreck."

"She was."

JD had wanted to call her this morning, just

to see how she was doing. In the end, he talked himself out of it and sent a text with a simple, Doing okay this morning? She'd answered with an equally simple, All right ☺. That had been the extent of their communication.

"Look." Ethan pushed back from the desk and stood. "Your and Carly's relationship, whatever that may be, is none of my business. Forget what I said."

JD also stood, eager to let the matter drop. "By the way, the mare's limp is better."

"That's good news. The owner will be happy."

They went outside, Hombre's toenails clicking as he skittered across the porch. Ethan inspected the mare, satisfied the doses of bute JD had been administering were doing the trick.

"One last thing," he said, dropping the mare's hoof. "And you can tell me to shut up if you want."

"What's that?"

"I get why you and Carly have decided to remain friends. Sometimes, though, being a friend, a good one, requires you to step up in ways you didn't anticipate."

"Not sure what you're implying."

"Trying not to cross a line might prevent you from being the kind of friend she needs.

Someone to talk to, for instance. And rely on. Just think about it."

"We'll see."

As the day progressed, JD repeatedly returned to his conversation with his boss. At a quarter to four on the dot, he drove the truck and trailer, loaded with six already bridled and saddled trail horses and the ATV, from Powell Ranch down the road to Sweetheart Ranch.

At the stables, the wedding party milled about, smiling broadly and chatting excitedly. With them was Sweetheart Ranch's on-staff wrangler and their three resident trail horses. The wrangler pitched in, helping JD unload the horses he'd brought.

"Appreciate your help," the wrangler said when they were done, and shook JD's hand.

As soon as everyone was mounted, instructions were given and stirrups adjusted for those who needed it. The group started off down the dirt road at a leisurely amble. Beyond the far gate, a glorious summer sunset and miles of open desert awaited them.

His work done for the day, JD returned to the trailer and started up the ATV. Easing it slowly down the ramp, he accelerated once he was clear of the stables and drove toward the main house. Any other day, he'd have brought Hombre. But as much as the dog loved riding in vehicles, the choppy roar of the ATV scared him.

As JD neared the house, he slowed and glanced at his phone. Four forty. The boutique was still open. His gaze traveled to the parking area in front of the house, where he spotted Carly's vehicle. She'd yet to leave for home. He had no reason to stop in and see her. And yet, a few minutes later his boots thumped loudly as he crossed the wide veranda to the front door, the ATV keys jangling in his hand.

Entering the foyer, he came to an abrupt halt. Maybe this was a bad idea. By showing up unexpectedly, he'd be sending Carly those same confusing and contradictory signals they'd discussed the other day.

"Hi, JD." Molly hailed him from behind the antique desk that served as a registration counter. "You here to see Carly?"

Busted. "I, um, don't want to bother her if she's busy."

"Nonsense. It's nearly five, and I doubt any customers will show up between now and then."

"You sure?"

"Go on. Get out of here." Molly waved him away, the same kind of smile on her face that his boss had been wearing that morning.

Did everyone suspect he and Carly were

more than friends? Little side trips like this one to see her at work weren't helping to erase their suspicions.

Like on his previous visits, he felt awkward and out of place as he moved carefully through the main house's elegantly decorated rooms. He much preferred the sturdy and basic surroundings he'd grown up with in Las Cruces.

JD suffered a pang of homesickness, as he often did when reminded of his childhood. He owed his mother a phone call. They usually spoke once or twice a week. She had a cell phone but refused to text, preferring, as she said, to hear the sound of his voice. He liked hearing her voice, too, and made a mental note to call her tonight.

She and Carly weren't unalike—both single mothers, both raising their children on their own while working full-time. Now that JD thought about it, his mother would probably love Carly. Whenever he mentioned her, always emphasizing they were just friends, his mother needled him for more information. Clearly, she knew him better than he knew himself.

The fear that he'd knock into something returned the moment he entered the boutique. Fortunately for him, Carly stood near the front with her back to him, moving cake toppers around, frowning and muttering to herself. Answering her own question, she lifted two cake toppers and swapped them out. Retreating a step to inspect her handiwork, she nodded approvingly and then broke into a radiant smile.

As JD stared, the floor beneath him started to ripple even as his chest filled to capacity, making breathing difficult. He wasn't having an attack. Not from Meniere's Disease, anyway.

Time for him to face the truth. All the denying his true feelings, all the insisting they were just friends hadn't stopped him from falling hard for Carly.

She promptly turned and spotted him. "Hi! What are you doing here?"

He needed a second to recover. "I delivered some horses to the stables for a trail ride. Figured I'd swing by while I was here and see how you're doing after last night."

"Great. We can chat while I'm closing for the night."

He followed her through the narrow aisle to the counter, remembering the day he'd stood there while she adjusted his bolo tie, the warmth from her fingers penetrating his shirtfront, the intense color of her eyes dazzling him.

No chance of that happening today. He stayed on the boutique side of the counter while she went behind it, tucking items in drawers and powering off the electronic register.

"I had a rough night, I'll admit," she said as she worked. "Took me a while to calm down enough to even try sleeping."

"Did Evelyn give you a reason for being late and not answering your calls?"

"Several. They stopped for fast food, supposedly because Rickie was hungry." Her skeptical tone implied she didn't totally buy the excuses. "Her phone battery died. Patrick Sr. is hard of hearing, which is why he didn't answer his phone when I called it."

"Couldn't she have used his phone to call you?"

"Exactly! But rather than argue I kept my mouth shut. I was too tired and too grateful to have Rickie home. I did, however, shut Evelyn down when she asked to visit Rickie again on Monday." Tapping a stack of papers into a neat pile, she glanced up at JD. "Do you think I'm overprotective? Insisting Evelyn text me every hour? Freaking out when they were late? Allowing visits only on my terms?"

"No. They destroyed your trust in them when they cut you off last year and believed Pat over you in the face of some pretty overwhelming evidence. They need to earn that trust back. So, they either play by your rules or they don't get to play at all."

"I agree." Carly huffed. "Evelyn accused me of having too much on my plate, and swore they were only trying to help out by lightening my load."

"That's a load of bull—" He stopped short, chuckling dryly.

"I said pretty much the same thing." She aimed her incredible smile at him, dazzling him all over again in a brand-new way. "She also said Rickie needs a strong male role model in his life. Apparently, because I don't have a boyfriend, he's lacking one."

"She actually said that?"

"I couldn't make this up if I tried."

"What about your dad?"

"I mentioned him. Evelyn still thinks Rickie should spend more time with Patrick Sr."

"She may not be wrong," JD conceded. "He seems like a nice enough guy."

"He's not the problem. I dislike Evelyn's tactics. I want her and Patrick Sr. to be involved in Rickie's life, but not if they fight me at every turn. Evelyn's called me twice today, even though I told her I was at work and unable to talk."

"She can be a little pushy."

"A little?" Carly abruptly sobered. "Ever since I found that gum wrapper, I can't stop thinking that these sudden visits with Rickie are a scheme to orchestrate secret visits with Pat."

"Would she do that?"

"She might. Evelyn has no reservations about advancing her own agenda."

"After the way he treated you? And Becca?" Anger seized JD with razor-sharp fingers, as it did every time he pictured Pat harming Carly and her friend.

"Keep in mind, she doesn't believe Pat is capable of violence. Apparently all those broken windows and holes in the walls just spontaneously appeared and he was merely defending himself against the guy in the bar parking lot. I have no doubt she and Patrick Sr. are convinced they'd be doing the right thing, reuniting their son with their grandson." Carly removed her purse from beneath the counter and fished a set of keys from the side pocket. "I just wish there was a way I could get her to back off a little. I'm open to ideas if you have one."

JD did. It sprang to mind as if hovering on the sidelines for just this moment. He hesitated telling Carly. For one, it went against everything they'd agreed to and everything he'd told himself. For another, they'd be sorely tempting fate.

Outside the boutique, he waited while she flipped around the sign from Open to Closed and locked the door. As they retraced his earlier route through the house, he barely heard her talking about Rickie's latest day care adventure and her weekend plans. His idea for a solution to her problem kept short-circuiting his concentration.

On the veranda, they paused to say goodbye. Losing the battle with himself, he asked, "What if you did have a boyfriend?"

She narrowed her gaze at him. "What are you talking about?"

"Me. Maybe if you and I started dating, that would be enough to get Evelyn off your back."

Carly studied him, her mouth pursed in concentration. "Is that your only reason?"

"Well...no."

"What else?"

JD swallowed. He'd started this, now he had to see it through. "I'd like to give us a try. But before you say yes, there's a lot to consider. One important thing being Evelyn's reaction. She didn't much like me when we met at West-World, and I'd hate to make things any harder for you."

"I can handle Evelyn." Carly dismissed her former mother-in-law with a wave. "You're my concern. I've said before I don't consider your health problems a deterrent to a relationship. You're the one with reservations."

He nodded. "We'd need to go slow. Maybe give ourselves a few weeks."

"Like a test run?"

"And agree that if things don't work out, we part with no hard feelings."

"Our friendship could take a real hit in that case," she said. "Are you willing to risk it?"

The question was a fair and important one. "Yes. If you are."

She debated, tapping her finger on her lower lip. The longer she took, the more JD's doubts escalated. What if his idea backfired? Evelyn could, and probably would, make Carly's life miserable. And he might lose a person he'd come to care for deeply.

What had he been thinking? This was a big mistake. Before he could speak, she cut him off.

"All right." A twinkle lit her eyes. "Let's do it. Let's date." She pulled him into an unexpected celebratory hug.

JD held her close, not sure whether he should be happy at this newest turn of events or worried they were making a terrible mistake.

CRADLING HER PHONE between her cheek and shoulder, Carly carried Rickie to the family room.

"So," Becca asked excitedly, "where are the

two of you going? And no skimping on the details. It's been a very long dry spell, and I'm living vicariously through you."

Smart, fun and striking, Becca had her pick of men. Any dry spell was by choice.

"An early dinner at the Cowboy Up Café in town," Carly said, "and then to the recreational bull riding at the Poco Dinero."

"Sounds like fun!"

"I hope."

"What's wrong?"

Why did Becca have to know her better than anyone else? "I worry JD will feel bad watching the guys compete. Giving up his rodeo career has been really rough on him."

"Didn't you say he chose the place?"

"Well, yes."

"Then, obviously, he's fine with going."

"Maybe."

"Come on, Carly. What's really bothering you?"

"Nothing," she insisted.

"Worst liar ever."

She wasn't about to admit her true concerns, even to her best friend—that her feelings for JD would grow by leaps and bounds and he may not reciprocate them to the same extent or decide that dating was a mistake.

"You know," Becca mused, "he might be

planning on entering the recreational bull riding when he's ready to return to competing—maybe he's scoping out the place. Kind of like a reconnaissance mission. Has he been to the Poco Dinero before tonight?"

"You think?"

"What I think is you need to quit fixating on JD's reason for choosing bull riding and focus on more important things like whether he'll kiss you again."

Carly laughed despite her concerns about the evening and lowered Rickie into the playpen. "No kissing. It's just a test date."

At Rickie's loud squawk of protest at being confined, Carly grabbed a musical stuffed bear from the many toys scattered on the floor of the playpen, activated the On button and handed it to him. He immediately banged the toy on the side of the playpen and burst into giggles. Poor Freddy the Teddy.

Confident her son was happily occupied, she scurried to the kitchen and made a final inspection of the toddler meals, snacks, juice and milk she'd left for him. There was enough for three children.

"I'm just glad you're dating again. And JD's such a nice guy." Becca sighed. "You're so lucky to have found him."

"We're going slow, remember? Don't get ahead of yourself."

"You keep selling, but I'm not buying."

Carly ignored Becca. "I'll get the chance to see if I'm really and truly ready for a new relationship. JD, too. He's convinced I'm not. And he'll get to see how well he handles dating with his health problems. I'm sure he'll do fine. He's doubtful."

"Excuse me while I stifle a yawn."

"Am I boring you?"

"To tears. Nothing you've described sounds very romantic."

"Not even dinner?" Carly asked.

"I have very high expectations for the two of you."

"Well, you need to lower them."

"I'm sorry, I must have missed something. Did you two sign a contract? Most people do when they enter into a business arrangement."

"Very funny. I'm in stitches."

All joking aside, Carly didn't disagree with her friend's assessment. JD had more or less proposed a plan, which she'd accepted. It did sound rather businesslike when put like that.

Hearing the doorbell, she told Becca, "I need to run. Mom and Dad are here. They're babysitting."

"Wait! Don't hang up yet. What do they think of you and JD dating?"

"I haven't told them yet."

Rickie had begun to shout, "Hi, hi, hi," from his playpen, something he'd recently started doing every time the doorbell rang.

"Why not?"

Carly hurried through the living room. "I don't want them getting the wrong idea. I said I was going out with a friend. Which is true."

"Should be interesting when he arrives. Any chance you'll be filming their reaction? I'd love to see the look on their faces."

"Good night, Becca."

"Call me tomorrow!"

Carly swung open the door at the same time her mom raised her hand to ring the bell again. "Sorry to make you wait. I was on the phone with Becca."

"How is she?" Her mom gave Carly a warm hug.

"She's fine."

Her dad kissed her on the cheek. "She still seeing that one man?"

"They broke up months ago. I told you." Carly smiled at her dad's forgetfulness. If something didn't directly affect him or the family, he immediately forgot about it.

"Where's my beautiful grandson?" Her mom started for the family room.

"Follow the noise," Carly called after her.

Rickie's delight at seeing his grandparents was adorable to watch. Grinning wide enough to show off his newest tooth, he held out his arms and squealed. Carly's mom hoisted him from the playpen and deposited him on the floor. She then knelt in order to engage him on his level. Carly's dad joined them, and she smiled to see her parents frolicking on the floor with her son. Rickie began tottering about the room, gathering books and knick-knacks and whatever he could get his chubby hands on, then dividing his bounty between Nana and Papa. They were thrilled with the game and showed endless patience.

Carly used the opportunity to finish her hair and makeup in the bathroom. When she returned ten minutes later, purse in hand and ready to go, Rickie was sitting on her mom's lap, a cloth book open to a cartoon picture of a whale. He stabbed the book with his finger while babbling nonsense.

Seeing Carly, her mom moved Rickie and the book from her lap to his papa's. With a "Here, take him," she accompanied Carly to the kitchen, where they went over Rickie's feeding-and-bedtime routine.

"What in the world made you decide to watch the bull riding tonight?" her mom asked. "Was it Becca's idea?"

"Actually, I'm going with someone else."

"Oh. Anyone I know?"

"Kind of." Carly intentionally dodged her mom's question. She had several of her own to ask and only a short time until JD arrived. "Have you and Evelyn started talking again?"

Guilt flashed in her mom's eyes. "Don't be mad."

"I'm not."

"I never discuss your personal life. I swear."

"She asks?"

Her mom conceded with a nod. "But I don't respond. Not a word. I think she's finally gotten the message."

"What does she ask about?"

"Your job. Your horse jewelry business. Who watches Rickie during the day. What kind of mother you are."

Carly vented her irritation on a defenseless dishcloth, wringing it to within an inch of its life. "What kind of mother I am!"

"She thinks you spoil Rickie." Her mother picked at a spot on the counter with her thumbnail. "And that you're overprotective."

"Because I was upset when she and Patrick

Sr. were late returning Rickie the other night and didn't answer my phone calls?"

"I knew I shouldn't have told you."

"No, no. I'm glad you did." Carly hung up the mangled dishcloth.

"Actually, I lied earlier," her mother said. "I do respond to Evelyn. I tell her that you're a wonderful mother and take excellent care of Rickie."

"She thinks I'm stretched too thin and need help."

"You have taken on a lot, what with a full-time job and the jewelry business."

"I make my jewelry from home and Rickie goes with me whenever I attend events. He's not being deprived or handed off to whomever I can recruit to babysit."

"Yeah." Her mother dragged out the word.

"What, Mom?"

"Don't take this wrong, but he spends a lot of time in day care."

"Oh, wow. Thanks so much for the show of support." Her eyes stung, and she blinked to stem the rush of tears. "Lots of children spend time in day care, and they grow up just fine."

"No, no. That came out wrong." Her mom draped an arm around Carly and squeezed. "I'm sorry, honey. I'm trying to be sympathetic and supportive."

"No more conversations with Evelyn about me, okay? I don't care what she says, just walk away or hang up."

"Absolutely. I promise. Nothing but sharing recipes and knitting patterns and talking about our latest ailment."

With only minutes to spare before JD arrived, Carly asked her most pressing question. "Evelyn and Patrick Sr. want to come over again this week, but I'm busy. When I told her no, she began nudging in that passive-aggressive way of hers."

"Yes…well…"

"Is something going on with them? Something I should know about?"

Her mom shook her head. "I don't think so."

"Then why, after a year of no contact whatsoever, not even a post on my Facebook page, are they suddenly desperate to see Rickie all the time?"

"You know how they are. They adore their grandchildren and love helping out."

"Is it possible Evelyn's using me being busy as an excuse?"

"For what?"

Secret meetings with Pat? But Carly didn't say that. "To strong-arm me into letting Pat have visitation or even shared custody."

"Absolutely not. She's accepted that Pat abdicated his rights."

"Has she?"

"I'm sure they're simply trying to make up for lost time," her mom continued.

"They're the ones who lost time by cutting off all contact with me."

"People change."

At that moment, the doorbell rang for the second time that evening. Carly spun, her nerves humming from both her emotional conversation with her mom and a sudden injection of excitement at seeing JD.

"Your friend is here." Her mom angled her head in an attempt to see around the corner. "You still haven't told me who she is."

Rather than answer, Carly headed for the living room, her mom dogging her heels. Rickie hollered, "Hi, hi, hi," from the family room.

Even before Carly had unlocked the deadbolt and turned the knob, her dad appeared, bouncing Rickie in his arms.

Carly groaned. There'd be an audience to greet JD and no chance for her to warn him. Not how she'd envisioned them making their big announcement.

Steeling her resolve, she swung the door wide. "Hello. Come on in. You're right on time."

"Evening." Removing his cowboy hat, he stepped over the threshold. "You look nice."

Her? He was the one who looked good. Incredibly good, with his Western dress shirt and pressed jeans. Her mom's openmouthed stare confirmed Carly wasn't the only one to notice.

"JD," her mom croaked. "It's you."

"Evening, Tilly." He nodded at Carly's dad. "Russ. Nice to see you both again."

"What are you doing here? Wait, *you're* Carly's—" She couldn't finish.

Carly drew in a fortifying breath. "Mom, Dad. JD is my date. We're seeing each other."

"Like in…" her mom sputtered "…boyfriend and girlfriend?"

"Yes. Like that."

"'Bout time," her dad said and winked.

CHAPTER TEN

JD AUTOMATICALLY TOOK Carly's arm as they walked out the door, only to reconsider. Too soon? He'd been the one to set the rules.

He didn't let go of her, however. Not until they reached his truck and he opened the passenger door for her. Her soft skin had felt too nice. Also, he wasn't made of stone.

"Sorry about my parents." She flashed him an apologetic smile. "They had no right bombarding you the way they did. I swear I wanted to scream."

She slid into the truck cab, tugging her legs after her. This was the first time he'd seen Carly wear boots, and he liked the look on her. Even with her short un-cowgirl-like blond hair, she'd fit right in with the crowd at the Poco Dinero *and* sitting next to him in the stands. He was eagerly anticipating that part. With luck, there'd be a big crowd at the bull riding tonight, and they'd have to squeeze in close.

"Not a problem." He started the engine and reversed out of her driveway.

"I didn't tell the folks about us."

"Us?"

"Our plan to test the dating waters," she quickly amended. "Just because I knew they'd start grilling you. In hindsight, I probably should have since they grilled you anyway."

"They're hardly the first parents to question me and my intentions."

"Really?" She swiveled in her seat to face him. "Do tell."

"You want to hear about my former girlfriends?"

"You've never mentioned any, and I've shared my entire history with Pat."

"There's not much to mention," he said. "I've had a few relationships. They didn't last."

"What went wrong?"

"Rodeo life isn't for everyone. They grew tired of spending weekends alone and waiting for me to settle down."

Funny, he'd wound up in one place after all. Though not by choice. Except—he shot Carly a glance—for the first time in his life, the prospect of settling down didn't make his feet itch.

"That's all I get?" she grumbled. "One measly tidbit?"

"We were discussing your parents."

She groaned. "Like pulling teeth with you."

"Why didn't you let your parents know we're dating?"

"Oh. That." Carly slumped back in her seat. "As I suspected, Mom and Evelyn have become friends again. I'd rather Evelyn found out about us from me and not Mom. That way, I can present the situation in the most positive light and gauge her reaction."

"Makes sense."

"Get this. Evelyn's been interrogating Mom about me."

"Interrogating how?"

"She pressed Mom about my job and my jewelry business. Who watches Rickie when I'm at work. She even asked what kind of mother I am."

They'd reached the center of town, and JD slowed to accommodate traffic. "What kind of mother you are?"

"Seriously, right?" Carly groaned. "I wish I knew what that woman's up to. I keep expecting her and Patrick Sr. to corner me about allowing Pat to visit Rickie or joint cust— God, I can't even say it for fear of jinxing myself."

"What does your mom think?" JD stopped at the light. "Has Evelyn hinted to her about Pat visiting Rickie?"

"According to Mom, Evelyn's resigned to Pat having abdicated his rights."

"What about Pat? Is he resigned?"

"I haven't spoken to him since shortly after the divorce. No reason to." Carly leaned her head back and closed her eyes. "This is what I get for letting Evelyn and Patrick Sr. back into Rickie's life."

"You're doing the right thing, Carly. Hard as it is. They're his grandparents."

JD reached over and patted her hand. He'd have preferred to hold it, but resisted.

"Yeah. That's what I keep reminding myself. They're good people. They weren't the ones who hurt me. They deserve a chance to know Rickie."

JD and Carly pulled into the Cowboy Up Café a few minutes later. There was almost always a familiar face or two whenever JD ate here, and tonight proved no exception. On the way to their booth, they stopped to say hello to a regular at the ranch and then the local livestock inspector.

JD noticed more than one raised eyebrow and curious stare aimed in their direction. The ranch regular whispered to her husband seconds before JD and Carly approached. Them having dinner at the café was bound to cause a stir. Until recently, they hadn't been seen together away from Powell Ranch.

He ordered the Saturday dinner special:

chicken fried steak with all the fixings. Carly chose a healthier fare, broiled tilapia and vegetables.

"Is Hombre sad about being left at home tonight?" Carly sipped her iced tea.

"He was moping in the corner when I left. I just hope he doesn't retaliate by tearing the bunkhouse apart. I let him swim in the stock tank this afternoon, trying to tire him out. I also gave him two of those peanut butter–filled toys."

"You're a softie, JD. Anyone ever tell you that?"

She had no idea just how much his heart had softened toward her.

"Shh." He pretended to hush her. "I have a reputation to maintain. Only you and my family know the truth."

"I bet you miss them."

"I do. I talked to my mother the other night. She's doing well. Keeping busy with church and my sister's kids. She loved the video you took of me and Hombre, by the way."

"Have you told her about me?" Carly asked shyly.

"Not about this." He pointed to her and then himself. "I'd rather wait and see how things go. My mother tends to get carried away."

"Believe me, I understand completely. Any

chance she'll come to Mustang Valley for a visit? I'd love to meet her."

"Not much of one. She sticks pretty close to home. But I'll see her over Labor Day weekend. Ethan gave me the time off."

Carly didn't inquire about his father—she had no reason to. JD had told her early on in their friendship that he'd had little contact with the man growing up and none in the last three years.

His father's abandonment had greatly impacted JD's opinion of marriage and how he intended to treat his future wife. He sure as heck wouldn't walk out and leave her to raise his children alone like his father had done to his mother. It was the main reason he'd avoided serious relationships while competing professionally. And why his old girlfriends had grown tired of waiting.

"I forgot to ask, how are you feeling today?" Carly speared a green bean.

"Good. I shouldn't embarrass you."

"You never embarrass me, JD."

He liked the sweet timbre of her voice nearly as much as he'd liked the soft feel of her skin. Did she notice him the same way he noticed her? He sometimes spotted her studying him. Tonight, for instance, when he'd walked into her house.

"Don't speak too soon," he warned her. "The night's still young. You could still end up pouring me into my truck and having to drive me home."

She shook her head. "We're going to have fun. Wait and see."

He was already having fun.

Conversation flowed easily, a big improvement from that Saturday after the wedding when they'd endured several long and grueling silences that cumulated in an argument. Carly had then broken down his barriers with a mere hug. He still remembered the feel of her in his arms and his anger melting away.

"I was a little surprised you suggested the recreational bull riding," Carly said, dabbing her mouth with a napkin.

"Why?"

"Will it bother you, watching other guys and knowing you can't participate?"

"No different than any other time I've been sidelined."

"Yes, but that was because of injuries. You knew you'd be competing again once you recovered."

"I refuse to live my life as if my rodeo career is over. I can learn a lot by watching and be that much more ready when I do return."

"That's more or less what Becca said." Carly

reached into her purse. "Wait. Did I forget?" She pulled out some business cards. "No. Whew."

"Drumming up business during the bull riding?"

She laughed. "Sort of. I brought a fresh supply of cards to tack to the bulletin board in the entryway. I stop in every couple of weeks."

"Ever considered selling your horse jewelry during the rodeo events? Lot of horse people there."

"Do they have vendor booths?"

"Not sure. We can find out tonight."

"Thanks, JD. That's a good idea. I'll talk to the owner if she's around, see if she's receptive."

JD insisted on paying for dinner when they were done.

"My treat next time," Carly said.

Yes. Next time. He smiled. "We'll take turns."

She beamed at him. "I like that."

JD couldn't turn away. Only when the waitress materialized with his credit card and sales slip to sign was the spell Carly had cast broken.

At the Poco Dinero a short drive away, JD and Carly wove their way through the rows and rows of vehicles, everything from compact electric cars to enormous dually pickups.

"Is it always like this?" she asked.

"So I hear."

He grabbed her hand as they hopped over a pothole, and he didn't let go when she was safely on the other side. He was tired of fighting with himself and tired of resisting. He waited for her to pull away. Instead, she gripped his fingers tighter.

Unusually warm evening temperatures had no effect on attendance at the Poco Dinero, as the overflowing parking lot and noisy, bustling crowd reflected. Many of the patrons had arrived that afternoon to watch the barrel racing and stayed for the bull riding. Every available inch of space the saloon had to offer was occupied, with people spilling outside to fill the stands, wandering about in the open areas or mingling along the arena fence.

Like at the café, JD and Carly ran into several people they knew. JD shook hands and clapped the backs of two old friends from the rodeo circuit who happened to be in town for a horse sale. Carly greeted a couple who'd recently been in the boutique shopping for his parents' thirty-fifth wedding anniversary.

Available seating in the stands was limited. "What about up there?" Carly squinted and pointed to a row near the top.

"Let's go."

JD captured her hand again as they climbed

the bleacher steps. The Poco Dinero's rodeo facility was small compared to WestWorld or nearby Cave Creek Memorial Arena. On the plus side, there wasn't a bad seat in the house, including the two JD and Carly finally snagged.

"I almost dropped my soda when that guy bumped into me." The can released a hiss when Carly popped the top.

JD had insisted she needn't skip having a beer just because he was abstaining—he didn't want to take any chances. Carly being Carly had refused, citing a mild headache. JD knew better. Either she didn't want to drink in front of him or was erring on the side of caution should she be called on to drive home.

He wasn't sure if he should be pleased at her consideration or annoyed that his health was affecting not just him but the people close to him, as well.

"You doing all right?" she asked.

"Great." JD had been a little concerned about climbing the bleacher steps. Glancing around, he was glad to realize the height didn't bother him. In fact, he hadn't felt this good in ages.

How could he not feel good, sitting next to Carly? When another person plopped down at the end of the row, everyone scooted to the left, putting her and JD that much closer.

"I haven't been to a rodeo since before I was pregnant." She surveyed their surroundings with keen interest. "Becca and I went to the Parada del Sol. She managed to wrangle us front row seats through her work, and we had a blast."

"This may not be quite as exciting. Amateur events don't compare to the real thing."

"They use the same bulls, right? I read that in the *Mustang Valley News*."

"They do. But the skill level of the competitors won't be the same. Still, we could be in for a few wild rides. Bulls are pretty unpredictable."

A loud commotion had them twisting in their seats. From their elevated vantage point, they could see the wranglers herding the bulls from the holding pen behind the arena and along the fenced-off aisle to the bucking chutes. The first three bulls were loaded into the chutes with, fortunately, little trouble. Raring to rumble, they kicked and snorted and pawed the ground.

How many times had JD seen this exact same sight? His muscles tightened in anticipation. He pictured himself straddling the chute, adjusting his hat and gloves and buckling his safety vest as he readied for his ride. A burst of adrenaline energized him, and he tapped a nervous rhythm with his boot heel.

Someday soon, JD would be on a bull again. He refused to believe his rodeo days were at an end—he had more incentive now than ever before. She sat right beside him.

"Listen up, all you cowboys and cowgirls," blared the announcer's voice from the speakers. "The bull riding will start in ten minutes."

The crowd collectively quieted.

"We ask that you find your seats before then and stay put. Remember, no one other than contestants, rodeo wranglers and Poco Dinero staff are allowed past the yellow barriers. One warning and one warning only. If you cross the barrier a second time, you'll be assisted out the front entrance by two big and mean security guards and not let back inside for the rest of the night." He paused until the laughter died down. "In all seriousness, bull riding is a dangerous sport. We want you to enjoy yourselves, and the best way to do that is to make sure our EMTs over there by that ambulance do nothing all night but twiddle their thumbs. Now, are you ready to get started?"

A deafening cheer filled the stands. When it finally died down, the first competitor's name and number were called. Scattered gasps went up as the bull exploded from the chute into the arena, twisting and spinning and bucking, doing his best to unseat his rider.

"I can't believe he's hanging on," Carly said, her gaze riveted on the action below, her hands clasped in front of her.

"Not for long." JD's prediction came true a second later when the competitor was hurled through the air like a beanbag in a child's game.

"Ouch," she squealed and then faced JD. "How'd you know?"

"He was off balance from the moment the chute door opened. I'm surprised he lasted five-point-nine seconds."

From then on, Carly insisted JD assess each rider, listing what they were doing right and what they were doing wrong.

"Do you know anyone competing tonight?" she asked after a particularly harrowing ride.

The cowboy had fallen directly beneath the bull's thrashing hooves, and the comically dressed bullfighters had rushed in without hesitation, putting themselves in grave danger. The first guy had shouted and waved his arms to distract the bull while the second guy ran to the fallen cowboy and pulled him to his feet. Fortunately, the man was unhurt and waved his hat to the crowd before jumping the arena fence.

"I've met a couple of the locals at the ranch," JD said and indicated a woman standing beside the chutes and adjusting her chaps. "I've run into her and her boyfriend a few times on the circuit."

Carly turned to him, her eyes wide. "She's a bull rider?"

"A pretty decent one, too. There aren't a lot of women in the sport."

"I can't begin to imagine. I'd be scared to death."

They both watched as the woman scaled the chute and lowered herself onto the bull's back.

"She's on Mash Up," JD said. "I've ridden him before."

"And?"

"He's no dink. She's got her work cut out for her."

"What's a dink?"

"A bull without a lot of buck in him."

Carly bit her lower lip, her attention glued to the woman.

The next instant, the chute door flew open. Mash Up entered the arena, though *charged* was a better description. The woman hung on, leaning back when the bull bucked and raising her feet to spur him in the shoulders.

"She knows what she's doing," JD commented. "Amateur events like this are about the only place women can compete."

"She has more guts than I do."

JD laughed. "She has more guts than a lot of the men here."

The woman managed to stay on until the buzzer sounded. Her score wasn't high enough to put her in the money, but the crowd loved her and showed their appreciation.

At the end of the bull riding, the top three winners were announced. The crowd vacated the stands and headed inside for drinks and dancing, creating a huge bottleneck at the door. Inside, the band was setting up on the small stage, checking the microphones and tuning their instruments.

JD really wanted to dance with Carly but hesitated asking her. As it turned out, they could barely find a place to stand, much less sit.

"You mind if we leave?" she shouted in his ear.

He shook his head and they jostled their way to the front door. Once outside, they stood for a minute breathing the fresh air.

"Did you see the dance floor?" she asked. "It was packed."

"We'll have to come back another night."

Her expression softened. "I'd like that."

They walked to JD's truck, holding hands

and hopping potholes like earlier. Only when he got behind the steering wheel did he think about the upcoming end of their date. Walking her to her door and…what then? Another kiss? Did that violate the moving-slowly rule?

The ride to her house lasted less than fifteen minutes, during which JD tried hard not to think about them together on her doorstep, inches apart and exchanging body heat.

A hug. That was what he'd do. Give Carly a nice platonic hug and then get the heck out of there before he was tempted to do more.

Pulling into her driveway, he parked behind her parents' car, shut off the truck and climbed out. She did, too. They met at her walkway.

"Thanks, JD. I had a great time."

"Me, too."

"It's been a while since I've gone somewhere other than Sweetheart Ranch or an arts-and-crafts fair. Sometimes I think there's no more to my life than Rickie and work." At the door, she asked, "Would you like to come in?"

"Naw. It's getting late. I don't want to keep your parents waiting."

"All right." She moved toward him. "Good night, JD."

"Night, Carly."

If he wasn't going to kiss her, he should go. Except he couldn't bring himself to move.

Moonlight had turned her green eyes nearly black, and they drew him in. He went willingly.

"I'll talk to you soon," she whispered. "We can make plans for our next date."

"Okay." Still, he didn't move.

"JD?"

"Uh-huh."

When he continued to stand there, she sighed with exasperation. "Guess I haven't made myself clear."

Standing on her tiptoes, she planted a tender kiss on his cheek. JD promptly forgot about going slow and wrapped his arms around her waist.

"That's more like it," she murmured and kissed him fully on the lips.

He let her set the pace for a little while. Then he took charge. She didn't appear to mind, increasing her grip on his neck. When they finally broke apart, they remained where they were, holding on to each other and staring into each other's eyes.

"Where's this going, Carly?" JD finally asked.

"I don't know."

"We should probably talk. Soon."

"We should."

"I don't want there to be any misunderstanding."

Before either of them could say more, the doorknob rattled and twisted. They separated a split second before Carly's dad yanked open the door, a bemused expression on his face.

"Am I interrupting?" he asked.

CHAPTER ELEVEN

CARLY FLOPPED DOWN onto the recliner in her family room, groaning with relief. Pulling the side lever, she raised the footrest and wriggled her aching toes. A grueling day at the boutique and then running errands, Rickie in tow, had left her completely exhausted. He still needed a bath, but Carly couldn't make herself budge.

"Give Mommy a few minutes, okay, sweetie?"

Rickie giggled.

What if they skipped a bath tonight? Would the world come to a screeching halt? Hardly.

She watched her son play on the family room floor. At the moment, he was banging out an earsplitting tune on a toy keyboard. Carly was too tired to object.

One more day of work and then she'd be off for the weekend. It couldn't come fast enough. Sweetheart Ranch, however, would be open and hosting six weddings, three each on Saturday and Sunday. Fourteen total for this week alone, hence the reason for Carly's exhaustion. With June being such a popular month to tie the knot, she'd handled countless last-minute emergencies, earning points with the owners, who'd thanked her profusely for going above and beyond.

Carly liked staying busy. It kept her from dwelling on JD, their *second* kiss after the bull riding and their new relationship. It seemed their hearts had known all along what their heads refused to accept: they were meant for each other.

But that didn't guarantee smooth sailing ahead. There were still obstacles to overcome.

JD had left shortly after Carly's dad opened the door and discovered them acting like a pair of teenagers caught necking. JD had been willing to stay and face the music with her, not that he'd used those words. Rather, she'd read them in his eyes. But she'd refused to put him through another third degree from her parents and told him they'd talk the next day. He'd gotten her message, bid good-night to Carly's dad and made a beeline for his truck.

To Carly's shock, her dad said nothing to her mom. She doubted his silence had lasted. Odds were he and Mom had engaged in a lively discussion on the drive home. They must have mutually decided not to pester Carly.

If only she and JD could have that talk he'd mentioned, she might fret less. But with the incredible number of June weddings happening at Sweetheart Ranch and a five-day-long barrel-racing clinic at Powell Ranch, they'd yet to find an opportunity to focus exclusively on each other. She'd considered asking him over for dinner one evening, but until her work schedule lightened, that wasn't an option. She could barely keep her eyes open past Rickie's bedtime much less have an important conversation.

They did find time to connect every day at least once and usually twice. Hearing JD's voice lifted her spirits and gave her the boost she needed to power through until five o'clock. Just this afternoon they'd made tentative plans for Saturday evening after JD finished at the ranch. Carly planned to nap when Rickie did in order to be well rested.

As if her thoughts had reached JD, her phone pinged. He wasn't the only person who texted Carly, but lately he texted her more often than anyone else, including Becca.

Carly picked up her phone from the side table and glanced at the display, fully expecting to see his name and picture—she'd taken several of him at the bull-riding event and saved the best one to his contact profile.

To her surprise, Evelyn's name appeared. Carly experienced a moment of confusion, followed by trepidation and didn't immediately open the message.

Her former mother-in-law had continued her same previous pattern for this past week, continually calling Carly and asking when she and Patrick Sr. could come for another visit. Carly had put her off, blaming her grueling work schedule. Evelyn would then counter that she and Patrick Sr. could help Carly by easing her load.

Carly kept trying to convince herself that Evelyn's intentions were well-meaning. But ever since she and Patrick Sr. were late returning Rickie, Carly's internal voice had been screaming at her to exercise caution.

The last time it happened, when Pat's drinking and violent tendencies had increased in equal proportions, she'd ignored the voice, and look where that got her. This time she was listening, and there would be no repeat. No one was getting hurt, most especially Rickie.

Yesterday, Evelyn had asked if Carly was punishing her. The question had startled Carly. Was she? Subconsciously? She'd ended the conversation by assuring Evelyn they'd get together soon, possibly Sunday.

Drawing in a fortifying breath, she tapped the icon and opened the message, only to read it twice.

We're in the area. Be there shortly.

She sat bolt upright. Evelyn and Patrick Sr. were showing up without calling first? No way!

Carly quickly typed a response.

Not a good time. Just got home from work and have a bunch to do ☹

Evelyn didn't respond. Growing impatient, Carly called her, disconnecting when Evelyn's voice mail kicked in.

Grumbling under her breath, Carly pushed up from the recliner and put Rickie in his playpen. He released a loud wail and shook the sides of the playpen like an angry prisoner rattling his jail cell bars.

"Sorry, sweetie. Mommy needs to tidy up the house really quick."

She spent the next ten minutes furiously putting away toys, loading the dishwasher, taking out the trash and running a comb through her hair, her mood continually souring. Evelyn had obviously tired of being put off and decided on a course of action. Not for one second did Carly believe they'd been in the area. They lived a good twenty miles away.

"Hi, hi, hi!" Rickie shouted as soon as the doorbell rang.

"Be right back. Hang tight, young man."

Carly brushed at a food stain on her blouse, a remnant from Rickie's dinner, and wished she'd changed into fresh clothes. Checking the peephole first, she opened the door to Evelyn and Patrick Sr. and gestured with her hand.

"Come on in."

Why fight? They were here. There'd be no stopping them now.

"We brought oatmeal cookies." Evelyn handed Carly a food storage container. "I made a batch this morning."

"Um, thanks."

"I know how much little Patrick loves them."

"I try not to give him too much sugar."

"My dear. Oatmeal cookies are healthy. Like eating cereal."

Not exactly. Carly tucked the food container under her arm.

Patrick Sr. offered her an apologetic smile. "Sorry to barge in on you."

Carly led them to the family room, where an excited Rickie waited. "I've been working late every night this week," she said. "I just sat down when you texted."

Hopefully, they'd take the hint and not stay long.

Evelyn hurried to the playpen, arms extended. "How's my beautiful baby boy?" She lifted him out and deposited him on the floor.

Patrick Sr. sat in the recliner while Evelyn coaxed Rickie onto the sofa with her. The three of them were soon playing a combo game of peekaboo and catch-the-ball.

"If you don't mind," Carly said, "I'm going to throw some laundry in the washer." She'd been planning on doing that tomorrow on her day off. Now seemed like a better time.

"Go right ahead, dear," Evelyn said without glancing up.

Eventually, Carly finished her chores and Rickie grew tired. Both of them were getting cranky. Carly hid it better than Rickie. He cried.

"It's his bedtime," she said.

Evelyn jumped to her feet with surprising speed. "I can change him and put him down."

"Sure."

One more battle Carly refused to fight. She fixed a bottle while Evelyn carried Rickie into the bedroom, where Carly had already laid out his pajamas. Evelyn then fed him in the rocking chair by the crib. Before long, Rickie nodded off, and she laid him in the crib.

Evelyn stared for several minutes, an expression of pure love on her face. "He's such an angel."

Carly began to wonder if she'd been wrong to question her former mother-in-law's motives. She clearly cared for Rickie. Emotions like the one radiating from her couldn't be feigned.

A thought hit Carly, one she hadn't considered previously and wouldn't have understood before becoming a mother herself. Evelyn's blindness to Pat's faults wasn't entirely out of obstinance or ignorance. She believed the best of her son because she loved him with all her being. To the depths of her soul. Like Carly loved Rickie.

"We should let him sleep," Evelyn finally said, and they tiptoed from the room.

When they returned, Patrick Sr. stood. Carly fully anticipated walking him and Evelyn to the door. Only Evelyn didn't reach for her purse. Pivoting, she confronted Carly.

"We need to talk."

Carly gnashed her teeth together, her brief tenderness toward Evelyn vanishing. "It's late. Can we do this another day?"

"We learned you've been dating that man. The one we met at WestWorld."

"From who?" Surely her mom hadn't broken her promise.

"Annalise saw you at that bar."

"The Poco Dinero?"

"I don't know what it's called."

Carly wracked her brain, finally recalling Annalise. She lived across the street from Evelyn and Patrick Sr. What were the chances she'd be at the bull-riding event on the same night as Carly and JD?

"Yes," she admitted with a tired sigh. This wasn't going according to plan. "JD and I are dating."

"Where do you think the relationship is heading?"

"It's still early. We've only gone out once." Technically. Meeting at Hombre's agility classes didn't count.

"But you like him."

More than liked him. "He's a wonderful guy and really good with Rickie."

Evelyn stiffened. "Isn't he ill?"

Where had she heard that? Maybe Carly's mom wasn't closemouthed when it came to JD.

"He has Meniere's Disease," she said. "It's a condition that affects his balance. It's not fatal or anything and completely manageable with meds and treatments and a few lifestyle changes."

"Is he the best choice for a potential father figure to little Patrick?"

Carly should have seen this coming the second JD's name was mentioned.

"Look, Evelyn. First off, JD and I are nowhere close to discussing a future together. Secondly, he's a big help to me, with Rickie, and my horse jewelry business, which, by the way, is what *you* told me I needed. And lastly—" Carly strove to kept her tone level "—who I date is none of your concern."

"Little Patrick is my grandson."

"That doesn't give you a say in my personal life."

"It does if that person is a potential danger to him."

Carly bit back her first impulse, to state that Evelyn need only look as far as her son for a danger to Rickie. "I assure you, JD is no risk to Rickie or anyone."

"You said yourself he has balance issues. You're not letting him drive little Patrick, are you?"

"I'm exhausted, Evelyn," she said with more bite than she'd intended. "I've had a rough week."

Evelyn responded by dropping the bombshell Carly had been expecting since their very first phone call.

"Little Patrick has a father. If you would only let him—"

"Absolutely not! Pat abdicated his rights."

"He's stopped drinking and is attending AA meetings."

"I'm glad for him," Carly said, "but it changes nothing."

"For you, maybe. It changes a lot for Pat. Being a father to little Patrick will help keep him on the straight and narrow."

Did she really believe that? Apparently. And it would explain her and Patrick Sr.'s sudden reappearance after a year. They wanted to use Rickie as a means to motivate Pat. Or manipulate him. Carly would have to think about that some more.

"The answer is no. Don't ask me again."

Evelyn made a sour face. "You're holding a grudge."

A huge grudge. "I'm keeping my son safe. Which is my number one duty as his mother."

"Pat swears he never hurt your friend." Evelyn whirled on her husband. "Say something, will you?"

Patrick Sr. cleared his throat. "Pat is very sorry. He takes responsibility for letting his drinking get out of hand and for his contribution to your marriage falling apart. That's part of the AA program, owning your mistakes."

Months of arguing and mountains of evidence hadn't changed their minds about their son. Carly would have more luck toppling a brick wall with a handful of pebbles.

"Again, I'm glad for him," she said. "But he's not getting within a mile of Rickie. Not until Rickie's much, much older and able to decide for himself if he wants to meet his father."

"You never used to be this difficult."

Evelyn could credit her son for the change in Carly.

"I wasn't a mother before. Now everything I do, every decision I make is in Rickie's best interest."

Evelyn stuck out her chin. "We still want to see little Patrick on Sunday."

"I'll call you."

"And we'd like to take him to the park."

"No. That's not possible."

"We have rights, Carly."

"You can visit Rickie. Here," she emphasized, "or not at all."

"Th-this isn't over."

"No, I don't suppose it is."

Evelyn and Patrick Sr. left in a huff. Carly closed the door behind them, the bones in her legs like rubber bands. Her former mother-in-law was right—Carly had changed. She'd learned to stand her ground. Still, it wasn't easy, and the last ten minutes had sapped every ounce of her remaining energy.

She flipped off the light and made straight for Rickie's room. In the dim glow of the night-light, she kissed him on the head and rearranged his blanket.

"I love you, darling boy."

In her bathroom, she showered, letting the hot water restore her. Finishing, she slipped on gym shorts and an oversize T-shirt. Was it too late to call JD? He'd likely be asleep by now.

The next minute, she changed her mind. He answered on the second ring, always there for her when she most needed him.

JD PROPPED AN elbow on the stall door and settled in for the early-morning call with his mother. He'd rather talk about his sister's gall bladder surgery recovery, but Sophia Moreno had returned to the topic of *his* health twice now during their conversation.

"Tell me, how's Lupe doing?" he asked, attempting yet again to change the topic. "Feeling better yet?"

"More and more like her old self every day. She has a follow-up appointment with the doctor on Tuesday. But what about you, *mijo*?"

"*Estoy muy bueno*, Mamá. No attacks."

"I worry about you."

"Worry about Lupe. She just had surgery."

"I loved the new pictures of Hombre you sent. He's getting so big."

JD thought of the demolished roll of paper towels he'd found this morning. "Can't grow out of his puppy phase soon enough for me."

"How is Carly? Have you seen her recently?"

"She's all right." It was just like his mother to make the leap from Hombre to Carly. "And no, I haven't seen her since last Saturday."

He shouldn't have mentioned they were dating when he'd last talked to his mother. She'd become ruthless in her quest for information.

"Why not?" she asked.

"We've both been busy. I might go to her house for dinner tomorrow."

"Eso es espléndito!"

"It's just dinner, Mamá."

"We'll see. Any more problems with Rico's grandparents?"

He told her about Evelyn and Patrick Sr.'s unexpected visit and how they wanted Carly to let her ex visit Rickie. "They called and said they were sorry and asked for another chance."

"Is Carly giving them one?"

"They're coming over on Sunday."

"She's a good person. *Una gema.*"

JD agreed. She was a gem. He might not have been as tolerant with Evelyn and Patrick Sr. after the stunt they'd pulled. Stunts, he corrected himself. They'd also shown up at West-World without any advance warning.

The stall's occupant, a large but delicate-boned thoroughbred whose owner used him for dressage, stuck his head over the half door to make friends with Hombre. JD absently patted the horse's withers as the two animals sniffed noses.

"She's decided to have her attorney prepare a visitation agreement. With luck, they'll sign it and stop giving her trouble."

Not for the first time, JD worried that he and Carly dating had caused Evelyn to increase her pressure tactics. Carly had insisted no when he'd brought it up.

"And if they don't sign?" his mother asked.

"Then they won't be seeing Rickie except at Carly's home for the foreseeable future."

JD doubted Carly would go so far as to deny her former in-laws visits altogether. The agreement was more a show of strength and to provide her with much needed peace of mind.

"When do I get to meet her?" His mother's voice had become infused with warmth. "Maybe you can bring her with you when you come home over Labor Day weekend."

"I don't think so." He and Carly weren't at the road-trip stage yet.

"I miss you, Juan Diego. You looked so

handsome in the wedding pictures you sent. I can't believe Carly is able to resist you."

Little did his mother know how much he was the one having trouble resisting Carly.

"I need to improve first before we get serious."

Her voice sobered. "I want that, too, *mijo*. You deserve to be happy. But if Carly is as wonderful as you say she is, she won't care whether you have Meniere's Disease or not."

She didn't. It was in Carly's nature to love unconditionally. But it was in *his* nature to be strong, capable, fit and healthy for the woman he loved. And a worthy provider. Not that Carly needed a man to support her, and not that he didn't like his job. But he'd been chasing a world bull-riding championship for half his life. Working as a barn supervisor, even at an upscale facility like Powell Ranch, didn't compare.

JD pushed aside the despair that hit every time he remembered the rodeo career he'd been forced to quit. His life felt unfinished, his potential unrealized. Accepting defeat—and it did feel like defeat—wasn't easy. There were days he refused and days when holding out for a miracle seemed a waste of time no matter what new treatments or techniques he tried.

"I'd hate to disappoint her, Mamá," he said, trying to explain yet again.

"I think you're more afraid of disappointment yourself."

Could she be right?

A movement at the end of the aisle caught his attention. The horse sensed it, too, and jerked his head up from where it rested on JD's shoulder. Hombre barked once and then began wagging his tail.

Gradually, Tanner emerged from the shadows cast by late-afternoon sun slanting through the overhead openings, and JD waved.

"Mamá, I have to go. Tanner's here."

"Adios, mijo. Yo también te quiero."

"I love you, too."

JD slipped his phone into his jeans pocket and then strode forward to meet his friend, Hombre tagging along.

"What brings you here?" he asked.

"Looking for you." Tanner gave him a brotherly nudge. "Let's get a move on. I talked to your boss already, and he's cutting you loose early. Says he'll meet with the equine chiropractor and handle the evening feeding."

JD hadn't seen much of Tanner since the wedding. He'd been away on his honeymoon trip and then immediately returned to the rodeo circuit.

"Where are we going?" JD asked.

"You'll see."

"Last time I went along with one of your harebrained ideas, we nearly landed in a Tulsa jail."

"It's nothing like that. And those horses were practically starving. We saved their lives."

JD shook his head. "Not sure the local deputy saw it that way. Or the owner."

They'd been heading home from a rodeo early one Monday morning after crashing at a buddy's house for the night. On the outskirts of the neighborhood, they'd spotted a trio of half-starving horses standing in a ramshackle corral, their hooves buried in five inches of mud. The sorry animals had been squeezing their heads through the openings in the corral rails and nibbling the tall grass on the other side. There hadn't been a single blade in the corral or a stalk of hay or a kernel of cracked corn. Tanner had taken pity on the horses and convinced JD to help him jimmy the lock on the corral gate and set the horses free to graze.

The idea had been Tanner's, but JD went willingly along. He refused to let any animal suffer needlessly if he could help it. He'd been glad the deputy released them with only a warning despite the owner's objection. The last thing they'd seen as they drove away was the animal control truck arriving. Tanner had called a few days later and learned the horses were being cared for at the county's large-animal shelter awaiting their owner's court date. He'd been charged with animal neglect.

"Come on, pal. Tell me where we're headed," JD insisted as they left the horse barn.

"The Poco Dinero."

"Bull riding?"

"Yeah. I'm entered, and I need someone to spot me."

"You're entered?" The announcement surprised JD. "Didn't get enough practice last weekend at the Steamboat Springs Rodeo?"

"I wrenched my shoulder. Been taking it easy this week. Figured I could use a test-drive before I hit the road again."

JD whistled to Hombre. "Let me put him in the bunkhouse and I'll be right back."

Tanner was sitting behind the steering wheel of his pickup, the engine idling, when JD hopped in. He'd fed Hombre and given him several toys that should keep him out of trouble until JD got home later.

Traffic was lighter than usual for a Friday night. During the drive, the two men discussed strategy, with JD relaying what he'd seen the previous weekend. Once there, they sauntered through the saloon, stopping to chat with some of the other competitors. Outside, Tanner signed up for the event and evaluated his competition while JD moseyed over to the holding pen.

The familiar sounds and scents—the sight of the cowboys conducting last-minute equipment checks, the sound of bulls lowing, the dust stirred up by shuffling hooves—sent his blood racing. He may not be competing tonight, but his body didn't know the difference.

He didn't just miss bull riding, he physically ached—the pain no less than if he'd lost a limb. The phone call with his mother had only increased his pain. Standing there, seeing what he desperately wanted and couldn't have, JD fought an overwhelming urge to run.

Tanner came up behind him. "You okay?"

"Nope."

"Look." His friend kicked at a loose stone, hands planted on his hips. "You don't have to help me. I shouldn't have asked."

"I want to. I will."

JD knew how important it was to Tanner, to any bull rider, to have someone he trusted in the chute with him. One missed detail, one loose knot, one unfastened buckle, could mean the difference between winning and losing. A good ride and injury. In rare circumstances, life and death.

"Thanks, man." Tanner put an arm around JD and jostled him like he would his brother.

The moment he removed his arm, a shift occurred inside JD. Like the earth resettling in the wake of an avalanche. Not his Meniere's Disease. Something else. His purpose. His dream.

He turned to Tanner. "Are all the slots filled?"

"No. Why?"

"I'm entering."

"JD, man. You can't."

"And, yet, I am." He didn't wait for Tanner to talk some sense into him—he hurried toward the registration table, dodging people right and left.

"You'll get hurt." Tanner jogged to keep pace with JD.

"You might get hurt. It's a risk we take every time we climb on the back of a bull."

"Don't do it." Tanner tugged on JD's arm, pulling him to a stop and looking him square in the face. "What if you have an attack? You could—"

"Carly and I are dating."

"You are? That's great. And no reason to kill yourself."

For Tanner, the answer was easy. He didn't live with JD's limitations. He could drive. Ride a horse. Rodeo for a living. He had perfect hearing. A wrenched shoulder didn't begin to compare.

"I won't ask her to spend her life looking after a sick man, which she'd wind up doing if I can't kick this thing."

"You're not sick."

"Yeah? Then how come you don't want me to compete tonight?"

They reached the registration table. JD gave his name to the young woman in charge, paid his fee and filled out the paperwork. Tanner had quit trying to change his mind.

"Go on." The young woman nodded at the fishbowl on the table holding small folded slips of paper. "Draw your bull."

JD hesitated a moment, nervous energy coursing through him. Then his hand disappeared inside the fishbowl.

He'd been late signing up. Only a few slips of folded paper remained. JD's fingers closed on one, and he withdrew it.

"Well?" Tanner looked over his shoulder.

JD opened the paper and read the name. He knew this bull, had ridden him once before a few years ago and had one of his highest scores ever. The bull might be getting a little long in the tooth by professional rodeo standards, but he'd still give JD a run for his money.

"Sonic Boom," JD said, smiling.

Tanner let out a long breath. "We'd better get you ready. I have some spare equipment in the truck." On the way to the parking lot, he said, "I sure hope I don't regret this."

JD stood ten feet tall after that, excitement tinged with just a trace of fear did that to him. His goal wasn't to win, or even to stay on the full eight seconds. He just had to get on that bull and ride without having an attack, proving his rodeo career wasn't over.

He and Tanner were on their way to the chutes—where they'd sit on or straddle the fence and watch the other competitors ahead of them—when his phone played the ringtone he'd assigned to Carly.

"Hello." He shouted in order to be heard over the noise.

"Hey. Did I catch you at a bad time? Sounds loud there."

"I'm at the Poco Dinero. Tanner's riding tonight."

"Oh. Okay." She paused.

"What's up?"

"Nothing. I was just calling about dinner tomorrow night. But we can talk later," she added.

"I'll call you when I get home, if it's not too late."

Tanner nudged him in the arm to get his attention and pointed. “There’s your bull.”

“Is that Tanner?” Carly asked. “What does he mean, your bull?”

JD debated lying or telling her the truth. He didn’t want to cause her worry. Then again, it was important to him she know he felt good enough to compete, even on this amateur level.

“I’m riding tonight.”

“What? JD, no!” She didn’t miss a beat. “I’m on my way.”

“You don’t have to come,” he said, but she’d already disconnected.

CHAPTER TWELVE

CARLY FIDGETED NERVOUSLY as she waited for Becca to open her door. Finally, *finally*, the knob turned. Carly didn't give her friend the chance to even say hello. Thrusting Rickie into Becca's arms, Carly yanked the diaper bag off her shoulder and dropped it on the floor.

"Thanks for watching him. Give him a bottle, change him, and he should fall asleep soon. If he cries, rock him or pace the room. That sometimes soothes him."

"Wait a minute." Becca blinked startled eyes at Carly. "If he cries?"

"Well, he's a baby. They do that."

Becca shook her head, her long black hair swaying. She and Carly looked as different as two people could. Besides their hair—Carly's short blond locks were a stark contrast to Becca's luxurious ebony mane—Becca also stood four inches taller than Carly and possessed the svelte figure of a runway model.

Yet the two were as close as any sisters. Becca hadn't hesitated a single second when

Carly called and pleaded with her to babysit Rickie so that she could track down JD at the Poco Dinero and convince him to see reason before he killed himself.

"You know I don't have a lot of experience with kids." Becca bounced Rickie in her arms.

He stared in fascination at her hair, eventually grabbing a thick strand and stuffing it in his mouth. Becca barely noticed. She may not have experience, but, in Carly's opinion, she was a natural.

"You'll do great. Call me with any problems. I shouldn't be late. But just in case, there are diapers, juice, milk, toddler meals, cereal and clean pajamas in the bag. Enough for a full day."

"A full day!" Becca's voice rose with alarm. "How long are you planning on being gone?"

"Two hours. Max. The extra supplies are just for emergencies." Carly shifted impatiently. "And I really need to hit the road if I hope to catch JD before he rides."

"Okay. Good luck. But I'm sure he'll be fine."

Carly kissed Rickie on the head and sped off. It wasn't lost on her how she had no hesitation whatsoever about leaving Rickie with her friend. Yet, at the moment, she was refusing Evelyn and Patrick Sr., his grandparents, to see Rickie unsupervised, much less take him anywhere.

They'd shattered her trust. It would be some time before they earned it back, whereas Becca would lay down her life for Rickie. Hadn't she put herself in harm's way and taken the blow intended for Carly?

Scenery sped by on her drive to the Poco Dinero. She mentally rehearsed what she planned to say to JD once she arrived. Had he lost his mind? What if he had an attack? If he didn't care about himself, fine. But he should think of his mother. His sister. His friends. Her. All the people who loved him and didn't want to see him hurt.

Okay, maybe she should leave herself off the list of people who loved him. He might take that the wrong way. Well, she did love him—it was true. As a friend. A good friend. Maybe she'd come to love him as more than that one day. If he lived long enough!

At the Poco Dinero, she parked illegally and ran inside. Weaving her way through the crowded saloon, she skirted the bar and ducked outside to the rodeo arena. There she stopped, her glance wildly darting in every direction. Where was JD?

Almost ready to give up and try the holding pens behind the stands, she suddenly spotted him on the other side of the arena, emerging from a tightly clustered group of cowboys. Pivoting, she hurried toward him, zigzagging like a character in a video game dodging laser fire.

"JD! Wait."

He turned, searching the sea of faces.

"Over here." Breathless, she narrowly avoided two people more interested in partying and having a good time than watching where they were going.

He stopped, recognition dawning in his eyes and then puzzlement. "Carly. I told you not to come."

At long last, she reached him. "I'm rescuing you."

He chuckled. "Am I in danger?"

Beside him, Tanner spoke up. "Evening, Carly. By the way, thanks for all your help with the wedding. We really appreciate it."

"Sure, sure." She didn't take her eyes off JD. "Can we talk? Somewhere more private?"

JD shot Tanner a look.

"Don't let me stop you. I've already had my ride. Fared pretty well if I say so myself." He rolled his shoulder. "Feel good, too."

Carly ignored him. Not on purpose. She was simply riveted on JD. "Please?"

"All right." He grabbed her hand and led her toward the stands.

Rather than go up the steps as she expected, they rounded the corner. There, they found space to breath and a modicum of privacy, the spectators above and beside them watching the competition and paying them little heed.

"Where's Rickie?" he asked.

"With Becca. She's babysitting." Carly's carefully prepared speech evaporated in a thin wisp. At a loss for words, she threw herself at him, letting her actions speak for her. "Don't ride tonight. Please."

He hugged her close. "I have to."

"No, you don't. No one's making you." She pressed her cheek to his chest, drawing comfort from his steady heartbeat.

"*I'm* making me," he said.

"What if something happens?"

"Carly. *Mi cariño*."

He'd never called her an endearment before. She liked the sound of it, though she wasn't sure of the translation. Didn't *mi* mean *my* in English? My something.

"I couldn't bear it," she said into his shirt. "You're too important to me." There. She'd admitted she cared for him without treading into *L* word territory. "And to your family. What about your mother? Does she know you're riding?"

"No."

"If Tanner were any kind of a friend, he'd have stopped you from signing up."

"He tried his best."

"And you refused to listen." That darn stubborn streak of his.

"How can I explain?" JD took hold of her shoulders and set her away from him, just far enough so that he could meet her gaze. "I'm not ready to accept that my rodeo career is over. I won't until I see for myself."

"By putting your life in jeopardy? JD, this is insane. You had an attack the other day when you were riding a horse. A gentle horse that didn't buck or rear or spin or try to trample you when you fell off like a bull will." Just saying those words out loud chilled her insides. "I'm asking you not to ride. For me."

"I've lost something. A part of myself. I have to try to get it back."

"Are you saying if you survive tonight in one piece, you're returning to the rodeo circuit?"

"Riding will let me know returning one day is possible. I'll have hope. Or, I'll have no hope whatsoever. Either way, I'll get my answer. And then maybe I can move forward with the rest of my life."

She didn't think he had to risk life and limb for that. But, apparently, he disagreed.

"I can't bear to watch."

He pulled her in for another hug. "Then don't. Wait for me outside."

"I'm not going anywhere." She pulled back from him, well aware she'd contradicted herself.

"Okay." He laughed.

She pouted. "JD, this isn't funny. I'm scared for you."

"I know." He smiled fondly at her. "You left Rickie and came tearing down here. I'm flattered."

"I might have blocked someone's car in the parking lot."

"I'll be fine, *mi cariño*."

That endearment again. "You swear?"

"Yes. I swear." They walked together to the stands, where they found her a seat near the bottom.

She couldn't quite let him go yet. Giving him a kiss on the cheek, she said, "You stay safe, and there's more where that came from."

"Now that's what I call incentive."

He left her to meet up with Tanner at the bucking chutes. Carly watched his retreating back, her heart constricting.

This was a mistake. A terrible one. She knew it in every fiber of her being. But what could she do? Overpower him? Hardly. He was bigger than her and considerably stronger.

She should have pretended to be sick. Insisted he take her home. Or pitched a fit. No, that would only have embarrassed them both. And the fact was, she and JD weren't in the kind of relationship where she could demand he do or not do something strictly for her.

Her torture didn't last too long. Five minutes later, JD's number was called. From where she perched on the very edge of her bleacher seat, she could see him and Tanner at the bucking chute, swinging their legs over the side. When the announcer said the bull's name, Sonic Boom, Carly gasped. That sounded dangerous.

JD suddenly disappeared down into the chute. Carly wrung her hands, twisting and tugging on her rings. If only they hadn't just watched the bull riding last weekend, she might have been less scared. But the memories of those cowboys being thrown and knocked around and trampled on were too fresh.

With a loud metal clang, the chute door sprang open. Carly jumped to her feet.

"Sit down," a person behind her yelled.

She did, holding her breath as she watched Sonic Boom live up to his name by charging into the arena at what indeed seemed like the speed of sound.

JD hung on for all he was worth—for as long as it took Carly to whisper his name five times. Then he popped off the bull and sailed in a near-perfect arc, landing face-first in the dirt. Rolling onto his back, he lay still.

The audience groaned in unison. Carly leapt up and ran pell-mell toward the arena. The cowboys on horseback herded Sonic Boom toward the gate at the far end as the bullfighters rushed to where JD lay prone.

Was he all right? Why wasn't he moving? Oh, my God, he'd been injured!

"JD!" she shouted at the top of her lungs.

Slamming full force into the arena fence, she clutched the top railing. She might have heaved herself up and over, but at that moment, JD crawled to his feet and grabbed his hat in one smooth motion.

He was all right! And unhurt. At least, he was walking unassisted. Her knees wobbled, and she held on to the railing for fear of collapsing.

Tanner met JD as he exited the arena, giving him a man-hug from the side. They were both smiling like a couple of idiots.

Carly ran to them. Well, to JD. "Are you okay?"

He opened his arms, and she charged him

with nearly the same force as she had the arena fence.

"Hey, careful," he said with a good-natured grin.

She instantly drew back to inspect him. "What?"

"I might have sprained my wrist."

"Let me see." She took his hand in hers, inspecting for swelling. "We need to get ice on this right away."

"Hey, Carly," Tanner said. "I'm here, too."

She barely acknowledged him, which he seemed to find quite amusing, given his belly laugh.

"It's just a sprain," JD insisted.

"I'm taking you home," Carly stated and grabbed his arm.

"Have fun, you two," Tanner called after them, but they were already halfway to the saloon.

JD UNLOCKED THE door to his bunkhouse. On the other side, Hombre alternately whined and scratched.

"Be warned," he told Carly before turning the knob. "He's been home alone for several hours. We could find a shredded couch cushion or a gnawed coffee-table leg."

"Don't worry." Carly inched closer to JD.

"I'm more concerned about getting ice on your wrist. The swelling's worsening."

It did hurt, not that he'd let on.

"Hey, boy." JD entered first, just in case he needed to run interference. Turned out to be the right move—Hombre went wild with excitement, hopping and yipping and jumping on JD. Reaching for the dog's collar with his uninjured hand, JD tried to settle him.

It was a waste of time. The second Hombre saw Carly, he broke free and spun in circles, only to stop abruptly and start barking.

"Enough, Hombre."

JD's command went unheeded.

"You silly dog." Carly stepped inside the bunkhouse. Kneeling down, she let Hombre shower her with affection. "Okay, okay. Enough face-licking. Now, Sit."

As if she spoke flawless dog-ese, Hombre instantly lowered his hind end onto the floor and sat, panting heavily.

"Hmm." JD stared, feeling betrayed. "He listens to you but not me."

"I have the mother voice. Works every time. Well, almost every time." She rose, her gaze traveling to the small kitchen. "Where's your ice pack? In the freezer?"

"I'll get it." To JD's vast relief, everything appeared intact and undamaged. Except for the dog toys he'd left. Those were unrecognizable. Good. His precautions had paid off. "What about Rickie? Is he going to be okay?"

"I'm sure he's fine. Becca would have called me otherwise." Carly pulled out one of the dinette chairs and sat. "I should check in, anyway. Let her know I'll be late."

"You don't have to stay."

"I'm not leaving." She sent him an impatient look and then dialed her friend. "Hi, Becca. How goes it?"

He listened to Carly's end of the conversation as he grabbed a cold pack from the freezer and wrapped it in a dish towel. He held it to his afflicted wrist, then lowered himself into the chair opposite Carly. Hombre crawled beneath the table and lay down, perfectly content now that his human had returned along with one of his favorite people.

"That's good," Carly said into the phone. "No, he'll be fine. He'll probably sleep until I get there." Her gaze sought JD's. "I'm not sure how long I'll be. An hour? JD hurt his wrist." She listened, rubbing her forehead. "Four or five seconds. All that matters is he's mostly unscathed." After a pause, she told Becca, "I'll text you when I'm on my way. And thanks. I owe you big-time." Another pause. "Absolutely. I insist. What colors? All right. See you shortly." She disconnected. "Becca wants a new charm for her horse to match the others I made for her. I should probably give her two—she's earned them."

"Rickie sleeping?"

"She made a bed out of blankets for him on the floor."

"The floor?"

"He'll be all right for the time being. I once let him sleep in the empty bathtub when he was being really fussy and insisted on playing with his bath toys. Next thing I knew, he'd curled into a ball and was sound asleep. I put a washcloth under his head, covered him with a blanket and kept an eye on him until he woke up." She suddenly noticed JD holding the cold pack. "Here. Let me help."

"I've got it."

"Men." She rolled her eyes. "That'll fall off."

JD relented and watched intently as she carefully and gently tended him. Though her ministrations were purely innocent, there was something intimate about sitting across from each other, knee-to-knee, her fingers dancing across his skin.

He sat there, unmoving and barely able to breathe. His wrist might have hurt when he first sat down. But not anymore. The only things he felt were Carly's soft caresses and his heart filling with emotions he wasn't ready to admit.

"All done." She'd used the dish towel to securely bind the cold pack to his wrist.

"Thanks." JD inspected her work. "You're a pro at this."

"You have any aspirin or ibuprofen?"

"In the bathroom medicine cabinet." He started to rise. "I'll get it."

"No." She stood first and placed a hand on his shoulder. "Let me. You just keep that cold pack on your wrist. You're lucky you didn't break it. And I still think you should see a doctor." She'd suggested as much on the drive over. "You may need an X-ray."

"I'll go to the urgent care clinic tomorrow if I'm worse."

She returned a few minutes later, hiding something behind her back. "I have bad news."

"Uh-oh."

"There isn't much left of your bath mat." She pulled what remained from behind her and showed him. "I hope he didn't eat any of it. There's pieces all over the bathroom floor."

JD bent at the waist and peered under the table at his traitorous dog. "My mother gave me that."

Hombre averted his head, refusing to make eye contact, and thumped his tail.

"Watch out he doesn't get sick," Carly said. "Depending on how much he swallowed, he could have a blockage. Take him to the vet immediately if he starts throwing up."

"Great. Just what I need. An expensive vet bill on top of replacing my bath mat."

She walked toward the wastebasket in the corner. "Should I throw this out?"

"Thanks."

When she was done, she brought JD a glass of water and set it, plus two ibuprofen, on the table in front of him. "Take these."

"Yes, ma'am." Hadn't he recently said he liked bossy women? He sure liked *this* bossy woman.

JD downed the pills in one swallow and finished off the remaining water. When Carly carried the glass to the sink, he tracked her every move.

"I can't remember if you told me, are Evelyn and Patrick Sr. for sure coming over on Sunday?"

"I'm calling her tomorrow morning and confirming." Carly returned to her chair and sat.

Sadly, there was no more knee-touching. No more touching of any kind.

"You going to mention the visitation agreement?"

"I haven't decided." She lifted a shoulder.

"Think I'll play it by ear. See how the visit goes first and what kind of mood they're in. Evelyn was very contrite during our last conversation, but she can change on a dime."

With his wrist on ice, there was no reason for Carly to stay. Any moment, he expected her to grab her purse and leave. Instead, she made herself more comfortable, crossing her legs and propping an elbow on the table.

"Tell me about your ride."

"My ride?" The request surprised him.

"How was it?"

"Short." He chuckled, remembering the embarrassingly low number of seconds he'd lasted appearing on the scoreboard.

She smiled. "Besides that."

He looked at her with interest. "You really want to know?"

"Now that it's over, yes."

He considered before answering. "Like I never quit. Like I was right where I belonged, doing what I was born to do. I had no doubt I was in for one of the best rides of my life. My grip was tight, my balance was perfect, I'd ridden the bull before and I knew exactly what to expect."

"What happened? Why did you fall?"

"Sonic Boom decided to give me a flying lesson. He must have sensed my overconfidence and swerved to the left when I anticipated him swerving right. Simple physics. It's what makes bull and bronc riding hard to do and fun to watch."

She assessed him critically. "Did you accomplish what you set out to?"

He nodded. "Rodeo is a part of me. I'm not ready or willing to give it up yet."

"When are you thinking of returning to the circuit?" Her voice contained a slight tremor.

"Don't worry. I'm not doing anything reckless or impulsive." He sat back in his chair. "I may have a lead on something."

"Define *something*."

"The Poco Dinero is hiring a new part-time rodeo event manager. I'm applying for the job."

"What does a rodeo event manager do?" she asked hesitantly.

"Oversee the barrel racing and bull riding. Coordinate with the bucking-stock rental company. Supervise the staff, hire bullfighters and wranglers. Make sure the grounds, arena and stands are maintained and the equipment is in good working order."

"Sounds like a lot for just a part-time position."

"About twelve hours per week. Fridays and Saturdays only, with the occasional Sunday."

At her raised eyebrows, he said, "I talked to the owner. She's interviewing me this week."

"Really?" Carly attempted to hide her surprise. "What about your job here at Powell Ranch?"

"I'd have to talk to Ethan. See if he'd let me adjust my schedule. He's been pretty flexible so far."

"Would you be working with the bulls? Riding? What if you have an attack? Will the Poco Dinero be responsible if you get hurt on the job? Is there insurance? Will you be required to sign a waiver?"

She was asking good questions. "I'll find out all that at the interview. I won't lie to the owner—I'll disclose my condition. Come up with a backup plan should I have an attack on the job."

"You think she'll be agreeable?"

"The best I can do is see what she says."

"It could still be dangerous, JD."

"No more dangerous than the job I have now."

"If you get the job, will you stay in Mustang Valley and not return to rodeoing?"

"I may keep Mustang Valley as my home base. But I'd return to rodeoing."

She lowered her gaze.

He reached across the table with his good

hand and folded her fingers inside his. "I refuse to allow fear of what might happen to rule my every waking moment. I'm improving. My attacks are coming less and less frequently."

"But they haven't stopped altogether."

"And they may never stop."

She sighed.

"I've lost so much, Carly, made so many sacrifices. I'm not letting Meniere's Disease rob me of rodeo. I'm not letting it rob me of a potential future with you, either. And before you say anything, yeah, I know that contradicts what I've been saying all along. The thing is, I've changed my mind recently."

"Because of one bull ride," she said flatly.

"Because of you, Carly. I'm glad you didn't give up on me and kept pushing."

She grimaced. "I didn't mean for you to get into a more dangerous line of work."

"I won't be riding any bulls."

"Not yet."

"You're right." He squeezed her fingers. "If I continue to do well and improve, I will ride again. That's a given whether I get the job at the Poco Dinero or not."

"Don't suppose I can convince you otherwise?"

"This is a step in the right direction. For me. For us. I can't keep treading water, waiting for something to happen. Not when I have the ability to make it happen. We're alike that way. Fighters for what we want."

Her gaze roamed his face for several long seconds. "I could say you're in this alone, that I can't bear to stand by while you take unreasonable risks."

"You could."

"Or I could say, whatever you're planning, count me in."

His pulse instantly accelerated. "Which is it, Carly? I need to know before this goes any further."

She braced her hands on the table. "I'm done."

His spirits immediately sank as if weighted with boulders. He'd been so sure of her answer.

"Done with staying safe and being cautious." She leaned forward, her jade eyes alight. "And you were right. I fight for what I want—which happens to be you."

JD shot out of his chair, sending it teetering. Carly rose, too. A moment later, they were in each other's arms, her sighs and his low moan mingling.

By now, they fit comfortably together, two halves of a whole. JD lingered, rushed and lingered again, sensing Carly's needs and striving to fulfill them. Several kisses and murmured phrases later, they separated.

"So, does this mean dinner tomorrow night is official?" she asked, skimming her lips along his jawline.

He circled her waist with his unafflicted arm. She'd be leaving soon. Until then, he'd enjoy every second. "Tomorrow and the next weekend and the weekend after that."

"Good," she said with a contented sigh. "Because as it turns out, I'm free."

He kissed her one more time for good measure before walking her outside to her car. They still faced countless challenges, but the odds had changed to much more in their favor.

CHAPTER THIRTEEN

CARLY SAT AT the table in her workroom, adjusting the stand supporting her tablet. Right, left and then up.

"Nope."

The angle cast her face in too many shadows and showed the marks on the wall where Rickie had colored with a supposedly washable marker. She tilted the stand and moved her chair.

"Much better!"

Now the background was filled with photos displaying her equine jewelry creations. If all went well, the potential new client would be impressed during their video call.

Carly checked the time. Twenty-seven minutes. Her nerves tingled in anticipation.

She was putting extra effort into this call. The woman frequently rode her stunning Arabian in parades and horse shows and even at rodeo halftime performances, both she and the horse decked out in full costumes. If she chose to purchase originally crafted accessories from Carly, it could mean a nice bump in sales. More, if the woman recommended Carly to her fellow exhibitors.

Carly had scrambled to find a babysitter at the last minute, preferring not to have a crying or overactive Rickie interfering with such an important call. But both Becca and her parents had plans, as did the teenager Carly had used once before in a pinch. She'd expected as much—it was Wednesday evening and the call with the potential client had been last minute.

When JD had volunteered, she'd immediately accepted his offer. Rickie adored him, and JD was really good with Rickie. Besides, how much trouble could they get into, playing in the family room while she talked? In return, she'd promised to feed JD. Even now, beef stew simmered in the slow cooker, a salad chilled in the refrigerator and a loaf of French bread sat on the counter, waiting to be sliced.

Carly laid out the sample pieces of jewelry she intended to show the client during the call, arranging them in a specific order on the table next to her tablet. They represented some of her best work, and she thought they'd fit well with the woman's various costumes. To prepare, Carly had visited the woman's website and pored over the photo gallery posted there.

"Hombre, Leave It!" JD's voice carried from the family room.

Carly smiled to herself. The dog must be stealing Rickie's toys again. He couldn't help himself—they looked too much like his own toys.

She continued readying for the video call, letting JD handle the situation. Things had been progressing well for them this past week and a half. So well, she sometimes worried it was too good to be true.

In addition to her dropping by the ranch twice with Rickie and them tagging along to Hombre's agility class, Carly had formally introduced JD to Becca. She'd given Carly her full approval. On Monday, Carly and JD had taken Rickie to Molly's house after work for his first horse ride, though Popeye was smaller than any horse.

While JD led the kid-friendly pony around the yard, Carly walked alongside, holding on to Rickie's waist. He'd been ecstatic, laughing and babbling the entire time. When they were done and Rickie was back on solid ground, he'd reached up and, holding Popeye's head between his hands, kissed the pony's nose. On the way home, they'd stopped at the market for ice cream—cones for Carly and JD, and cups for Rickie and Hombre.

JD also had his interview with the owner of the Poco Dinero for the part-time rodeo event manager. According to him, the interview had gone well. The owner had called this morning to schedule a second interview and let him know she was considering him and one other candidate. JD was the most qualified, experience-wise, but the owner was understandably concerned about his health issues. JD was being cautiously optimistic.

Carly, too. She knew how much he wanted the job and was determined to support his choices regardless of her own concerns. Besides, why fret about what hadn't happened? Better to wait and see if he got the job before worrying herself into a frenzy.

Her advice to herself had turned out to be good. Carly hadn't been this happy in a long, long time. JD still expressed concerns that she might not be emotionally ready for a romantic relationship or could wind up taking care of a sick man. But Carly felt more than ready, something she was sure had everything to do with JD being "the one."

In fact, she'd been feeling so good and optimistic about the future, she'd decided to let Evelyn and Patrick Sr. take Rickie to the park. Not this Saturday. The one after. Maybe. If they asked. And as long as they continued to respect her wishes without complaints and without pulling any fast ones on her.

Carly was very proud of herself for how she'd been standing up to Evelyn. She'd been making her point and getting Evelyn to agree to her terms without engaging in verbal battles. Considerable progress over the old Carly.

Conducting one last review, she went out to the family room. JD tossed one of the tennis balls he'd brought with him. Both Hombre and Rickie ran after it. Ran! Rickie had only just learned to walk a short while ago and already he was a track star.

Hombre reached the ball first, and they both came hurtling toward JD, Rickie crying, "Dada, dedoda."

Was he saying *Daddy*? No, impossible. He must be babbling like always. It wasn't as if she'd been teaching him to say the word, whereas she'd painstakingly taught him to say *Mama*.

JD spied her and rolled to his feet. "You all set?"

She was relieved to see his sprained wrist had fully healed. There was a chance, like usual, she'd overreacted the night he'd been injured.

"Ready as I'll ever be," she said.

"Nervous?"

"A little. She seemed very nice when we spoke on the phone yesterday and scheduled the video call."

He slung an arm around her shoulder and squeezed. "You'll do great."

Rickie ran over to them, the tennis ball forgotten, and hugged both their legs. A lump formed in Carly's throat, and she swallowed, surprised by the sudden rush of emotions. This was exactly the kind of scene she'd imagined with her and Rickie and JD but hadn't allowed herself for fear of being disappointed.

Afraid she might start crying and ruin her makeup before the video call, she pulled away. "I should get a water. In case my throat gets dry or I start coughing."

Five minutes before she was scheduled to place the video call, Carly kissed Rickie and told him to behave for JD. She'd half hoped he'd be sleepy and ready for bed but knew that wasn't going to happen. Not with JD and Hombre there.

"There's a bottle of juice in the fridge and some teething biscuits on the counter if he wants them or starts fussing," she told JD.

"Quit worrying. We'll be fine."

They would be, too. She was sure of it. Standing on tiptoe, she gave JD a quick peck on the cheek. "Thanks."

He held her a moment, his gaze locked with hers. “Good luck.”

Was this a glimpse into their potential future? The kind of life they could have together? The thought filled Carly with joy and made concentrating on business hard.

The client—potential client, she should say—answered on the second ring with a cheery hello. As JD had predicted, everything went wonderfully. The woman loved Carly’s creations and placed an order for two ankle bracelets, ten mane charms, four necklaces and two brow bands. Carly jotted down notes and dashed off a few sketches as they talked. They also discussed charm selection, semiprecious gemstones and completion dates.

As they were wrapping up the call, the doorbell rang, shattering Carly’s concentration. Who could that be? She wasn’t expecting anyone. The sound of JD’s footsteps let her know he was answering the door.

“Hi, hi, hi,” Rickie squawked loudly.

Carly apologized to her new client, who was very understanding.

A minute later, Carly’s mood plummeted and her anger rose when she heard Evelyn’s voice.

“Oh. You’re here. Where’s Carly?”

Her former in-laws! What did they want?

Had they sent another text saying they were in the area? Possibly. Carly had left her phone in the kitchen so as not to be disturbed.

"On a video call," JD answered. "We can't disturb her."

Rickie continued shouting, "Hi," over and over.

"I'll call you in a few days with any questions," Carly told the woman, "and to give you a progress report."

"Wait."

All her hopes of ending the call vanished. The woman had several more questions, which Carly tried to patiently answer while keeping one ear trained on the conversation between JD and her former in-laws.

Eventually satisfied, the woman thanked Carly and they said goodbye. Carly hurriedly disconnected and rushed into the family room, fighting to keep a lid on her anger.

"Evelyn. Patrick Sr. This is a surprise."

She expected to find three adults conversing—if not politely, then at least civilly—while Rickie played or was being held by a grandparent. Instead, JD sat in the recliner, cradling his head with one hand. Rickie clung to him, tears streaming down his face. Hombre sat beside the recliner, constantly nudging JD's other hand with his nose.

Shock rippled through Carly, her mind quickly fitting the pieces together. Poor JD. He'd had an attack…and at the worst possible time.

Evelyn wheeled on Carly. "Thank goodness we got here when we did. Your boyfriend almost collapsed and might have dropped little Patrick if not for us. Patrick Sr. had to grab him by the arm and help him into the chair before he fell." She emphasized the words *he* and *him* to indicate JD. "Little Patrick could have broken a leg or hit his head and suffered a concussion."

Carly went over to the recliner, immediately determining that, despite his tears, Rickie was fine and unharmed. Probably more scared that anything, either from JD swaying or, Carly guessed, his grandmother's raised, infuriated voice. Carly stroked his hair and spoke soothingly, which had the desired effect of calming him.

"Are you okay?" she asked JD.

"I'm sorry."

He looked miserable. His face drained of all color and his eyes closed, he breathed slowly and evenly as if timing himself. She imagined he was desperately trying not to throw up on Rickie and in front of everyone.

"Can I get you something?" she asked gently. “A glass of water? A sports drink?” Had he said that helped? She couldn’t remember. “An ice pack for your neck?”

“Water,” he croaked. “Thanks.”

“What about little Patrick?” Evelyn demanded, glaring at Carly.

“He’s okay for now.”

In fact, he looked perfectly content right where he was. Carly wondered if, not unlike Hombre, her son was helping JD stay focused and ride out his attack.

She was just returning from the kitchen, a glass of water for JD and the bottle of juice for Rickie in hand, when Rickie suddenly called out, “Dada, dadoda,” followed by a sharp yelp.

Hastening her steps, she came upon Evelyn attempting to take Rickie from JD. Rickie refused to let go, and the harder Evelyn tugged, the tighter he clutched JD.

“Evelyn. That’s enough.” Carly placed the glass of water beside JD and gave Rickie the bottle of juice, which he shoved in his mouth.

“He won’t let go of Rickie,” she said, red-faced.

Clearly, it was the other way around. Rickie wouldn’t let go of JD.

“He’s upset,” Carly said.

“Of course he’s upset. He was almost dropped.”

Carly placed a hand on JD’s shoulder. “You

want me to—" She was about to say "help you into the bedroom," but reconsidered. JD would detest appearing like he needed assistance walking. "You want to go into the other room?" she asked instead.

He attempted a weak smile. "Maybe. In a minute."

Hombre whimpered and licked JD's hand. He stroked the dog's head in return.

"What about little Patrick?" Evelyn demanded.

Her former mother-in-law wasn't going to rest until Carly rectified the situation. Problem was, her solution wouldn't sit well with Evelyn. Well, too bad.

Reaching down, Carly lifted Rickie into her arms. He wasn't happy but let go of JD. When Evelyn extended her arms toward Rickie, he shook his head and, continuing to drink his bottle, hugged Carly's neck as hard as he had JD's.

Evelyn's expression darkened.

"Will you be okay for a bit?" Carly asked JD.

He nodded and took a long swallow of the water. "Don't worry about me."

"Good." To Evelyn and Patrick Sr., she said, "Let's go to the living room where we can talk."

As she led the way, she glanced over her shoulder at JD. He'd drained the glass and was now leaning his head against the back of the recliner, petting Hombre, breathing deeply and moving his lips as he silently counted or perhaps chanted.

It pained her leaving him to fend off the attack by himself, but she had little choice. The situation with Evelyn and Patrick Sr. couldn't wait a moment longer.

"We realize who you choose to date isn't any of our business."

Carly shook her head. "No, it's not."

Evelyn sucked in a breath and started again, "We're concerned."

"About?"

"We're not the bad guys here, Carly."

"I wouldn't say bad." Carly's glance traveled from Evelyn to Patrick Sr. "You are pushy."

"We only have little Patrick's best interests at heart."

"I'm sure you do. *Your* idea of his best interests."

Evelyn snapped her mouth shut.

She and Carly sat together on the living room couch, Rickie between them. He'd finally settled and lay on his side, his head resting in Carly's lap. He'd finished his bottle and was beginning to drift off. Six fifty was normally too early for his bedtime, but he did sometimes konk out after a crying jag. Carly wished she could put him to bed but refused to leave her former in-laws alone with JD.

Sneaking a glance in the direction of the family room, she wondered how he was faring. Had his attack subsided? The last two had been over fairly quickly. Considering all was quiet, she figured he was resting. He might also be listening to her conversation with Evelyn and Patrick Sr. She would, were their situations reversed.

"You haven't explained why you're here. And please don't say you were in the area," she added.

Evelyn cleared her throat. "We'd like to take Rickie to his cousin's birthday party on Saturday."

"You could have called. There was no need to show up unannounced."

"We thought asking in person would be better."

Of course. Carly was very familiar with this Evelyn-tactic. Harder to deny a face-to-face request.

"I'll check my schedule and get back to you tomorrow. What time is the party? I should be free during the day."

Evelyn didn't miss a beat. "We'd like to take little Patrick ourselves. Without you."

Carly swallowed a surprised laugh. Was she kidding? "I'm sorry. The answer is no."

"Be reasonable."

"I am. Some people in my shoes wouldn't allow you see their child without a court order. Eventually, someday, you can take Rickie again. To the park or the fast-food restaurant. Not for an entire afternoon to Glendale, thirty-something miles away."

"You're being selfish."

"Selfish would be saying Rickie can't go at all. He can, with me along."

From the family room, Hombre yipped. JD could be heard telling the dog to be quiet.

Evelyn scowled. "He has some health issues."

"JD," Carly corrected her. "His name is JD."

"Little Patrick seems fond of him."

"He is," Carly agreed. "And JD's fond of him."

"He called him *Daddy*."

Ah-ha. This would account for Evelyn's scowl. "Rickie babbles a lot."

"I heard him clear as day."

Carly would have been annoyed at Evelyn if the same thought hadn't occurred to her earlier.

"Okay. Let's assume he did call JD *Daddy*.

Children learn words by hearing other people speak them. Since I've never called JD *Daddy*, in front of Rickie or otherwise, I must have read it to him in a book."

Evenly averted her head, but not before Carly noticed a flicker of alarm in her eyes.

Suddenly, she knew! "You've been talking to Rickie about Pat."

"No!" Evelyn's denial was much too quick and much too forceful.

"We agreed you weren't to mention him."

"I didn't."

Carly shot Patrick Sr. a glance. His guilty expression told her everything.

Biting her tongue, she held in the furious rant threatening to erupt. Continuing to argue with Evelyn would just cause her to dig in her heels and put Carly in a tough spot.

"Since neither of us has said *Daddy* in front of Rickie, he couldn't have learned the word and must have been babbling."

If she'd expected her former mother-in-law to back down, she was gravely mistaken.

"Well, it does raise several important questions."

This Carly had to hear. "Such as?"

"Is *JD*," Evelyn said, emphasizing his name, "fit to be a father figure to Rickie, what with his health problems?"

Carly wouldn't give Evelyn the satisfaction of knowing JD had posed the same concerns. "As I've said before, we've only been dating a short while. Too short to consider marriage."

Right. Tell that to her heart. Lately, she'd been seeing herself in every bride who entered the boutique and comparing their purchases to ones she'd make.

"We'll stick to the present, then," Evelyn said. "He was watching little Patrick while you worked, right? And then he had a spell or whatever you call them. The results might have been disastrous for little Patrick." She absently reached over and rubbed Rickie's leg.

Carly was again reminded that her former mother-in-law cared greatly for Rickie. And while her actions were sometimes questionable, they were motived by love.

The thought gave Carly pause. The truth was, she hadn't actually seen what happened. Evelyn could well be painting a more dramatic picture, as she often did. Then again, Carly had previously witnessed JD topple during an attack. If he'd been holding Rickie when that happened, her son could have been hurt.

"I hear your concerns, Evelyn. But keep in mind, I was in the other room, not miles away. Also, JD and Rickie were playing on the floor.

He only stood and picked up Rickie because you and Patrick Sr. arrived."

Evelyn's cheeks reddened, telegraphing her opinion of Carly's response. "That doesn't change the fact, if you're relying on him to help parent little Patrick, he's unreliable at best and a potential danger at worst."

"I'll consider your points, I promise." Carly prayed for this conversation to end and for her former in-laws to leave. Rickie had fallen fully asleep by this time, and she was utterly drained. Making a show of looking at her watch, she said, "Wow, it's getting late."

Evelyn made one last attempt as she and Patrick Sr. got to their feet.

"Will you please let us take little Patrick to the birthday party? He'd have a chance to meet his cousin and aunt and uncle."

Carly really wanted Rickie to meet the other side of his family. "Will Pat be there?"

"No!"

Another vehement reply that left Carly uneasy. "As I said before, Rickie can go as long as I go, too."

"I'll let you know," Evelyn answered brusquely. Her demeanor changed entirely when she whispered a gentle goodbye in Rickie's ear.

After they left, Carly carried Rickie into the

family room, where JD was still sitting in the recliner and stroking Hombre's head.

"How are you doing?" she asked.

"Better."

She was glad to see his color had returned. "Let me put this little guy to bed. I won't be long."

"No rush."

Another missed bath for Rickie. Carly was beginning to feel like a failure as a mother. He slept through the diaper change and putting on clean pajamas. Carly bent and kissed him good-night. When he murmured and smiled in his sleep, love filled her to bursting and she didn't feel like a failure at all.

Returning to JD, she patted his shoulder before perching on the sofa adjacent to the recliner. "You hungry?"

"Not yet. My stomach's… Food's not a good idea at the moment."

"I have some over-the-counter anti-nausea medicine in the bathroom cabinet."

"Helped myself to some while you were talking to Evelyn and Patrick Sr. Hope you don't mind." He gave her the serious look she was coming to recognize. "We need to talk."

Obviously, he'd heard her conversation with her former in-laws about him. "If you're thinking of breaking up with me because of what happened, mister, think again. Not happening."

"Evelyn isn't wrong. I could have dropped Rickie."

"Don't let her get in your head," Carly insisted. "I know from past experience how easy that is."

"Okay."

He wasn't giving up on them—she could tell that much from his tone. He also had his doubts. She blamed the attack and scene with her former in-laws. It had sapped JD's energy and damaged his confidence in them and their future success as a couple.

"I should probably hit the road," he said.

"Are you able to drive yet?" At his hesitation, she suggested, "I have an idea. I'll pour me a lemonade and you some ginger ale. We can sit on the patio for a little while."

"I'd like that. Thanks for being so understanding."

"That's what people who are seeing each other do. Be understanding." She rose from the sofa, prepared to help him stand if necessary. It wasn't.

"You're taking on a giant burden with me."

"Same goes for you. I have a ton of baggage. Including two difficult former in-laws."

He smiled, and some of Carly's earlier tension evaporated.

While he and Hombre went outside, she fixed their drinks. Joining JD on the patio, she handed him the ginger ale and sat beside him in the empty chair.

"To us." She tipped her glass of lemonade in a toast, which he returned.

"To us."

"Now distract me from my troubles with Evelyn and Patrick Sr. by telling me how pretty I look at sunset."

"Not pretty." He reached over and covered her hand with his. "Beautiful."

She sighed. "Much better."

They chatted when they had something to share and enjoyed companionable silence when they didn't. She told him about her call with the new client and the big order the woman had placed. He updated her on his sister's post-surgery recovery. Together, they watched the falling dusk turn the sky from gold to gray and the full moon, an enormous silver disk, rise in the eastern sky.

"I've been thinking of getting one of those child GPS devices," Carly said. "If I eventually let Evelyn and Patrick take Rickie places without me. I read an article about them in a parent magazine."

"Child GPS device?"

"They're for tracking your child's location in real time. I could always hide it in Rickie's diaper bag. That way, if they're late, or even if they're not, I can verify his location on my phone and, hopefully, worry less."

"That's actually a good idea."

"I'm not being too obsessive?"

"If a GPS device gives you peace of mind, why not? And who knows? You might find out for sure if Evelyn's up to something."

He was right. She'd look into buying one the first chance she had.

Sooner than she was ready, JD got up and announced he was hitting the road. Carly packed him some leftovers to take: a food container with stew, another one with salad and two thick pieces of French bread wrapped in plastic.

She walked him outside to his truck. "Can I call you next time I need a sitter?"

"Call me anytime." He set the leftovers on the passenger-side floor. "Sorry I ruined our dinner plans."

"Now I have an excuse to invite you over again. How about Saturday? Assuming Evelyn doesn't call me about the birthday party."

"I have my second interview with the owner of the Poco Dinero at two."

"Swing by after that. Rickie should be up from his nap."

"It's a date."

She did so like the sound of that. "Maybe we'll have a reason to celebrate."

They kissed tenderly before he climbed in his truck and drove away, Hombre riding shotgun. Returning inside, Carly decided against eating so late and drank a protein shake she found in the cupboard. Changing into her nightclothes, she flipped on the bedroom TV, thinking a mindless sitcom would help her relax until she grew tired enough to fall asleep. Three commercial breaks into the show, her phone rang, triggering a burst of nervous anger. Her phone seldom rang this late barring an emergency.

Evelyn's name and number appeared on the display. "Really?" Carly said to the phone and sat up. "I thought we were done for the night."

Skipping any greeting, she answered with, "It's well after eight."

"Patrick Sr. and I were talking." Evelyn didn't bother with a greeting, either. "About your friend JD."

"You were." Carly failed to keep the sarcasm from her voice.

"We can't, in all good conscience, permit him to take over the role of little Patrick's father. Not when little Patrick already has one. And especially not when the man is clearly sick."

"Permit him," Carly blurted. "Are you joking?"

"We never wanted Pat to abdicate his rights," Evelyn went on as if she hadn't heard Carly. "We encouraged him to take his time and think about it before signing the paperwork. But your friend threatened to press charges and left him no choice."

Carly's grip on the phone tightened until her hand cramped. "Pat's assault on her was what left him no choice."

Again, Evelyn continued as if not hearing Carly, "We've agreed to lend Pat the money so that he can fight the custody agreement."

Carly's gut roiled. Yes, she'd been expecting something along these lines for weeks—that didn't lessen the impact.

Holding in her rage, she kept silent. Knee-jerk reactions often backfired. Also, it was possible this idea was solely Evelyn's and Pat had no clue. Until Carly learned for sure, she'd refrain from inciting her former in-laws or giving them reason to retaliate.

"However," Evelyn said, jarring Carly from her musings, "if you agree to let Pat see Rickie, he won't move forward with any legal action."

Forget keeping silent. Carly's blood boiled. "Are you blackmailing me?"

"Absolutely not!"

"It certainly feels like you are."

"We're merely asking you to be reasonable. Little Patrick needs his father."

"Put Patrick Sr. on the phone."

"What! No, I won't."

"Let me talk to him or this conversation ends now."

A moment later, he came on the line with a hesitant "Hello."

"Are you in agreement with what Evelyn is saying?" Carly asked.

There was a long pause followed by, "Pat's changed. He's really trying. And he misses his son. Surely you can understand that."

Patrick Sr.'s little speech sounded rehearsed. That, or Evelyn was speaking in his ear and telling him what to say.

"Please, Patrick. You know what your son's capable of and that what he did to Becca is no fabricated story. You also know Evelyn's orchestrating this whole thing. Help me do what's right."

"They're my family. My son and my wife."

"Your loyalty to them is admirable but misplaced. Tell Pat I'll see him in court." Carly started to hang up.

"Carly, wait." Evelyn was back on the phone.

"Pat can help you. Take some of the burden off you. Think about it."

"Good night, Evelyn."

Carly sat on the edge of her bed, fuming. Sooner or later, she and her former in-laws were bound to have this conversation. But it happened sooner rather than later, all because Rickie had babbled a string of nonsense syllables resembling *Daddy.*

Scrubbing her cheeks and groaning, she pushed to her feet. There'd be no sleep for her now—her thoughts were firing nonstop and all over the place. She considered calling JD, only to change her mind. He'd be tired after his attack and had probably gone straight to bed.

She'd talk to him in the morning—right after she called her attorney and put the woman on the alert.

CHAPTER FOURTEEN

JD SAT ON his couch, feet planted square on the floor in front of him, hands resting on his thighs, eyes closed and the back of his head supported by a pillow. Yet, instead of blocking out his surroundings and "finding his zen" as he often joked with himself, images of Carly kept appearing.

Okay, that made sense in a way. Being with her did bring him inner peace and well-being—another joke. But that wasn't the purpose of him meditating.

The soft *beep, beep, beep* of the timer derailed his train of thought. JD reached over and pressed the Stop button. So much for his daily session. He should have quit sooner.

On the floor beside him, Hombre panted and thumped his tail.

"Yeah, I'm done." JD rose from the couch and crossed to the kitchen. Hombre tagged along in the hope food was forthcoming. "That's what I get for calling Carly right before I started."

He'd let her know that he was home after his second interview with the owner of the Poco Dinero and would arrive at her place around five o'clock. When Carly had asked how the interview went, he told her it was good and that he'd fill her in during dinner. He, in turn, asked her if she'd talked to Evelyn since the surprise late-night conversation. Carly said yes, Evelyn had called today, and then echoed his comment about filling him in later.

There'd been an odd quality to her voice JD hadn't heard before. When he'd questioned her, she insisted nothing was wrong. He remained dubious and would wager money Evelyn had given Carly more grief. Grief about him.

In the kitchen, he downed his medication with plenty of water. There would be no repeat attack tonight if he could help it.

"Should I make an appointment with the doctor?" he asked Hombre. "To discuss surgery or implant options?" He tugged on an earlobe. "Maybe another hearing test."

The dog wagged his tail, same answer as always.

JD's previous resistance to more invasive treatments was waning. The positive—a potential future with Carly—was outweighing the negatives—lengthy time off work, hefty insurance co-pays and no promises he'd be any better off than he was now.

Interesting that he hadn't been willing to consider surgery or an implant when it was just about returning to rodeo. What did that say about him and his feelings for Carly?

"You ready, *amigo*?"

Hombre popped off the floor, dancing and spinning in circles.

"I'm excited, too." JD stopped at the door and studied Hombre. "I read somewhere that talking to your pet is a sign of intelligence. You think that's true?"

Hombre snapped at a fly that had gotten in the bunkhouse—he missed by a good ten inches.

"Hmm. At least one of us is smart."

On the drive to Carly's, JD decided to stop at the market for one of their bouquets of fresh-cut flowers and a frozen ready-to-serve chocolate cream pie. He should have done this the other night, especially since Carly had gone through the trouble of fixing a nice dinner they weren't able to enjoy.

Because of the extreme summer heat, the market had set up a dog station outside the store. Customers could leave their four-legged companions in the shade and in the care of a local animal shelter volunteer who would watch them while the customer shopped inside.

"He's a good doggy," the teenage girl said when JD returned.

"When he isn't chewing." JD dropped a donation in the jar and then collected Hombre, who instantly forgot his new acquaintance in favor of a truck ride.

"You think I'm doing the right thing?" he asked the dog when they were back on the road. "I'm pretty sure Carly's the one. No, I'm very sure. But am I the one for her? Evelyn wasn't wrong. I do have issues."

Hombre looked away as if to remind JD of Carly's warning not to let Evelyn get in his head.

"The last thing I want is to cause Carly problems. She already has enough on her plate. What if Pat comes after her for joint custody? I doubt Evelyn was bluffing."

When Carly had told JD about the phone call, she'd referred to Evelyn's threat as a blackmail attempt. While a strong word, it wasn't entirely off base.

"Just because Carly hasn't heard from Pat's attorney yet is no guarantee she won't."

Hombre scratched himself and, when he was done, looked around as if bored.

"She could do a lot better than me. Yes," he

interjected before Hombre could comment in his dog way, "I care about Carly and what we have is really special. But, and I'm just speculating here, maybe we shouldn't have started dating. I'm complicating her life. Heck, I might be ruining it."

Hombre swung his head around and stared at JD with soulful eyes.

"Yeah, I feel that way about her, too. And Rickie. He's a great kid. Which means if she and I are going to have any shot at a life together, we need to find a compromise with Evelyn and Patrick Sr. One we can all live with and that puts Rickie's welfare and safety first."

What if that compromise was JD no longer being in the picture? Could he leave Carly for Rickie's sake?

Apparently losing interest, Hombre lay down and snoozed the last five minutes of the drive to Carly's. The second JD pulled into her driveway, Hombre sprang up and began whining excitedly. He didn't wait for JD to come around and open the passenger-side door. Instead, he scrambled out after JD, leaping from the cab onto the ground and then sprinting to Carly's front door.

"No, Hombre," JD scolded when the dog started scratching the door and barking.

So much for their agility classes improving his bad behavior.

The next second, the door flew open. Carly didn't hesitate. She greeted JD with a hug and a warm kiss that made him forget all about his concerns. The instant they separated, Hombre scooted between them and dashed into the house, full speed ahead.

"Where's Rickie?" JD asked, guessing at Hombre's destination.

"In his playpen."

Which, surprise, surprise, was where they found the dog. He'd jumped into the playpen with Rickie, and the two were tumbling about amid all the toys.

Carly stopped JD before he could reprimand the dog. "I want a picture. This is just too cute."

"We're enabling him."

"Relax, Mr. Grumpy."

How could he not oblige her? The smile she beamed at him melted his resolve.

While Carly put the flowers in a vase, complimenting him on his choice and fussing over the arrangement, JD helped her set the table for dinner. "You're spoiling me," he said when she removed a meat loaf from the oven.

"It's not what you think. Bridget from work sent this home with me yesterday when Molly mentioned you were coming over for dinner. Along with garlic mashed potatoes and grilled green beans. Leftovers from the Literary Ladies luncheon."

"Like I said, you're spoiling me."

Bridget, Molly's sister and head chef at Sweetheart Ranch, was reputed to be an incredible cook. This would be JD's first time sampling her cuisine. From the incredible aromas filling the kitchen, he anticipated being in for a treat.

Dinner proceeded far better than it had the other night. Carly secured Rickie in his high chair before they sat to eat. She kept him occupied and relatively quiet with his own plate of mashed potatoes and cut-up meat loaf. He didn't like green beans.

"I registered for a table at the Cave Creek craft fair in October," Carly said.

"Let me know if you need any help."

"Count on it. You may wind up sorry you offered."

JD didn't think that would be possible.

"Oh, oh. I landed a new client today. A friend of the woman I video chatted with. She's interested in brow bands and ankle bracelets."

At least a couple good things had come out of that miserable evening.

Carly paused, fork poised in midair, happiness radiating off her like sunshine. “Things are going really well for us lately, aren’t they? My jewelry business. Your potential second job.”

He wanted to share her enthusiasm, to be confident no obstacles lay ahead that they couldn’t overcome. But having Meniere’s Disease had upended his entire life in a single day and made JD a realist.

“You barely mentioned the interview with the Poco Dinero owner,” Carly said. “How’d it go?”

“We hit it off. I felt good when I left. But you never know. She wasn’t the easiest person to read.” He summarized the near hour-long interview. “She did agree to me taking off Labor Day weekend to visit my mother, which I really appreciate.”

“Has she already spoken with the other candidate?”

“She didn’t say, and I didn’t ask.”

Carly harrumphed. “He’s underqualified.”

“Yeah, well, he doesn’t have a debilitating health condition.”

“You’re going to jinx your chances of her hiring you with an attitude like that.”

He shrugged. “I won’t lie to her. Or imply I’m capable when I’m not. That’s not the way I operate.”

"I wasn't implying—"

"I know." He reassured her with a grin. "We tossed around possible plans B and C. Her assistant manager could cover for me if I have an attack. It's just that… I hate forcing my employer to make concessions for me. It eats at my craw. Hard enough at Powell Ranch."

"I understand."

"Maybe I shouldn't have applied for the job."

Carly set down her fork. "The owner's narrowed down the candidates to you and one other person. Clearly, she has faith in your ability to handle the job."

"Dada, dadedo."

They both looked over to see Rickie throwing pieces of meat loaf onto the floor for Hombre, who instantly lapped them up. Rather than be annoyed, Carly burst out laughing.

"More enabling," JD grumbled. "Not funny."

"No, no. JD, listen. Evelyn blew her stack the other night because she thought Rickie was calling you *Daddy*. He wasn't. He was just trying to say *dog*. Wait until I tell her."

JD didn't respond.

Carly's laughter gradually died. "What's wrong?"

"It doesn't matter what Rickie said, whether he was calling me *Daddy* or saying *dog*."

"I disagree."

"It changes nothing, Carly. Evelyn will still be upset about me, and not without reason."

"She'd be upset about any man in my life who isn't Pat." Carly pushed her plate away. "But she doesn't get a vote. I'm the one who decides."

"What did she say today when she called? Is Pat pursuing joint custody?"

"Not at the moment."

"Okay. That's good." JD knew Carly well enough to realize there was more to the conversation with Evelyn. "And?"

"And nothing."

"Carly."

"I don't want to talk about it."

He reached out and cupped her cheek. "What kind of relationship do we have if you won't level with me?"

She swallowed, taking her time to respond. When she finally spoke, a tremor shook her voice. "Evelyn said I will be hearing from Pat's attorney early this week. Unless…" She faltered.

"Unless what?"

"She will not manipulate me. Not ever again." The tremor had vanished, replaced by determination.

"How exactly is she trying to manipulate you?"

"Typical Evelyn-tactics. Strong-arming."

Suddenly, JD understood, and his gut clenched in fear and dread. "You either stop seeing me or Pat takes you to court."

Tears filled Carly's eyes.

JD threw down his napkin and pushed back from the table. His appetite had fled.

"Where are you going?" she asked.

"We agreed when we started dating that we'd go slow to test the waters. If any of the problems we faced became too much, we'd stop seeing each other. Well, Evelyn is one of those problems, and she's become too much."

"If you walk out now, you're letting her win."

"There is no win or lose, Carly. There's only me protecting you and Rickie from that worthless excuse for a husband and father." He grabbed his cowboy hat hanging on the back of the chair. "I won't be the reason you lose even partial custody of Rickie. I couldn't stand to look at myself every day in the mirror if that happened. I couldn't stand to look at you."

With that, he started for the door.

JD DIDN'T GET very far. Carly stopped him halfway to the living room door and pulled him around to face her.

"Wait. Don't go. Not yet."

It wasn't as if JD could leave anyway. Hombre had refused to abandon Rickie and remained behind, sitting beside the high chair. JD considered whether the dog was simply being stubborn or was actually smarter than JD.

Carly gazed at him with pleading eyes. "We just found each other, and I won't give you up. Not at the first little bump in the road."

"This isn't a little bump."

"We can figure things out as long as we don't act rashly. I told Evelyn she could take her blackmail threats and shove them where—"

"I'm not more important than your son. No one and nothing is."

His remark stole some of her bluster. "You're right. Rickie's safety comes first. But I also swore I'd never let Pat or Evelyn or anyone push me around and dictate my life. That's important to me. And if for one second it looks like my full custody of Rickie is in jeopardy, then, yes, we'll stop seeing each other. I promise you."

Thoughts whirled and clashed inside JD's head. He wanted to be with Carly, today and fifty years from today. More than any woman he'd known. More than he'd believed possible. And she made a valid point about not letting others push her around.

But what he wanted didn't trump Rickie's

safety and well-being. Until Pat had proven himself trustworthy and reliable beyond question, he remained a potential danger to Rickie.

"You fought tooth and nail to get free of Pat and to protect yourself and your son," JD said. "You found a home and a job that provide you with security. I won't let you sacrifice all that for me."

"Your concerns are valid, even though I think we can overcome them. Honestly, they make me care about you that much more."

He took Carly's hand. "If Pat were to gain joint custody of Rickie and abused him, you'd blame me for making you choose."

"I'd blame *him*."

"You say that now. But what if Rickie comes home with a bruise?"

She shuddered and hugged herself. "Which is why I won't let Pat near him. Not if I can help it."

"Set your feelings aside for a moment," JD said. "What are the odds Evelyn will eventually give up and leave you alone?"

"What are the odds Pat will win in court? Very low. He has a proven violent history."

"He's also made significant strides toward rehabilitating himself. A judge will take that into consideration. And then there's the matter of my health," JD continued. "If we're together, Pat can claim I'm a danger to Rickie. And, truthfully, maybe I am. The other night I was holding him. What if I was driving with him in the vehicle or riding a horse with him and I had an attack?"

Carly squeezed her eyes shut in an obvious fight to maintain control. "You're doing a lot better."

"I won't let myself be a weapon Pat can use against you. If we stop seeing each other, he and Evelyn will back down."

"I disagree. She might give me a little breathing room if we break up. But I'd bet anything, six months or a year from now, she'll be up to her old tricks. Lying to me. Pressuring me to let Pat see Rickie. Threatening me with a custody battle."

"She may, she may not. The difference is, she won't have me to use against you."

Carly covered her face with her hands. "I'm sorry. I'm being selfish and unfair to you. It's only that my heart is breaking."

"Mine, too, *mi cariño*."

"I'm furious with Evelyn." She ruthlessly wiped her nose with the back of her hand. "I just don't understand why, after a year, she and Pat changed their minds. He wanted zero to do with Rickie before. Heck, he wasn't even happy about the pregnancy. He probably would have abdicated his rights without Becca pressing charges against him."

"Remember, he's stopped drinking and is going to AA meetings. That could make a big difference. Cause him to regret past mistakes."

She sniffed and blinked back tears. "I wish everything you said didn't make so much sense."

"Me, too."

Rickie chose that moment to start crying, his wails escalating to shrieks within seconds. Hesitating only briefly, Carly went over to the high chair and, talking softly to him, lifted him out and propped him on her hip.

"Shh, baby."

With her free hand, she pressed his head to her chest. His crying promptly subsided into hiccups.

The sight of them hit JD like a mule kick to the belly. He'd been letting himself imagine seeing Carly and Rickie like this every morning when he woke up and every afternoon when he came home from work.

He should have known better than to get caught up in an unrealistic fantasy. Look what happened to his ambition of becoming a world rodeo champion. A mere three weeks away from qualifying, he was struck down and had yet to recover. Why had he believed a future with Carly would be any different?

As if sensing JD's despair, Hombre trotted over and nudged his hand, much like he did during an attack. Well, JD supposed, he was exhibiting many of the same symptoms. Lightheadedness and disorientation, sweating, stomach roiling.

Carly stared sadly at the dog as if saying goodbye to a dear friend. "Poor Rickie is going to miss Hombre."

"You can borrow him anytime."

"We'll see." She swayed back and forth, rocking Rickie and stroking his back. "Might be hard on me."

Hard on JD, too.

All at once, Rickie lifted his head and extended a hand toward JD. "Dada, dada."

Carly gasped. "Rickie!"

Reason told JD that the boy wasn't calling him *Daddy*. But, for one precious moment, he let himself believe it was true. The sharp stab when reality returned nearly felled him. Carly, too, by her stricken expression.

"Maybe he's trying to tell us something," she said softly.

"He doesn't know any better."

"But what if he does?"

"Carly."

"You're right," she conceded with a heavy sigh. "We'd only be postponing the inevitable."

She carried Rickie outside, keeping her distance from JD. At his truck, she surprised him by putting her free arm around his waist and resting her cheek on his shoulder.

"I don't want this to be a forever goodbye. If things change..."

"Carly. *Mi cariño.* If things change, I'll be here in a flash knocking your door down."

But things wouldn't change, not for a long while. And on some level, they both knew that.

JD folded her and Rickie in his arms, committing every tiny detail about her to memory. The soft feel of her skin. The heady floral scent of her hair. The pressure of her arm as she gripped him tight.

A part of him longed to kiss her one last time. If he did, however, there was a good chance he'd never leave. Difficult as it was, they were making the right decision. The only decision.

"See you, Rico." JD cupped Rickie's head and brushed his thumb along the boy's smooth hair.

He plucked at JD's cowboy hat and tried to pull it off.

"Rickie. No, honey," Carly gently scolded.

"Here." JD removed his hat and gave it to Rickie. "He can have it." The kid already owned a big piece of JD, might as well have his hat, too.

"Thank you." Carly's voice cracked.

"Take care." He pulled away from her before he lost his nerve. "Come on, boy. *Vamos.*"

Hombre walked as if carrying a hundred-pound pack.

Carly hurried inside rather than wait and watch while JD reversed out of her driveway. Hombre scratched at the passenger window and barked at her retreating back.

"I know how you feel, *amigo*. I don't want to leave, either."

During the drive home, JD tried telling himself he was no worse off than he'd been a couple months ago, before that first day when he'd called Carly *gorgeous*. Possibly better off. He may never return to the rodeo circuit, but he had a decent job at Powell Ranch. And if he landed the part-time job as rodeo event manager at the Poco Dinero, he'd be earning more money and working on the fringes of the sport he loved.

Who was he kidding? JD was infinitely worse off than he'd been, and he doubted he'd recover. Carly was his heart. His life. His motivation—even more than his love of rodeo—to kick his Meniere's Disease. Worse, he'd lost Rickie, too. The pain from that was almost as acute.

For the first time, JD related to Pat. If

Rickie were his son, he'd move mountains and threaten whoever got in his way in order to have visitation rights or joint custody.

At the stop sign, JD battled the pressure building in his chest. "I deserve this," he told Hombre. "I knew better than to get involved with Carly, and I did it anyway."

Hombre ignored him.

"Go ahead, bring on the mad. I'll barely feel it after the beating I'm giving myself."

The dog did just that. Later on, to express exactly how he felt, he chewed up JD's favorite pair of boots and left them in the middle of the kitchen floor for JD to find.

He didn't punish the dog. He simply picked up what remained of the boots and tossed them in the trash, the symbolism not escaping him.

CHAPTER FIFTEEN

THE BRIDE AND groom poked through the array of cake toppers, laughing together at the comical couples—her oohing and aahing at the adorable ones, him groaning at the absurd ones. In between, they affectionately linked fingers or gazed at each other with such adoration, a painful lump rose in Carly's throat. Swallowing it was impossible, so she straightened the books of sample invitations rather than continue to stare.

She and JD had been this couple once. On their way to becoming them, at least. Was it only two and a half weeks ago? It seemed more like two and a half months. Years, even. Feelings as strong as the ones they'd shared didn't fade because they'd stopped seeing each other. They lingered, perhaps forever, and stirred tender reminders during unexpected moments.

God, how she missed him. Missed *them* and what they'd had together.

Sadly, their friendship had also taken a severe hit and was unlikely to survive. She'd been to Powell Ranch only once since their breakup for a horse photo shoot. Seeing JD, struggling to make small talk when what she really wanted to do was hold him close and kiss him senseless, had been agonizing. She'd avoided the ranch after that and anywhere else around town she might run into him like the park or the market, unwilling to further torture herself. She found herself looking for his truck before pulling into parking lots or while idling at intersections.

"Scaredy-cat," she murmured under her breath.

But was she really? Becca had assured Carly repeatedly that, rather than avoiding him, she was wisely giving the two of them necessary time and space to heal. Seeing him would serve no purpose other than to pour salt in an open wound.

Carly reluctantly agreed with her friend. If she and JD had a prayer at recovering and moving on with their lives, they needed to keep their respective distances.

That didn't stop the memories and regrets from flooding her every time an obviously-in-love couple entered the boutique. Personal pep talks had no effect. Her misery refused to abate.

"We'll take this one."

Hearing the voice behind her, she spun around, her leg bumping into the table. The bride presented a cake topper, a miniature groom joyously lifting a miniature bride off her feet. Carly approved. It was one of her favorites.

Clearing her throat, she said, “Good choice.”

She led them to the sales counter where their other purchases waited: a silver cake cutter and vintage-style silver teaspoons engraved with *Happily Ever After*. Those last items were gifts for the maid of honor and bridesmaids.

“Are you all right?” the bride asked Carly while she rang up the sale.

“Me? I’m fine.”

“You seem…upset.”

This wasn’t the first time a customer had commented on Carly’s emotional state. It wasn’t even the first time today. She’d come up with a response that usually worked well.

“I’m just so happy for you both. I love helping couples find the perfect accessories for their big day, and I tend to get a little emotional. Sorry.”

“Don’t be,” the bride assured her, beaming. “I think it’s sweet. You must have the best job in the world.”

“That I do.” Carly placed the carefully wrapped and boxed items in a bag with the

Sweetheart Ranch logo on the side. "Congratulations, again. If you need anything, let me know. I'm here Monday through Friday."

"Thank you so much."

The bride impulsively hugged Carly when she came out from behind the sales counter to escort them to the door. The groom was more reserved and simply nodded pleasantly.

They weren't gone long when Molly appeared. She stopped by the boutique daily to review any pertinent business and deliver packages and mail. Carly had noticed Molly increasing her stops in the weeks since her and JD's split.

Molly had generously offered Carly a few days off work, but she'd declined. At home by herself all day with only Rickie for company, she'd sink into further depression. She also feared her parents might come over and try to cheer her up.

Twice in the days after Carly and JD's breakup, her mom had tactfully brought up the subject of counseling or an abuse support group for Carly. In the past, she'd resisted. Hard. This time around, however, she'd reconsidered. Maybe she was holding on to a lot and needed help processing. As a result, Carly started seeing an affordable therapist her attorney had recommended. She had her second session later this week.

Funny. All the prodding she'd received after her divorce from Pat hadn't gotten Carly the counseling she'd surely needed, but breaking up with JD had. What did that say about her? About her feelings for him?

"Was that the couple having the Labor Day–themed wedding?" Molly asked, setting a mug of caffe latte on the sales counter for Carly. She'd been bringing by pick-me-ups every afternoon. Usually coffee or tea and sometimes a pastry fresh from Bridget's oven.

"That was them."

"They're having mini hot dogs and cheeseburgers at their reception, and beer instead of champagne. Isn't that fun? Apparently they met at a mutual friend's Labor Day cookout."

"Yeah. Fun."

"Really?" Molly sent Carly an arch look. "Because you're wearing just about the most hangdog expression I've ever seen."

She forced her mouth into the shape of a smile. "Better."

Molly winced. "Now you look scared."

Carly flattened her lips, more to stop herself from crying than anything else.

"Everything okay?" Molly sat in one of the two ornate chairs and patted the cushion next to her. "Let me rephrase that since I know everything's not okay. What can I do to help?"

Obliging her request, Carly dropped into the empty chair. There were no customers in the boutique at the moment and no appointments scheduled for the rest of the afternoon.

"It's nothing, really. But thanks for the offer."

"Your former in-laws giving you grief?"

"Nope. Been extremely well behaved since JD and I stopped seeing each other. And not a peep from Pat's attorney."

Carly's mother had been the one to call Evelyn with the news. While Carly still had reservations about their renewed friendship, she hadn't been able to bring herself to inform Evelyn and left the task to her mom. Had she tried, the words would have stuck in her throat, at which point she'd have burst into tears.

She'd refrained from asking her mom about Evelyn's reaction, preferring ignorance. The only thing Carly had said to Evelyn and Patrick Sr. when they came to visit Rickie last weekend was that any discussion of JD was absolutely off-limits—they weren't to so much as mention his name.

Patrick Sr. had murmured an apology. It wasn't enough, not by a long shot. Evelyn, to Carly's mild surprise, hadn't gloated. If anything, she'd appeared chastened. Had Patrick Sr. warned her to be quiet or, perhaps, Carly's mom? She hadn't been able to look her former in-laws in the eyes during the entire visit. She'd barely been able to tolerate being in the same room with them.

"I know you're still hurting and probably don't want to hear this…" Molly finished her coffee and set it aside. "JD was right. Rickie comes first. And it says a lot about his character, making the kind of sacrifice he did."

Expounding on JD's qualities didn't lift Carly's spirits in the slightest. Rather, it drove them further down. She'd been forced to give up a kind, generous, wonderful man who'd made her incredibly happy.

"I believe things happen for a reason," Molly continued. "Maybe the timing was wrong for you two. Could be vastly different a year from now or even a few months. Don't give up hope entirely."

Unable to continue discussing JD, Carly changed the subject. "I bought one of those child GPS devices for when Evelyn and Patrick Sr. take Rickie. It works with an app on my phone."

"I thought you were only letting them visit him at your house."

"I've reconsidered."

Molly blew out a long breath. "You're a better person than I am, Carly. A lot better. I probably would have moved."

"The thought did occur to me. But if I'd continued playing hardball with Evelyn and Patrick Sr., we'd have wound up in front of a judge, and they would have likely won. This way, I get to mostly call the shots."

"I suppose. But still…"

"They're allowed to take Rickie to the park for one hour and no longer. If they're late, or go somewhere else, or I find out they've let Pat see Rickie, the agreement's off and the only way they'll get to see Rickie again after that is with a court order."

"I'd be watching my phone the entire time they were gone."

"Trust me. My eyes will be glued to that app." She set her empty mug on the counter. "I never realized how truly dysfunctional Pat's family was until lately. I feel really sorry for them."

"We're lucky. We have amazing families."

"We are."

Carly mentally counted her blessings. She had a beautiful, healthy son. A good job and a thriving side business. A wonderful relationship with her parents. A best friend who would slay dragons for her. A nice, comfortable home. A few dollars in the bank.

What she didn't have was the love of her life. JD had broken up with her in order to safeguard her many blessings.

"By the way," Molly said, "how's the horse jewelry business going?"

"Good. My online orders are growing." And staying busy in the evenings was helping her to not dwell on how much she missed JD.

"Growing enough that you'll eventually quit Sweetheart Ranch?"

"Hardly." Carly produced her first genuine smile in the last two and a half weeks. "I love working here."

"And we love having you." Molly stood and gathered the empty coffee mugs. Whatever else she'd intended to say was cut off by a customer hurrying into the boutique.

"Is it too late?" the woman asked, her face flushed and her breath coming in rapid bursts. "I rushed over from work."

"Not at all." Carly also stood. "Come in, and welcome. How can I help you?"

Molly left after assuring the customer she was in capable hands. Carly helped the woman select a bridal shower gift for her cousin. Going through the motions, she offered suggestions and responded appropriately when asked a question, all the while attempting to hold herself together.

Hopefully, one day, she'd be able to wait on customers without thinking of JD and what might have been. Except she wasn't sure if she looked forward to that day or dreaded it.

JD PULLED AROUND to the rear of the feed store. One hand gripping the steering wheel, he executed a one-eighty and backed up his truck to the loading dock.

"Wait here," he told Hombre, who sat in the front seat, panting and wearing his usual dog grin.

Between the two of them, Hombre was the only one happy these days. He still looked for Rickie around the ranch, but less and less often. Not like his owner. JD checked every vehicle coming and going, waiting for Carly's car to appear and his hopes sinking when it didn't. She'd come by the ranch only once since they'd parted ways—no, since he'd ended things, he needed to be clear on that—and hadn't returned since.

What had he expected? That they'd resume their previous friendship and act like they hadn't kissed, hadn't fallen hard for each other, hadn't started making plans for a future? That seeing each other wouldn't rip the bandage off old hurts and trigger a fresh onslaught of pain?

"Howdy, JD." Owen Caufield, the owner of the feed store, emerged from inside the loading area and clasped JD's hand when they met up. They hadn't seen each other since Tanner's wedding. "Wasn't sure you'd make it by today."

"Sorry to be late," JD said. "We had a slight emergency at the ranch."

"I heard some guy collapsed while watching his wife ride in the arena."

JD shook his head. "Kind of scary. One minute, he was standing there and the next minute he'd collapsed and someone was calling 9-1-1. The EMTs seemed to think he had a heart attack."

"I hope he's all right."

"He was sitting up on the gurney and talking when they loaded him in the ambulance, which, I guess, is good."

"Molly called. She said the wife rode with him to the hospital."

News traveled fast in Mustang Valley. JD hadn't told anyone that he and Carly split, yet within two days, everyone he met was giving him sympathetic looks. Carly was like him, not a big talker when it came to personal stuff. Someone from Sweetheart Ranch must have loose lips.

"I wound up taking care of the wife's horse," JD said, "which is why I'm a little late."

"Probably not the kind of excitement you like having at the ranch."

Together, they loaded the two-dozen fifty-pound bags of vitamin-enriched grain. When they were done, JD reminded Hombre to "Stay put," and then went inside the store. The dog would be fine there in the shade with the truck windows rolled down.

Inside at the counter, they completed the purchase. JD signed the bill of sale, the amount to be added to the ranch account. Just as they were finishing, the bell over the door rang, announcing a new customer.

"Well, well, partner. Didn't see your truck out front."

JD turned and spotted his good friend Tanner moseying toward him. "And I didn't know you were home."

"Got in a few days ago."

They greeted each other by clapping shoulders. Owen excused himself to wait on a young woman needing assistance with a pair of boots on the top shelf.

"How'd you do?" JD asked. "Leave the competition in the dust?"

"Not exactly. Second place. Joe Whitefeather

had a better run than me." Tanner shrugged. "By almost two points."

"It happens."

"He's a tough competitor. Making a real name for himself."

"You are, too."

"We'll see."

Tanner had been away for almost a week, competing in the Western Stampede Rodeo. He and JD had met for a beer before Tanner left, with JD giving him the lowdown on him and Carly. His friend had offered to skip the rodeo and stick around, but JD refused. Tanner hadn't yet cinched a spot in the National Finals Rodeo this coming December. Every rodeo mattered.

"What brings you into the store?" JD asked. "Seeing as it wasn't me."

"I'm here to pick up a new competition bridle for Jewel. It's her birthday this weekend."

"I thought she retired from barrel racing."

"She did. But she was in here a couple of weeks ago, saw the bridle and fell in love. I'm going to surprise her. She'll probably yell at me for spending too much money. But then she'll show me how much she loves me." He winked.

JD tried to ignore the stab of jealousy slicing through him. His friend deserved every bit of happiness coming his way. A beautiful wife and adorable daughter, a bull-riding comeback and a shot at a championship title, and a career waiting for him at his father's company whenever he chose to quit the circuit. JD might have had those same things—a wife and family, a shot at a title, a successful post-rodeo career—if not for his Meniere's Disease.

Not that he begrudged his friend a single thing, but why JD and not someone else? His mother had told him to be grateful for what he had, that there were plenty less fortunate people than him. She was right, of course. Didn't make him feel any better. Or any less lonely.

God, he missed Carly. Every minute of every day. And Rickie, too. He'd become pretty fond of the kid and could have easily seen himself as a stepfather.

Together, he and Tanner wandered over to the tack section. Besides livestock feed and supplies, Owen also sold saddles, bridles, riding equipment, halters, boots, cowboy hats, accessories like hat bands and belts and wallets, and a small selection of Western clothing.

"What do you think?" Tanner held up the bridle for JD's inspection.

"Very nice."

Silver conchos and turquoise-colored stones ran across the brow band and along the head-stall, giving the bridle an eloquent and expensive look.

"Too much?" Tanner asked.

"Naw. It's what she wants, right?"

"Yeah." He broke out in a wide sheepish grin. They returned to the counter, where Tanner paid and Owen bagged the purchase. "You have time for a cold one?" Tanner asked JD while shoving his wallet into his back jeans pocket. "My treat."

"Can't." He hitched his head toward the rear of the store and the loading area. "Hombre's agility class is at six."

"Another time, then."

"Count on it."

Tanner hesitated, giving JD a long once-over. "You doing all right, buddy?"

"Hanging in there." He was, too. Pretty much. For someone who'd been knocked down by life and then had the tar kicked out of them.

"Can I help?"

"Just have that beer with me when I'm not in a rush."

"Any attacks?"

"Nope." His longest record yet, and he couldn't celebrate it with the one person he cared most about.

"That's great." Tanner squeezed his arm encouragingly. "Maybe you've got this thing beat."

"I'm just having a good spell."

"But it's true. You can get better, right?"

"I can have long periods of remission. But I need to go more than a few weeks without an attack for that. More like a few months."

"For what it's worth, you did the right thing. Breaking up with Carly."

If one more person told that to JD, he was going to punch a hole in the nearest wall. What he said to Tanner, however, was simply, "Yeah. Thanks. Look, I need to run. Class is starting soon."

"I'll call you."

Hombre apparently sensed they were headed to the park the minute JD climbed into the truck cab and started the engine. His excitement increased the closer they got. By the time they turned into the parking lot, the dog was whining and scratching at the window.

JD reached for the leash on the passenger-side floor. "Come on, boy." Only one more class remained in their session. He hadn't yet decided if he'd register again in the fall.

They were cutting across the large span of green toward the dog area when JD caught sight of a family near the picnic area. Normally, he wouldn't pay strangers much attention, but the stroller reminded him of Rickie's. At the same time, Hombre started pulling hard on the leash, his whining increasing. When JD tried to restrain him, the dog pulled to the point he began choking.

"Slow down, *amigo.* What's going on?"

JD looked then. Really looked. Three adults sat at the picnic table, and a boy about Rickie's size and age sat in one of the men's laps. Suddenly, the woman stood, and JD drew up short.

Evelyn! He'd recognize her anywhere.

Quieting Hombre, he stared intently. Any last shreds of doubts were erased when Patrick Sr. moved into view. They must be having a visit with Rickie. Carly had briefly mentioned something about it when she'd last stopped at the ranch.

But who was the other man? JD squinted, noting the resemblance to Patrick Sr. Same hair, though Patrick Sr.'s was threaded with gray. Same build. Same belly laugh.

JD's blood ran instantly cold. Pat! It had to be.

Rather than risk being spotted, he changed direction and headed toward the playground area. The slides and jungle gym would provide cover while affording him an unobstructed view of the picnic area.

Luck was on his side—the playground was mostly empty. Half hidden by the slide, he waited, studying the group. Having never met

Pat, he couldn't be positive. Carly would know, however.

Removing his phone from his pocket, he zoomed in and snapped several pictures, texting them to Carly without any message. He then called her, grinding his teeth together until she finally answered.

"JD. Hi," she said tentatively.

"Did you see the pictures I just sent you?"

"No. What pictures? Is something wrong?" Confusion tinged her voice. "Wait a sec, my phone's beeping now."

"Look at them. I'll hold."

"Okay." A few seconds later, he heard a muffled gasp. "Oh, my God!"

"Is that Pat with Evelyn and Patrick Sr.?"

"Yes. Where did you get these?"

"I'm at the park now," he told her. "They're in the picnic area."

Her words spilled out in a panicked rush. "They lied to me. They swore they wouldn't let Pat see Rickie—" A sob cut her short. "I feel like a fool. I assumed because the child GPS showed they were in the park, everything was fine."

"What do you want me to do, Carly?"

"Stay there. Please. Keep an eye on them. I'm on my way now."

"I'll meet you in the parking lot. You're not

confronting them alone, you hear me? If they leave before you get here, I'll call you and then follow them in my truck."

"I'm on my way out the door." She hung up without saying goodbye.

JD continued waiting behind the slide, the dog agility class forgotten. Hombre watched, too, the fur along his back standing straight up as if he knew his little friend Rickie was in potential danger.

CHAPTER SIXTEEN

CARLY PULLED INTO the parking lot, tires squealing, and zoomed into the first available space. JD stood waiting for her just inside the main entrance. During the entire fifteen-minute drive to the park—no, from the moment she'd seen the pictures—pure electricity had flown through her.

What a fool she'd been. For weeks she'd given Evelyn and Patrick Sr. generous access to Rickie. First out of guilt because she'd falsely accused them of letting Pat see Rickie—something she now knew to be true. And, secondly, because they'd promised to abide by her terms. The sense of betrayal, of being used, of being *manipulated* wounded like a sharp blade to her heart.

Hombre started barking the moment he saw Carly. She all but ignored him, her mind on the picnic area and Pat sitting with her defenseless young son.

No, no, no! Another surge of electricity ignited every nerve ending in her body.

By the time she reached JD, her breathing was labored, less from exertion and more from agitation. "Are they still there?"

"Yes." He glanced over his shoulder toward the park. "They haven't come this way. I've been watching."

"Thank you, JD." Carly gave him a brief, impulsive hug. "If not for you, I might not have found out about Pat until it was too late."

"Pure luck. I was walking by."

Hombre tugged hard on the leash as they crossed the green expanse in the direction of the picnic area. Carly imagined him sensing where they were headed and the importance of their mission.

For reasons she couldn't explain, the dog's presence reassured her. Maybe it was his unconditional love and devotion to Rickie. Just like JD's.

She sent a silent prayer of thanks heavenward for JD being in the right place at the right time and for his enduring friendship despite the tumble their relationship had taken. The prayer was followed by a plea for strength and courage. Confronting Pat and his parents wouldn't be easy. She was grateful to have both JD and Hombre by her side.

They soon neared the picnic area, and the sight of Pat caused her legs to falter. She hadn't seen her abusive ex in over a year. Fear she'd suppressed and ignored all that time rose up from where it lay hidden to squeeze her insides with icy fingers.

He can't hurt you. He won't dare hurt you. Not in a public place and not with his parents there.

But, then, he had tried to strike her in front of Becca before her friend intercepted the blow.

"You okay?" JD tugged Hombre to a stop and put his hand on Carly's shoulder.

"I don't know," she answered weakly.

"I won't let anything bad happen to you, Carly. Count on it."

He wouldn't, and she trusted him with the same level of conviction she didn't trust Pat.

Gulping large quantities of air, she said, "Give me a second."

"Take your time." He'd yet to remove his hand, and she swore she felt a stream of strength flow from him into her. "I'm here for you."

He was. Physically and emotionally and in all the ways that truly mattered. Had been from the beginning. Not just when they'd started dating but from the moment they'd met and become friends.

She'd been the one to let him down. He'd deserved more from her, and she should have fought harder for them. When he'd suggested they end things, she'd done no more than put up a token fight and hadn't bothered to explore even one option.

Turning toward him, she stood on tiptoe and briefly kissed him on the mouth. "Consider that a warning."

"For what?"

"We're having a heart-to-heart when this is over. About us."

The next time they set out, she took the lead, confidence building with each step.

Pat sat at the picnic table, his back to her. Carly wavered momentarily as fear battled for control. It was met head-on by determination and fury. She had Rickie in her sights and no power on Earth would stop her.

He fussed inconsolably, his whines reaching Carly's ears even from a distance and propelling her forward. She heard Pat tell him repeatedly, "That's enough, son," while Evelyn tried to bribe Rickie with a cookie and a soothing "Be a good boy."

Carly's every instinct urged her to rush in and snatch Rickie away from Pat. Only by exercising incredible willpower was she able to approach him and his parents with measured strides and unshakable composure.

When Carly was ten feet away, they finally noticed her and JD. Pat twisted in his seat, one arm anchoring Rickie to him. Evelyn and Patrick Sr. drew back in surprise. Whatever expression Carly wore triggered a ripple effect of shock and guilt, dimming smiles and widening eyes.

Rickie spotted her and called, "Mama, Mama!" while holding out his arms.

She marched toward him.

"C-Carly," Evelyn stammered. "You're... you're here." Her glance cut to JD and her tone cooled. "Can we keep this to ourselves and not involve anyone else? Making a scene won't help matters."

Exactly the line she'd used to control and manipulate Carly when she and Pat were married. Except Carly wasn't that meek and mild person anymore. At this moment, she was a mother grizzly whose cub was in danger.

The first words out of her mouth startled even her with their ferocity. "Do I need to call the police?" She extracted her phone from her purse, hoping her fingers didn't tremble. "Because I will."

"The police," Evelyn exclaimed. "What for?"

Carly's laser gaze narrowed on Pat. "Kidnapping."

Through wasting time and refusing to be deterred, she skirted Evelyn and dove in, catching Pat off guard and swiping Rickie away from him. At the first sensation of her son's warm chubby body pressing against her, relief buckled her knees. She had a hold of him and would never let go again.

Pat hefted a leg over the bench seat, freeing himself from the clutches of the picnic table, and stood. "Now, wait a minute."

Patrick Sr. came out from behind the table. "Can we all just take a deep breath and relax? There's no need to get the police involved."

"There sure is a need to get my attorney involved," Carly spat out. "And the courts."

"I just wanted to see my son, Carly." Pat raised his open palms to her in a gesture of supplication. "You can understand that."

"Whether you want to or not doesn't matter. You abdicated your rights."

"Under duress," Evelyn added.

Carly turned on her. "Because he assaulted my friend."

"I've changed," Pat insisted. "Since getting sober, I'm a different person. I want to be a father to little Patrick." He flashed the smile that, until he'd started drinking and doing his talking with his fists, had always melted her resolve.

Carly stared, waiting to feel the shift in her that had always accompanied that smile. It didn't happen. If anything, her determination increased. "Surprise, Pat. I'm a different person, too."

She looked over at JD, warmed and assured by the pride and respect shining in his eyes. She needed no other incentive and, the next second, started for the stroller sitting next to the picnic table.

Settling Rickie into the seat, she made quick work of fastening the buckles. Before she could finish, however, a hand clamped on to her wrist. It wasn't JD's.

The fury residing just beneath the surface promptly exploded. She straightened and glared at Pat's hand.

"Don't. You. Dare. Touch. Me."

His grip remained firmly in place. "You're not leaving with my son."

"Oh, yes, I am."

JD suddenly materialized beside them. In a voice that could level a steel tower, he said, "Leave her alone."

Pat thrust Carly's arm aside and whirled to glare at JD. "Or what? You going to fight me?"

"If it comes to that." JD dropped Hombre's leash.

Pat retaliated by puffing up and bringing his nose to within an inch of JD's, his features contorting into a mask of hatred and rage.

"Bring it on, loser. I'm ready for you."

Dread immobilized Carly. JD and Pat weren't really going to fight, were they? She'd witnessed Pat's temper often, knew him capable of inflicting physical injury. Besides backhanding Becca and shoving her into the wall, there'd been that altercation in the bar parking lot and the basketball player in high school whose nose he'd broken.

She realized too late she'd been wrong. Pat had no qualms whatsoever engaging JD here, regardless of who might be watching.

"No!" she hollered. "Stop it."

Rickie erupted in sobs. Hombre jumped onto the stroller and began licking his face in earnest, but Rickie kept crying.

The next instant, JD's face drained of color, and he swayed unsteadily.

Pat laughed. "Easier than I thought." He refocused his stare on Carly. "Next time, find yourself a boyfriend with some backbone."

Eyes closed, JD reached out and grabbed... nothing. It hit Carly then—he was having an attack! She'd been too focused on Pat to notice.

Hombre abandoned Rickie in favor of JD, alternately barking loudly and nuzzling his hand. JD grabbed the dog's collar, not to silence him but to steady himself.

"JD, are you all right?" She reached for him.

He held up a hand to ward her off. "I'm okay."

Clearly, he wasn't. "Sit down." *Before you fall down*, she silently added.

He shook his head, his jaw clenched as he fought for control. How he must hate this, having an attack at the worst possible time. Worse even than at Tanner's wedding or in front of a rodeo arena full of spectators.

"That's right," Pat sneered, attempting to loom over JD even though they were of similar height. "I heard you were sick."

"Back off," JD choked out. He might have been swaying, but he stood his ground.

Pat didn't listen. "That boy is mine. Not yours. And if you try to take him from me, you'll be sorry. I won't settle for just a piece of you."

Hombre had stopped barking and was now growling at Pat, his head lowered and teeth bared.

Rather than be afraid, Pat cranked his leg as if to kick the dog.

"What's wrong with you?" Carly demanded.

It was just like Pat to pick on those weaker and more vulnerable than him. Carly. Becca. Hombre. JD, in the midst of an attack. How could she have ever loved a man like him?

All at once, JD pulled himself together. Seeming to draw on all his limited strength, he got up close to Pat. "You go near Carly or

Rickie again, and so help me you'll live to regret it."

How was it possible? JD had been on the verge of passing out.

Love. The answer filled Carly with joy. He was battling his attack in order to help her. Defend her. Protect her. And Rickie. All right, and his dog, too. The thought brought a tiny smile to her lips.

"Yeah?" Pat sneered. "Why don't you just try me?" He stabbed the air with his finger. In Carly's direction, not JD's.

"Carly, please." Evelyn went over to her son and patted his back as if he were a small boy and not a grown man. "Be reasonable. Haven't you put Pat through enough already?"

"Me put *him* through enough?"

Unbelievable. Evelyn was still convinced her son was innocent of any wrongdoing even in the face of indisputable evidence. Nothing Carly did would change that. Only when Evelyn was ready to accept the truth about her son would she cease enabling him.

Reaching her fill, she returned to the stroller and finished buckling in Rickie. She was glad to note the color returning to JD's cheeks. His attack hadn't been terrible, as far as attacks went.

Hombre continued to watch Pat, his ears lying flat and his front feet braced.

"This isn't over." Pat was evidently intent on having the last word. "Not by a long shot."

"That's enough, Pat. Leave them be."

The warning didn't come from Carly but rather Patrick Sr. And it was delivered in a tone that brooked no argument.

"This doesn't involve you, Dad. Stay out of it."

"I won't stand by and watch you kick someone when they're down and unable to defend themselves. I didn't raise you that way. Neither did I raise you to strike a woman."

"I told you, I didn't hit—"

"I'm sick and tired of you lying to us. I won't tolerate it another minute."

"Now, wait."

"And you can forget going after custody. You won't be getting a dime from us."

"Patrick!" Evelyn cried. "Don't say that."

He faced his wife. "Our son has an ugly side. Has since he was a teenager. Pretending he doesn't won't change that. The help he needs from us is to make sure he gets counseling, stays sober and continues attending AA meetings. Not violating a custody agreement."

"You're overreacting, Dad," Pat said, infusing a healthy dose of indignation and disgust in his voice.

"Past time I did."

"You'd take their side over mine?" he demanded.

"I'm taking Rickie's side," Patrick Sr. said with an authority Carly hadn't heard before. "What kind of grandfather would I be if I didn't?"

"Fine. I don't give a rat's hind end." Pat dismissed everyone with a sound of disgust. "I never wanted the kid, anyway. I only went along because Mom kept nagging me." He stormed off then, presumably to his parents' car. No one stopped him.

"What about us?" Evelyn asked, her composure crumbling. "I won't lose my grandson. Not again. I spent a year without so much as a single picture because Pat insisted."

Pat insisted? Carly had been told it was Evelyn and Patrick Sr.'s choice to stay away. She shouldn't be surprised that she'd been lied to about that. Yet, she was.

"Whether and how much we get to see the boy will be up to Carly," Patrick Sr. said.

He looked at her then, and she sent him a grateful smile. She wouldn't be making any decision about her former in-laws today, and he appeared to accept that.

"Come on, dear." He slung an arm around Evelyn's shoulders. "We've caused enough trouble."

She folded in on herself, shrinking in size. "Can I say goodbye to little Patrick?"

Acceptance was hard. No mother wanted to believe their child capable of cruel, violent deeds. Carly understood—she'd had to do a lot of her own accepting when she'd divorced Pat. No wife wanted to believe their husband capable of cruel, violent deeds, either.

"Go ahead." She nodded at Rickie, whose crying had subsided the instant Pat had walked away. Coincidence? Hard to say.

Gratitude filling her eyes, Evelyn went to the stroller and bent over Rickie, giving him a kiss on the head and murmuring, "Goodbye, my precious angel. I love you."

He raised his little hand and crinkled his fingers. "Bye, bye."

Evelyn broke into wracking sobs, and Patrick Sr. led her away. Nearby people may have been watching. Carly wanted to care, but she'd gone numb. Later, when everything had a chance to sink in, she'd probably break down and cry or scream into a pillow.

She afforded her former in-laws only the briefest of glances before pulling JD over to the picnic table and insisting he sit. He was the one who mattered the most. The one who deserved her attention and consideration.

He was the one who'd won her heart completely.

"Doing better?"

JD heard Carly clearly as opposed to ten minutes ago when she and everyone else had sounded like they were speaking through thick layers of insulation.

Pat had stormed off. JD recalled seeing his retreating back through a watery haze. The exact details of their heated exchange remained sketchy. Threats had been hurled. Challenges issued. Lines drawn. Patrick Sr. and Evelyn had left, too—though, by then, JD had started feeling normal again.

"Yeah," he said. "Much better."

"Honestly, JD. You were amazing."

Carly clutched his arm. Not in the aggressive way Pat had held her, but as if she'd found safe harbor.

He liked the idea of being the solid, heavy object she anchored to after a dangerous journey in stormy seas.

"I was worried I might chase Pat off by vomiting all over him rather than intimidating him with my impressive manliness." Another day, another time, JD would have laughed at his joke. He wasn't enough out of the woods to risk upsetting his still-queasy stomach.

"Here. Wait." Carly reached into one of the

stroller's many pockets and extracted a bottled water. "I forgot I had this."

He emptied the contents in a few swallows. "Thanks. That helps." He crumpled the bottle in his hands. "Was it my imagination or did Patrick Sr. actually step up and take charge?"

"Wow. He was pretty awesome, right? I didn't think he had it in him."

"Why the sudden change? From what you've told me, he's always been kind of a pushover."

"Maybe seeing Pat bullying you gave him a wake-up call."

JD considered that. "Maybe. Didn't change Evelyn's opinion."

"Patrick Sr. standing up to her had an effect, though. She gave in to him like that." Carly snapped her fingers. "Did you hear what she said about Pat insisting she have no contact with Rickie? That explains why they cut off all contact after Rickie's birth." Carly's features hardened. "What a selfish, cruel thing to do to your parents."

JD had stopped being shocked at Pat's actions. "And your son."

"I may let them visit Rickie again," Carly continued. "Not right away. In a month or two. I'm not punishing them. But they need to know I'm serious. Plus, I want assurances Pat won't be causing me trouble or pursuing joint custody."

"Supervised visits?"

"Of course. For now." She settled more deeply into her seat and laid a hand on JD's knee. "Did you see Evelyn saying goodbye to Rickie? She really does love him."

They both glanced at the sleeping boy, his head resting at an impossible angle that had to be uncomfortable. And, yet, he appeared perfectly content. JD, on the other hand, experienced sympathy twinges in his neck just looking at him.

Hombre slept as well, now that the excitement had died down. He lay at JD's feet, chin on his paws, the picture of an innocent, docile pet. If JD hadn't seen the dog growling and baring his teeth and ready to pounce, he wouldn't have believed it possible.

For all the trouble he could be, Hombre had really come through for JD, proving his loyalty, intelligence and devotion. What was the occasional chewed object compared to that?

By now, dog agility class was over or would be over soon. JD made a mental note to call the instructor and apologize for missing with no notice.

"I suppose I should head home." He really

didn't want to leave—Carly's hand felt nice on his knee. But he had no reason to stay.

"Not yet. Please."

"You don't have to worry about Pat. I doubt he's coming back. And if he does, he'll have to come through me first." An idea suddenly occurred to him. "You want to take Hombre home for the night? Apparently, he's a decent guard dog."

"I'm not afraid. If Pat were to show up on my doorstep, I'd call the police. I think he knows that." She turned and smiled tentatively at JD. "I have something important to tell you. About us."

Ah. The heart-to-heart she'd mentioned earlier. "Okay."

"I'm not sure where to start. That's not like me."

He eased the awkwardness by brushing a lock of her short blond hair aside. "There's no hurry."

"I'm sorry Pat was such an aggressive jerk. I never dreamed anything like that would happen."

"You have nothing to be sorry about. He's a piece of work." JD called him a whole string of worse names in his head. "I'm glad you got away from him when you did. There's no telling where you'd be today if you hadn't."

"I wouldn't be here."

"Safe and out of his reach."

"With you, sitting on a picnic table in the park and me about to bare my soul."

"Carly. Let's not—"

She reached up and put a finger to his lips. "Me first. When I'm done, you can have your say."

He couldn't resist grinning. "There's that bossy woman I like so much."

She smiled in return, only to immediately sober. "What you did today… It wasn't just standing up to Pat. You were having an attack, and you pulled yourself out of it. For me."

"Much as I want to be the hero, that's not how it happened. I can't spontaneously stop an attack. I might be able to minimize the symptoms with coping techniques, if I'm lucky. Today was one of those rare times when the attack lasted only a few minutes. Had it been a full-blown one, you'd just now be scraping me off the ground."

"Can you honestly say that's true?"

He took his cue from her and cradled her cheek. "If you choose to believe I fended off an attack through sheer will and determination, then okay. Anything to get you to look at me like you are now. But, for the record, it's not physically possible."

She placed her hand over his. "You stood by me, JD. You're the only one who's ever done that besides my family and Becca."

"I wasn't about to let Pat hurt you."

"Not that. You could have walked away and done nothing when you saw Pat with Rickie."

He shook his head. "No decent person would."

"I made a mistake, letting you convince me breaking up was the best decision. Yes, you did it for Rickie." She cut him off before he could respond. "And you were right. Sort of. Except it made no difference in the end. Evelyn and Patrick Sr. were still taking Rickie to secret meetings with Pat."

"We didn't know, and you couldn't take the chance."

"I suspected Pat had seen Rickie, at least once, so shame on me. I learned something today I should have figured out weeks ago." She let her hand drop to look him in the eyes. "You and I, we're stronger together than we are apart. And I don't want to be apart from you anymore, JD."

"I still have—"

"Stop using your health as an excuse."

Her remark knocked him for a loop more than his Meniere's Disease could. Was she right? Had he been using his condition as an excuse rather than admitting his fear that he wasn't good enough for her?

After everything they'd been through, he owed Carly his complete honesty.

"You could do a lot better than me. I'm a washed-up bull rider working at a horse ranch."

"You're not washed up. Will you quit saying that? You had to retire from rodeoing because of circumstances beyond your control. And you like your job at Powell Ranch, right?"

"Yeah."

"What about the Poco Dinero? Did the owner hire that other guy?"

"Nope." He smiled at her. She did have a knack for seeing the positive in every situation. "I start this weekend."

"What? Eeek! How could you not tell me?"

"Well, we weren't speaking much."

She aimed the same you're-in-trouble glare at him he'd seen her use often with Rickie. "You haven't been riding any bulls these last few weeks, have you?"

"No, ma'am. You can ask the owner."

Her demeanor softened. "Is it so bad? Working at two jobs you like? A lot of people hate their job."

She was right. JD could think of several right off the top of his head worse than that.

"How'd you get so smart?" he asked.

"If I was that smart, we'd still be dating."

He wasn't such an idiot that he didn't see she'd thrown the door wide-open. He could either step through it and into a future with Carly, or he could return to his risk-free but lonely life.

JD stood and prepared for a wave of dizziness to hit. When it didn't, he took hold of Carly's hand and swallowed, searching for the right words. The ones that would leave no doubt as to his feelings and intentions.

"JD?" Worry bloomed on her lovely face.

He tugged her to her feet. This wasn't going to be easy.

"You're right. I've been making excuses. I love you, Carly."

She swallowed a soft gasp.

"I have from the moment we met. I kept telling myself I wasn't ready for a relationship, and that was true. I'd been handed a difficult challenge, and I was still coming to terms with it. I may always struggle—"

"I don't care," she said, cutting him off. "I love you, too, JD."

He laughed. She always spoke her mind, that was for sure. A lifetime with her would never be dull or boring—and everything he could possibly hope for.

"You're also right about us being better and

stronger together. I want to date. And I want you to meet my mother and sister and the rest of my family."

She let out another squeal. "I can't wait!"

"Mamá is going to love Rico." He wrapped Carly in his arms. "Like I already do. I won't try to take the place of his father—that decision is his to make when he's older. But if things go the way I think they will, the way I hope they will, I'd like to raise him as my son."

"Oh, JD." Throwing her arms around his neck, Carly kissed him over and over.

When she finally slowed, he held her close, treasuring the moment. "We're going to be good at this dating stuff, aren't we?"

"Really good." She sighed contentedly.

"How will your parents feel about us?"

"Ecstatic. They were devastated when we stopped seeing each other. Mostly because I was devastated."

"I'll try my best to make you happy, *mi cariño*."

Hombre must have sensed something exciting was happening, for he suddenly woke up and sprang to his feet, a series of yips escaping.

"Which reminds me," JD said. "Hombre and I are a package deal."

"Trust me." Carly peered up at him, her expression radiant. "Rickie wouldn't have it any other way."

They kissed again, their future bright and brimming with hope when only an hour ago it had been dark and dismal. JD wasn't quite ready to get down on one knee. A proposal would come eventually, though, and he planned to make it the very best day of their lives.

EPILOGUE

Fourteen months later

JD GAZED DOWN the aisle of Sweetheart Ranch's wedding chapel, his gaze riveted on the arched doorway. Anticipation mingled with excitement and a healthy dose of nervousness. The day he hadn't dreamed possible was finally here.

His lungs refused to fill, the result of the room becoming void of oxygen. When he wiped his forehead with a white linen handkerchief, it came away damp. His stomach had constricted to the size of a golf ball.

Not from an attack. Thanks to an implant, JD's last one had been over seven months ago. His doctor considered him to be in remission. JD remained optimistic but realistically accepted he could relapse at any given moment. If that happened, it happened. JD refused to let his condition defeat him.

"Don't fade on me now," Tanner said and

gave JD's back a solid brotherly pat. "You got this, pal."

His friend's show of support wasn't unlike those in the countless times right before JD lowered himself down onto the back of a bull. Those days were over, however. He wouldn't be returning to the rodeo circuit—soon or ever.

He didn't mind. Powell Ranch had recently expanded, building a second horse barn and a large competition-training center for barrel racing and reining horses. JD's increased duties had come with a new title and pay increase. More important, he loved his job.

He'd left his part-time stint as rodeo event manager at the Poco Dinero a few months ago. Much as he'd longed to remain connected to the rodeo world, he simply didn't have enough hours in the day, thanks to a brand-new passion.

He and Hombre had become something of an internet sensation. It was Carly's doing. She regularly posted videos of the pair to their YouTube channel, something she'd set up and continued to manage. Together, they'd turned Hombre's extensive repertoire of tricks and his role as JD's support dog into a rewarding campaign that focused on increasing awareness of balance disorders and raising money for related charities.

He and Carly attended rodeos whenever they had the chance. These days, they took Rickie with them. At two and a half, he was old enough to enjoy watching the "horsies" and "cahboys."

When Carly accepted his marriage proposal, JD's life became complete. He knew without a trace of doubt he wouldn't be where he was today without her unwavering belief in him and unfailing support.

Equaled only by the belief and support of his friends. Next to Tanner stood Ethan Powell. JD would be forever grateful to his boss, who'd pulled him into a bear hug when JD asked him to be a groomsman.

Hearing a subdued sob, he glanced at the front pew where his mother sat, a handkerchief pressed to her mouth. Next to her was his sister Lupe, her husband and their two children. Many of JD's extended family had flown or driven to Mustang Valley in order to attend the wedding. Also filling the groom's side of the chapel were dozens of JD's former bull- and bronc-riding buddies, along with their plus-ones. Looking at them, JD added *throat closing with emotion* to his other symptoms.

Not to be outdone, Carly's family, friends and even a few clients had also arrived in droves. Her mother occupied the front pew on the bride's side along with her sisters' husbands and children. Becca stood across the altar from JD, having already made her trip up the aisle and taken her place as Carly's maid of honor next to Carly's sisters.

Of course, JD and Carly were tying the knot at Sweetheart Ranch. There had been no other choice for a venue, not as far as they were concerned. She loved working in the boutique. And though her equine jewelry business continued to grow, she'd decided to remain at the boutique until she and JD gave Rickie a little brother or sister in the not too distant future.

As the chords of recorded string quartet music filled the chapel, two more members of the wedding party made their appearance. Entering through the arched doorway, they proceeded up the aisle toward the altar, and a murmured round of oh-mys and look-at-thems and delighted laughter erupted among the guests. Pictures were snapped and videos recorded—and not just by the hired photographer.

Rickie walked alongside Hombre, holding on to the dog's collar. He wore black shorts, a white shirt, black cummerbund, bow tie, suspenders and a boutonniere. Hombre's black-and-white wedding shirt and vest, complete with a bow tie, matched Rickie's. Attached to his back was a frilly white pillow and tied to the pillow were two gold wedding bands.

They'd practiced this walk up the aisle over and over. Every one of those practices had gone badly, mostly because of Rickie and his temperamental fits. Carly often complained that he was in the throes of the terrible twos. Hombre, on the other hand, had not only outgrown his puppy phase, he was very used to performing in public. Besides the videos, he and JD had appeared at numerous local events and been on television twice.

Today, however, Rickie behaved perfectly, and the pair were a hit. As Carly had predicted they would be when she'd first suggested Rickie and Hombre be ring bearers.

Evelyn had made the pillow attached to Hombre's back. The offer had come as a surprise to JD and Carly. Her former in-laws hadn't been invited to the wedding, but they were involved grandparents, enjoying their monthly visits with Rickie. Repairing the damage had taken considerable time, the lost trust slow to rebuild. But apologies had been made, steps taken, lessons learned and respect given. Rickie reaped the benefits, enjoying a happy relationship with both sets of his grandparents.

Pat had moved to California last year. Beyond that, Carly and JD knew little else, and they didn't ask. Things were better that way.

When Rickie and Hombre reached the altar, the dog obediently sat at a hand signal from JD. Rather than stand with Tanner, as was the plan, Rickie held up his arms to JD and pleaded to be picked up. Faced with a decision, JD lifted his soon-to-be stepson and balanced him against his chest.

"What do you say, partner, how about you help me marry your mamá?"

Rickie wrapped his arms around JD's neck and buried his face in JD's tux jacket.

Everyone in the chapel let out a collective sigh.

Suddenly, the string quartet music faded, replaced by the strains of "Here Comes the Bride." Carly appeared in the doorway, a glowing vision in white and pink. Russ beamed at her and patted her hand where it rested in the crook of his arm, besotted as any father of the bride.

JD couldn't tear his gaze from her. With each step she took toward him, his smile grew. She'd been right, they were better together than apart and their life would be amazing.

At the altar, she and her father waited until the minister asked, "Who gives this woman to be married to this man?"

After Russ's answer, Carly passed her bouquet to a teary-eyed Becca and reached for JD's hand. With the other, she cradled Rickie's head.

As the three of them embraced, JD allowed his myriad emotions to sink in. A few moments from now, he would go from being a man alone to being a husband and father.

"I love you, *mi cariño*," he whispered. "You and Rico. I swear here and now I'll do my best to make you happy."

She gazed up at him, her features reflecting the same joy filling JD's heart. "I love you, too, and always will."

At their feet, Hombre yipped.

Rickie lifted his head and said, "I wuv you and you" to Carly and JD.

The minister chuckled. "Well, then. Let's quit dillydallying and get the two of you married. Or, should I say the three of you?" He winked at Rickie.

JD liked the sound of that. Twenty minutes later, in front of a chapel full of cheering guests, he and Carly were pronounced man, wife and son.

* * * * *

Get 4 FREE REWARDS!
We'll send you 2 FREE Books plus 2 FREE Mystery Gifts.
KELLY RIMMER
Unspoken
SUSAN MALLERY
California Girls
FREE
Value Over
$20
HEATHER GRAHAM
A LETHAL LEGACY
JUDE DEVERAUX
A Justified Murder
Both the Romance and Suspense collections feature compelling novels written by many of today's bestselling authors.
YES! Please send me 2 FREE novels from the Essential Romance or Essential Suspense Collection and my 2 FREE gifts (gifts are worth about $10 retail). After receiving them, if I don't wish to receive any more books, I can return the shipping statement marked "cancel." If I don't cancel, I will receive 4 brand-new novels every month and be billed just $6.99 each in the U.S. or $7.24 each in Canada. That's a savings of at least 13% off the cover price. It's quite a bargain! Shipping and handling is just 50¢ per book in the U.S. and $1.25 per book in Canada.* I understand that accepting the 2 free books and gifts places me under no obligation to buy anything. I can always return a shipment and cancel at any time. The free books and gifts are mine to keep no matter what I decide.
Choose one: Essential Romance (194/394 MDN GNNP)
Essential Suspense (191/391 MDN GNNP)
Name (please print)
Address
Apt. #
City
State/Province
Zip/Postal Code
Mail to the Reader Service:
IN U.S.A.: P.O. Box 1341, Buffalo, NY 14240-8531
IN CANADA: P.O. Box 603, Fort Erie, Ontario L2A 5X3
Want to try 2 free books from another series? Call 1-800-873-8635 or visit www.ReaderService.com.
*Terms and prices subject to change without notice. Prices do not include sales taxes, which will be charged (if applicable) based on your state or country of residence. Canadian residents will be charged applicable taxes. Offer not valid in Quebec. This offer is limited to one order per household. Books received may not be as shown. Not valid for current subscribers to the Essential Romance or Essential Suspense Collection. All orders subject to approval. Credit or debit balances in a customer's account(s) may be offset by any other outstanding balance owed by or to the customer. Please allow 4 to 6 weeks for delivery. Offer available while quantities last.
Your Privacy—The Reader Service is committed to protecting your privacy. Our Privacy Policy is available online at www.ReaderService.com or upon request from the Reader Service. We make a portion of our mailing list available to reputable third parties that offer products we believe may interest you. If you prefer that we not exchange your name with third parties, or if you wish to clarify or modify your communication preferences, please visit us at www.ReaderService.com/consumerschoice or write to us at Reader Service Preference Service, P.O. Box 9062, Buffalo, NY 14240-9062. Include your complete name and address.
STRS20R